"Deputy Commander," said the president, "OPERATION KLICK is now in place. How soon will the Arrow be ready for liftoff?"

"We'll start the final modifications immediately and be ready by early Friday morning."

"Very good. Now, give it to me straight, Commander. What are our chances of completing this successfully?"

"Well, sir, if Kapolski can't do it, nobody can."

"That's not what I asked you," the president spoke sharply.

"Mr. President, a mission of this length and magnitude had never been undertaken before, but I believe it will work."

The president sighed heavily. "It damn well better. Well, then, as Admiral Farragut once said in the heat of battle, 'Damn the torpedoes and full steam ahead.'"

# THE LAST FLIGHT OF THE ARROW

Daniel Wyatt

BALLANTINE BOOKS • TORONTO

All rights reserved under International and Pan-American Copyright Conventions. Published in Canada by Random House of Canada Limited, Toronto.

**Canadian Cataloguing in Publication Data**
Wyatt, Daniel, 1952-
   The last flight of the Arrow

ISBN 0-345-36594-1

1. Avro Arrow (Turbojet fighter plane) - Fiction
I. Title

PS8595.Y37L3  1990     C813′.54     C89-095495-x
PR9199.3.W93L3  1990

Printed in Canada

First Edition: April 1990

# PROLOGUE

"Sandbag leader, this is maple tree. bandits at angels one-five, crossing coast at hastings. vector one-ten and buster."

Squadron Leader Stanley Croft III of the Royal Air Force pressed the radio transmitter button on the left side of the cockpit. "sandbag leader here," he acknowledged. "will vector one-ten and buster." Then he took a quick look around at his squadron. "sandbag leader here, chaps. make sure your oxygen masks are on and functioning. we're climbing up to angels one-seven."

The Hurricane fighter squadron turned to starboard and commenced a full-throttle climb. When they reached seventeen thousand feet they leveled off.

"section leaders, keep your mates under control and don't get overanxious," bellowed the squadron leader.

1

A veteran of the Battle of Britain since its inception only weeks before, Croft was the commanding officer, the mother hen, of this Polish Air Force squadron. Only twenty-three years old, tall, handsome, unattached, he was out for a good time. In the air, however, this Englishman with the cockney accent was a dedicated fighter pilot. During the month of July he had commanded an RAF squadron with astounding success. His squadron had collected eleven kills, four of which had been his own. Then, just three weeks ago, Croft had been sent to lead these undisciplined, ragtag Polish pilots, most of whom could not speak English.

Pilot Officer Bogdan Kapolski, the leader of the Red Section, scanned the sky looking for German bandits. The twenty-year-old Polish youngster, Danny to his mates, checked his rearview mirror on top of the windscreen, then peered out through the perspex of his cockpit. He looked down to both sides, up, then right and left, and the whole cycle again. The sun shone brightly on his right through the canopy, left open to disperse the engine heat that had a habit of building up in the cockpit. As he peered through his goggles, he blotted out the bright orange ball with his right thumb in order to check for enemy fighters. The Krauts could be anywhere, maybe coming back from escorting a bombing run over England. If they were they'd be short of fuel and not wanting to fight. Easy prey.

"GET IN TIGHTER, CHAPS, YOU'RE TOO LOOSE. TIGHTEN UP THAT FORMATION, BLUE LEADER. YOU'RE TOO RAGGED!"

What a group these Poles were, too wild even for Croft. They could sure guzzle the brew. There was no way he'd take them on a drinking binge to his favorite watering holes. They were too well known for wrecking a place. In the air they were an entirely different breed.

Sometimes, in haste, they would go after a lone German aircraft only to be caught by a favorite Luftwaffe trick. Many more German fighters would be up above, ready to pounce on the fliers who were foolish enough to fall for the bait. The Poles were a constant headache to Croft, almost a liability, but he did appreciate their stirring willingness to fight. They were not afraid of anything. Some English fighter pilots said that the Poles hated the Germans so much that they had forgotten how to be scared. Other English pilots simply thought the Poles were nuts.

The eyes and ears of the world had been glued to the newspapers and radios for news from Britain, the nation that stood gallantly alone against the Nazi war machine. Hitler had conquered Europe without much resistance and had now turned his rage on Britain. But the Germans would have to knock off the stubborn Royal Air Force before an invasion was feasible. All odds were against Britain, and as the battle progressed through the summer it looked steadily worse for the English. The RAF commander in chief of Fighter Command, Air Chief Marshall Hugh Dowding, had his back against the wall. The Germans had been flying over in droves, like swarms of hornets, and Dowding couldn't replace his downed pilots fast enough. British war factories couldn't build Spitfire and Hurricane fighters to keep up with the frightening demand. Even the U.S. ambassador to Britain, Joseph Kennedy, had predicted that Hitler would occupy London by the middle of August. Well, August had come and gone, and the British were holding out. But Hitler was still knocking at the door.

The British were a stubborn lot. Their resolve stiffened all the more as the summer of 1940 wore on; they refused to cave in. They did have one distinct and formidable weapon at their disposal, Radio Direction Finding, or simply radar. Radar masts dotted the Channel coastline near Dover and could be seen easily by the Germans from the French coast on a clear day. It was these masts that detected enemy aircraft almost as soon as they hit the English Channel.

Kapolski, one of the few English-speaking squadron pilots, repeated Croft's last English order in Polish to the red section. "PRZYCIAG LEPIEG!" he blurted into the radio transmitter.

Kapolski glanced across and back to starboard, just in time to see Andrzej Zebrowski pull in closer with his beat-up Hurricane, so close that Kapolski could actually count the rivets on his mate's machine. The fighter was covered with patches hastily plastered on after too many close calls with German bandits. After one skirmish, a week before, Zebrowski counted twenty-one machine gun holes on his fuselage alone, and another fifteen on the wings. But it didn't matter. The Hurricane was still flying and still able to slug it out with the enemy.

Zebrowski gave his leader the thumbs-up sign. They both smiled as Zebrowski pushed his goggles in place. The others pulled in too, Radkiewicz, Mikolajczyk, Zankowski. They were dog-tired after answering to scrambles day after day, but they were still alert, ready to shoot down Krauts on a moment's notice. This was the squadron's fourth scramble today.

"SAMOLOTY OD PORTU," shouted one of the Poles over the R/T.

Croft studied the sky. "WHAT'S HE SAYING, RED LEADER?"

"SPITFIRES OFF PORT, SANDBAG," Kapolski answered. "THEY MUST BE THE SPITS OUT OF DUXTON."

"GOOD. PERFECT VISIBILITY NOW, CHAPS, SO KEEP

YOUR PEEPERS OPEN." Croft flipped his goggles down over his eyes and slid the canopy closed.

"KRAUTS AT TWO O'CLOCK, SANDBAG LEADER! TALLY-HO!" Kapolski suddenly broke in. In Polish he added, "OPOWIADAC SOBIE," as he slid his canopy closed with a hard thud.

Croft sensed what the Poles were up to and tried to stop them. "HOLD YOUR SECTIONS, LEADERS, UNTIL WE MOVE IN CLOSER. DON'T GO CRAZY NOW. TURN YOUR GUNSIGHTS ON. HOW MANY ARE THERE? I WANT A COUNT!"

There was no response. As Croft glanced to both sides of his fighter he saw he had been talking to himself. Where were the rest of the pilots? Even the Spit-fires were gone. He looked wide-eyed in front, below, then behind. They were nowhere to be found. As he glanced down over his starboard wing he saw to his utter horror that every squadron pilot, including the Spitfire pilots from Duxton, were diving in 180-degree turns to attack from behind. There were approximately forty Heinkel bombers escorted by a dozen Messer-schmitt 109 fighters. He noted that the Spitfire pilots were positioned in small orderly groups, line astern. In contrast, the Poles looked totally disorganized.

"Blasted Poles!" Croft screamed. "Stupid sods! Those idiots are going to be the death of me yet!" "MA-PLE TREE!" he yelled, hitting the R/T, "THIS IS SAND-BAG. WE SEE THE BANDITS. TALLYHO." He banged right rudder and eased the joystick to the right.

Two thousand feet below, the 109s scattered in all directions to avoid the diving Hurricanes and Spitfires. The Heinkel bombers opened up with their machine guns. Kapolski had instructed his mates to go in and pick a fighter target. After a few minutes of aerial com-bat the 109s would shed precious fuel and would be unable to complete their escort mission. The fighters would be forced to fly back to France, leaving the bombers without any support.

Kapolski saw a 109 bank right and dive toward a cloudbank. He followed right on his tail, even though he knew that a 109 could easily outdive a Hurricane. From a distance of three hundred yards he fired a short burst that went wild, then heaved back on the column. The 109 pilot leveled off and continued turning starboard. On a hunch, Kapolski banked right, making it look as though the German had given him the slip. Once the German had disappeared into the clouds, Kapolski broke to port and gradually tightened his turn. He could feel the G-forces build up against his body as he completed a full 360-degree turn.

Suddenly, the Messerschmitt burst out of the cloudbank, only five hundred yards away! Kapolski's hunch paid off. Now it was a game of aerial chicken. Who would break away first?

Kapolski picked out the yellow hub on the 109's prop as the two mighty fighters closed in on a six hundred mile-per-hour rate of closure collision course. Then, at a distance of 150 yards, the 109 pilot started climbing, leaving the whole underbelly of his aircraft as a target.

"RED LEADER, YOU GOT ONE COMING HEAD ON!" shouted a voice over the R/T.

Oblivious to anything but the German fighter, Kapolski climbed quickly. His right hand gripped the stick so solidly that his fingers were sweating inside his glove. He lined up the German in his sight and held the firing button on his joystick steady for a three-second burst. "Take that, Kraut!" he yelled into his oxygen mask, as a smoky trail of tracers edged a path towards the Messerschmitt.

His aircraft shook violently as his machine guns tore away at the German's starboard wing and bottom fuselage in a neat, perfect line. A total of thirteen pounds of lethal RAF .303 ammunition tore into the Messerschmitt at the rate of eighty rounds per second. A black cloud of continuous smoke poured off the wounded engine. The smell of cordite stung the air inside the Hurricane cockpit. Kapolski broke away violently to port and down as the German thundered through the air, only fifty feet above. Partway through his turn, the Pole looked through the perspex and saw the 109 spiraling to earth in a slow spin.

Kapolski steered his machine into a slow, lazy turn to watch for a chute. Nothing appeared. He felt no sympathy for the Messerschmitt pilot as he watched the German aircraft career into an open field near a winding creek. One less pilot on the Kraut payroll and kill number five for Kapolski. That made him an ace.

A sudden burst from his R/T snapped Kapolski to attention.

"PULL AWAY, YOU GOT ONE ON YOUR TAIL!"

"I WILL. BACK ME UP."

"STRZELAG, STRZELAG!"

"WEZ TO SZWABY."

"WHAT ARE YOU CLODS SAYING! DAMN IT, SPEAK ENGLISH, YOU GUYS! RED LEADER, THIS IS SANDBAG LEADER. WHERE ARE YOU?"

Kapolski pushed his mask closer to his face. "I READ YOU, SANDBAG. THIS IS RED LEADER."

"THE BANDITS ARE GETTING AWAY OVER THE CHANNEL. LET'S GO GET A PIECE OF THE BOMBERS."

"SANDBAG LEADER, THIS IS RED LEADER. I JUST GOT A 109 AND HE PLOWED A FARMER'S FIELD!"

"GOOD SHOOTING, ACE, NOW GET BACK TO THE REST OF THE PACK. LET'S GET THE BOMBERS. THERE'S NO FIGHTER SUPPORT."

"WHERE ARE YOU?"

"NORTH OF EASTBOURNE AND HEADING THREE-FOUR-ZERO."

"I READ YOU, SANDBAG."

Kapolski banked the fighter and looked out the portside as his shoulder harness and safety belt pressed hard against his already sore and tired body. He saw the Channel off in the distance. He eased the column forward and climbed steadily through the thin layer of cloud that blanketed the southern coast. The hunt wasn't over yet.

TINIAN, MARIANA ISLANDS, MAY 24, 1945

The voice of the aircraft commander, Edmund Schult, came over the intercom. "COMMANDER TO CREW, START UP IN FIVE SECONDS."

Schult ordered the flight engineer to start number one engine. The left outboard engine cranked and sputtered, sending out an enormous quantity of flame and white smoke through its exhaust stacks. When it was running smoothly, the inboard started, and performed the same way before it too ran smoothly. Then the other two engines fired and soon all four were humming evenly. The engines were 2,200-horsepower Wright R-3350-23 Duplex Cyclone 18-cylinder radials with two exhaust-driven turbochargers on each. The sound of nearly 9,000 horsepower echoed through the fuselage.

Schult's aircraft, nicknamed *Billy Bee*, moved out and followed the slow line of other B-29 Superfortresses rolling past the 462nd Bomb Group area to Runway Baker.

One by one the mighty bombers, fully loaded with bombs, ammo and high-octane fuel, took off. Schult pointed his seventy-ton bomber east and waited for the preceding bomber to take to the air. He and his pilot,

Walter Price, and the other crew members ran through the final part of their checklist.

"TURRETS IN PROPER POSITION?"

"CHECK."

"BOMB BAY DOORS?"

"CLOSED."

"FLIGHT CONTROLS?"

"CHECK."

"TRIM TABS?"

"NEUTRAL."

"HYDRAULIC SYSTEM?"

"PRESSURES RIGHT UP."

"VACUUM?"

"CHECK."

"SERVO SWITCHES?"

"OFF."

Schult powered up the engines. "WING FLAPS TWENTY-FIVE DEGREES?"

Price answered quickly. "WING FLAPS TWENTY-FIVE."

"HOW DOES THAT CHECK OUT, GUNNERS?" The two blister gunners checked to see that the flaps were in the proper takeoff position.

"OKAY, COMMANDER."

"EVERYTHING'S ALL RIGHT HERE."

"JASON, HOW DOES YOUR PANEL LOOK?"

"WE'RE HEATING UP A BIT ON ALL FOUR, BUT WHAT ELSE IS NEW?" answered the flight engineer.

"ANY DANGER?"

"WE'RE OKAY. NOTHING OUT OF THE ORDINARY."

"HOW'S THE REST OF THE CREW? ANY PROBLEMS?"

"NO SIR," came the check-in from the positions, one after the other.

"WINDOWS AND HATCHES CLOSED?"

"CHECK."

"RIGHT ON, COMMANDER."

The bomber ahead of them was over the far end of the runway now and starting to take to the air. Schult got the final clearance from West Field tower.

"OKAY, THIS IS IT," he announced to the crew.

He gunned the throttles. *Billy Bee* leaped forward and barreled down the runway, the G-forces pressing the occupants back in their seats.

Forty minutes after he'd begun the preflight check Schult and his crew were airborne over the ocean. They were over Saipan now, on a heading of 337 degrees, 620 miles from Iwo Jima. Their air speed was 180 knots, their altitude 4,700 feet. They were in the centre of three rows of Superfortress bombers, over 500 planes, that stretched out over several hundred miles. The bombers were carrying payloads of 10,000 pounds of lethal incendiaries and were heading for Tokyo.

The commander hit the intercom. "COMMANDER TO GUNNERS. YOU CAN TEST YOUR GUNS."

Sitting in the center of the aircraft's fuselage, in the gunners' compartment, was Ben Spencer, a red-haired, six-foot, twenty-one-year-old Canadian war correspondent for the *Vancouver Daily News*. He sat on the floor, his back against the bulkhead that led towards the radar room. He was busily writing, taking notes of what he had seen up to that point. The pressurized cabin was warm, but he was heavily dressed. He had a survival vest, food rations, a first-aid kit, and a drinking-water package strapped under his brown overalls. A parachute pack and a one-man life raft were on top. Next came a flak suit which seemed to hang on him like a hundred-pound bag of potatoes. He also wore a canteen, a .45 automatic pistol in a leather holster, and GI boots, and he was sitting on his fur-lined flight jacket. All this just in case the bomber was shot down. How did the bomber crews ever get used to so much bulk surrounding their bodies?

There were three gunners in the same compartment; a short, stocky left blister-gunner named Albert Groves; a skinny, nervous, prematurely balding right blister-gunner named Chester Wilkins; and, seated above Spencer in the central fire control position was Ben Woodman, a drawling Southerner, who always wore his sleeves rolled back to expose his large biceps.

Spencer had met Schult briefly an hour earlier under the nose of the aircraft. He was a stern, tight-lipped officer with a protruding chin and high cheekbones. He appeared to be in his thirties. The other crew members were much younger, probably in their early twenties.

As the aircraft droned on in the bomber stream, the writer had trouble staying awake, as did the gunners. Spencer was fast asleep well before the sun had set.

"COMMANDER TO CREW. SEARCHLIGHTS AHEAD. KEEP YOUR EYES OPEN FOR FIGHTERS AND BAKAS."

Spencer woke up with a jolt and knelt over the left blister. It was nighttime, and the gunners' compartment was dark except for a dim light by each gun position. Groves, Wilkins and Woodman scrambled to their seats. Woodman, high above the others, stuck his head into the astrodome and peered northward, towards the Japanese capital. To his amazement, the sky was glowing with hellish-orange flames. Tokyo was already burning.

"Hold on tight, Ben, this is it," Groves announced to the writer.

The Japanese coastline was now directly below them. Their I.P., Initial Point, of the bomb run, in this case the famous Mt. Fuji, was coming up ahead. Schult sighted the snow-covered landmark and banked the aircraft. The orange brilliance of the sky over Tokyo was reflected off the silver fuselages of the bombers surrounding them.

The minutes passed and then Spencer witnessed their first casualty. A B-29 was spotlighted in a hail of enemy searchlights and blasted out of the sky by antiaircraft fire. The plane went down in a crumpled, fiery mess and exploded.

Spencer swallowed hard. It's a madhouse down there, he thought. Look at the smoke clouds. Good Lord, they're higher than our planes. What was that smell? It was like pork. Barbecued pork. Good God, it was the smell of burning bodies, must be thousands of them. The *Billy Bee* was close enough to smell the bodies nine thousand feet below. It must be hell on earth down there.

''ALL BOMBS GONE,'' the bombardier announced over the intercom. Now lightened of its bombload, *Billy Bee* shot skyward.

Then without warning the aircraft leaped violently to its port side, sending Spencer and Wilkins to the left side with a hard thud.

''Buckle yourself to the bulkhead!'' Groves yelled.

As Spencer scrambled to obey, every loose piece of equipment, paper and leftover food flew about the compartment. The aircraft started shaking.

''We're caught in the turbulence!'' Woodman cried to Spencer and the gunners below. ''Hang on!''

The next forty seconds seemed like forever. Even a roller-coaster ride wasn't like this. Spencer felt sick to his stomach, so he gulped heavily to keep his K-rations down. He succeeded until the great bomber took a sudden violent dive. It was then that he tossed the entire contents of his stomach all over his flight boots and his papers on the floor.

With a jerk the aircraft started climbing again. *When will it end?* The plane continued to jitter and shake through the climb.

Suddenly there was an eerie calm. Searchlights and some exploding shrapnel were still filling the sky, but the turbulent ride was finally over. The aircraft banked easily to starboard. Schult was in control of the mighty machine.

An earth-shattering slam followed the temporary calm. Then came a series of smaller bangs that wouldn't let up. Commander Schult sent the radio operator to investigate. He found the bomb-bay doors knocked off their front hinges, probably from the firestorm turbulence. The drag from the doors, Schult reasoned, would gobble up their remaining fuel supply.

No sooner had this damage been reported than the *Billy Bee* was rocked by another explosion, a tremendous flaming burst of flak off port.

"CAPTAIN, NAV HERE," called the navigator. "THE PORT WING HAS A HOLE IN IT, AND THERE'S GAS POURING OUT OF IT."

"KEEP AN EYE ON IT."

They flew on for another ten minutes. "CAPTAIN, IT DOESN'T LOOK GOOD," the flight engineer broke in. "WE'VE GOT LEAKS IN TWO TANKS. I THINK EVEN AN EMERGENCY LANDING ON IWO IS OUT OF THE QUESTION. WE WON'T MAKE IT."

"I GUESS WE DON'T HAVE MUCH CHOICE BUT TO GET OUT."

"Forget the life rafts." Schult spoke coolly to his assistant. "We're going out individually. I don't want to take a chance plunking this bird down on the water in the dark."

"COMMANDER TO CREW, WE'RE OUT OVER THE WATER NOW, AT SIX THOUSAND FEET. WE'RE MAKING A DISTRESS CALL TO AIR-SEA RESCUE. CHECK YOUR PARACHUTE PACKS AND MAE WESTS. WE'RE GOING TO HAVE TO ABORT SOON. WAIT FOR THE ALARM. ONCE YOU BAIL OUT AND ARE FREE OF THE AIRCRAFT, PULL THE CHORD. WE'RE TOO CLOSE TO THE WATER FOR THE USUAL TEN-COUNT. MAKE LOTS OF NOISE ONCE YOU HIT THE WATER SO THAT WE CAN BE FOUND. GROVES?"

"HERE, CAPTAIN."

"FILL OUR VISITOR IN ON WHAT HE HAS TO DO."

"YES, SIR."

Groves pushed the microphone away from his face and quickly ran over the operating procedures of Spencer's parachute pack. "Don't worry," he said finally to the worried writer, "just jump, and pull the ring here," he pointed, "once you're free of the aircraft. I guess you never expected this to happen, did you?"

"No way!" Spencer swallowed hard.

"Are you all right?" the gunner asked.

Spencer swallowed hard again. "Just a little sick."

"OKAY, CREW. GET TO YOUR EXITS. GO."

The alarm rang throughout the bomber, and the three gunners whipped their headsets off.

When Spencer made his way to the aft section with the radar operator and three gunners, he was astonished to see several holes about the size of gallon paint cans punched through the fuselage. The rushing slipstream produced such a racket they could hardly talk.

"Damn, when did that happen?" Spencer screamed to be heard.

Groves leaned forward. "Flak!" he shouted. "Probably just before we got it on the port wing."

"Okay," Woodman yelled, "Groves, you first. Go!"

Groves pulled on the door handle, and it flew open. He jumped through without hesitation. Next went Wilkins, then the radar operator. Only Spencer and Woodman remained.

"Don't worry!" Woodman shouted at the correspondent. "You'll be all right. Once you hit the water, detach the chute. Your Mae West will keep you afloat. And make lots of noise so the sub can find you in the dark. Now get going!"

Then he pushed Spencer out the door.

# CHAPTER ONE

At Malton Airport near Toronto, a group of workers and press people gathered anxiously outside a hangar of the world-renowned A. V. Roe Corporation. They were waiting for the company's pet project, the multimillion-dollar Avro Arrow fighter-interceptor, to make its maiden flight.

The eyes of the world were watching and waiting breathlessly as the Avro test pilot manned the articulate controls of the CF-105 Avro Arrow. This day had been long awaited by a large group of people that included the Avro management, the plane's designers, assembly line technicians, ground crew, the live TV and radio audience, the Royal Canadian Air Force, the Americans and even the Russians.

Following the Arrow's rollout on October 4, 1957, *Aviation Week*, an American-based aircraft magazine, had said:

15

*The fighter makes Canada a serious contender for the top military aircraft of the next several years. The Arrow's power, weight and general design leave little doubt of its performance potential.*

*Important features of the present version of the CF-105 include 1) afterburner takeoff weight of about sixty thousand pounds with Iroquois engines; 2) maximum takeoff weight of about sixty thousand pounds; 3) area-ruled fuselage; and 4) very thin wings with conical leading edges and blunt trailing edges.*

*As far as ceiling is concerned, Fred T. Smye, president of Avro, has stated that the Arrow will be able to intercept and destroy aircraft flying at seventy-five thousand feet. There was no explanation as to the altitude in a zoom climb, or whether the Arrow actually had to reach seventy-five thousand feet for its missile armament to destroy the hostile aircraft, but it does give some indication of the Arrow's altitude capability.*

A week earlier, the first Arrow flight had been canceled because of a hydraulic leak. But today all systems were go.

An announcement over the plant P.A. system had invited all nonessential personnel to drop their workload, grab their coats, and catch the maiden flight. Needless to say, the plant emptied. Someone on the assembly line jokingly quipped that if the unfinished aircraft and equipment could get up and walk, they'd be out on the tarmac too.

Twenty-eight-year-old Lance Tiemans had been employed by Avro as an aeronautical technician for the past three years. It was a position he thoroughly enjoyed and was very proud of. The pay could have been better, but all in all, he was having the time of his life; unmarried, in a field right up his alley, and enjoying life to the fullest.

From the time he was ten years old Tiemans had dreamed of flying fighter aircraft. At that time, 1940, the Canadian daily newspapers were full of the daring exploits of British and Canadian pilots in the Battle of Britain. The Royal Air Force against the Luftwaffe; Spitfires and Hurricanes against the Messerschmitts; legendary pilots like Douglas Bader, Robert Tuck, and Adolph Galland. Tiemans had wished he were there with them, flying those legendary fighters for the Allies.

His dream had not unfolded exactly as he had planned, but it was close enough. This very day was the maiden flight of Canada's first supersonic all-weather fighter-interceptor, an aircraft he had been specially trained to work on. He knew every inch of the plane's engines. The Arrow wasn't just Avro's or the country's aircraft; it was also his. As Tiemans stood erect on the tarmac with the other members of the ground-crew staff, his excitement showed on his face.

As the thousands of onlookers waited, the pilot slowly taxied to the south end of runway 32. It was the longest runway at Malton and had recently been extended to eleven thousand feet just to accommodate the Arrow. All eyes were on the Delta-winged CF-105 Arrow Mark I as it waited for clearance from the tower.

The lines of the all-Canadian-built Arrow were beautiful. The front end came to a fine point and extended far beyond the pilot in the clamshell canopy. The swept-back wings on a fifty-foot span seemed to envelop the whole aft section, and indeed dominated the entire aircraft. The nose sat up slightly in a distinctive fashion. Just twenty-five years earlier many pilots were flying prop-driven biplanes in combat roles and now Canadian aeronautical technology was on the threshold of building a fighter that neither the Americans nor the Russians could beat.

Britain's best World War II fighter, the Supermarine Spitfire, would fit nicely into the aft section of the Arrow, while the Avro Lancaster, Britain's best bomber during the same period, was eight feet shorter than this aircraft calmly waiting to jolt loose and thunder down the extended runway at Malton. *Impressive. Elegant. Large. Awesome.* What words could properly describe Canada's new supersonic fighter that stood a graceful seventy-seven feet in length and an overpowering twenty-one feet high? What words indeed?

Two jet fighter chase planes (a CF-100 Canuck and an F-86 Sabre) were already in the air and set to monitor and record the Arrow's maiden flight. With the approaching chase planes as a signal, the test pilot let go the brakes and started to roll down the runway. Three thousand feet down the strip he lifted the nose gear off. The crowd held its breath. With a mighty spine-tingling roar from its dual Pratt & Whitney J75 engines, the Arrow was airborne in one smooth, graceful motion. The crowd cheered, elated with the breathtaking spectacle before its eyes.

A large smile broke across the face of Lance Tiemans. His deep-set eyes, bloodshot from staying up late with his drinking buddies the night before, watched the aircraft soar into the distance, closely followed by the chase planes. Tiemans stole a glance at the other members of his crew. They were all beaming like small, innocent children with a brand new toy; a $300 million toy.

As he pulled up the collar on his long, leather coat, Tiemans thought back to the proud day of October 4, 1957, when the Arrow was first exhibited to the world. The crowd of twelve thousand people, Avro workers, the press, and certain dignitaries, had been stunned, completely spellbound by their first sight of the fighter outside the Avro hanger. Tiemans could still remember the words of the defense minister of Canada as he spoke from the platform:

*"This event today marks another milestone, the production of the first Canadian supersonic airplane. I am sure that the historian of tomorrow will regard this event as being truly significant in the annals of Canadian aviation.*

*The supersonic era of flight is just beginning. Many of today's aircraft are regularly breaking the sound barrier, but this is done at the extreme peak of their performance. Supersonic flight is still not a routine matter. Present aircraft travel at these exceptionally fast speeds for only a relatively short period of time.*

*The Avro Arrow, however, has been designed from the outset to operate supersonically throughout as much of its mission as is deemed necessary . . ."*

The trio of planes flew over the Avro plant several times at different altitudes, at the same time communicating with each other and the Malton tower. After thirty-five minutes of aerial testing, the Arrow pilot obtained clearance from the tower to land. As he made his approach to Runway 32 at 180 knots, he dropped the landing gear in full view of the crowd. The tires screeched as they met the hard, concrete surface and smoke streamed off the rubber. Right away the parachute popped to slow the mighty machine down to a crawl.

The Arrow taxied up to the Avro hangar. When the pilot shut down the engines and climbed from the cockpit, the jubilant crowd descended upon him and hoisted him on their shoulders.

Tiemans was still grinning when a tall chubby redhaired man in his thirties stepped in front of him and blocked his view. He was wearing a greatcoat and had a camera strung sloppily around his neck.

"Good morning," said the man in a firm, professional manner. "I'm Ben Spencer from the *Tribune*."

Tiemans paused. "Oh yeah, I've heard of you. You're the fellow who's written several columns on the Arrow." His voice was higher than usual. "Well, what do you think? Mind you, you can't tell too much from a thirty-minute flight at eleven thousand feet." Tiemans watched as the crowd finally set the pilot down.

Spencer shrugged. "No, I guess not. But I think it's great. I once read somewhere that if a plane looks good, then it performs good too. Isn't that right? Like the Spitfire or the Sabre. The Arrow will too. Anyway, I'll get down to business. You're the pilot's crew chief, aren't you?"

Tiemans nodded. "That's right."

"Well, after this little merriment is over," said the reporter, as he turned for a moment to the now-quieting crowd behind him, "can I get the pilot and your crew together for a snapshot? It's going to be front page news tomorrow. Then maybe you can fill me in some more."

"Sure, no problem. I see you take your own pictures," Tiemans said, as Spencer checked the light readings on his meter.

"Most reporters don't, probably because they can't. But I like to."

"Nice camera."

"Thanks."

"While you're busy with your equipment, I'll get the ground crew together. You want to talk to the test pilot too?"

"If you can arrange it, sure."

OTTAWA, ONTARIO, 1010 HOURS (EST)

The prime minister of Canada and his finance minister were discussing the future federal election in the prime minister's office in the Center Block of the Parliament buildings in Ottawa.

"Well, Alex, we're only a few days away from the election. Tomorrow I'll hit southern Ontario, Toronto, Hamilton. Thursday, it's Windsor. We're going to get a majority this time around, but just how big remains to be seen. The Big Blue Tory Machine is on the move. Look out, Liberals!" The prime minister leaned back in his chair and laughed out loud, his voice echoing in the chamber. His finance minister, Alex Kralick, seated in front of the P.M.'s desk, looked pleased that his boss was in good spirits.

The prime minister was at an age when most other men would have been retired. But this tall politician with the curly white hair had the vigor of a man half his age. He was out to change Canada, perhaps the world, and nothing was going to stop him. He was looking for a solid mandate from his people to move Canada ahead, kicking and screaming, into the 1960s.

The Conservative party was indeed on a roll. Only last year they had been elected to the Canadian parliament, passing the Liberals with a small lead. For the first time in over twenty years the Conservatives were in power. But the prime minister desperately wanted a substantial majority. With an election only days away, the Gallup Polls predicted that the Tories just might be given a majority mandate to work with. Both the prime minister and Kralick were happy with this pending situation.

The Ottawa–Washington telephone hotline rang, a loud, coarse tone. The prime minister, knowing in advance who was on the other end, picked up the receiver.

"Yes."

"Mr. Prime Minister?"

"Yes, Mr. President."

"Good morning."

"And a good morning to you. How's the weather in the capital?"

"A little on the chilly side, I'm afraid, but spring is just around the corner." The president paused on the other end. "I know you must be busy, so I'll make this brief."

The prime minister grinned at Kralick. "I always have time for a diplomatic chat with our good neighbor to the south."

"How's the campaign coming?"

"It's full steam ahead. The Gallup Poll says we're going to win it."

"Great. I hope you get the majority you're expecting."

"Thank you."

"How's that fighter aircraft coming along?" asked the president.

The prime minister's grin dissolved, for he was surprised at the change in conversation. "It's being tested today," he said, "just outside Toronto. It's the maiden flight."

"I'm anxious to hear about the results."

"So are we, for several reasons."

The president coughed. "I haven't been able to get rid of this cold. Anyway, keep me posted, will you? That aircraft has some possibilities that we might be interested in." He coughed again, then cleared his throat.

"Really? It's costing us a fortune," the prime minister said, brushing his hand through his thick head of hair.

"I know it is. Anyway, we should get together in the near future for some defense talks and then we can discuss the Arrow further."

"Anytime."

"Excellent. We'll be in touch. *Soon.*"

RCAF STATION DIXON, ALBERTA
0834 HOURS (1034 EST)

From a vantage point outside an operational hangar, Bogdan Kapolski, a flight lieutenant with the Royal Canadian Air Force, watched the CF-100 fighter-interceptors from B-Flight practising circuits and bumps. The top-notch group could touch and go with precision. A cold wind whistled down from the north, almost right through the pilot's RCAF parka. It had to be ten below Fahrenheit without the wind. The clean, white snow, freshly plowed only hours before and piled off the runways and taxi strips, glinted in the sunlight as Kapolski slipped his fur-lined hood up over his head.

While the other pilots from A-Flight were in the crew room shooting the breeze and waiting for their stint in the air, Kapolski preferred to be by himself, even if it meant being outside.

He was several years older than most of the other pilots, and he didn't seem to have much in common with them, outside of flying. He was tall, husky and edging forty. Stress lines were starting to carve their way into his face, and his brush cut was receding more and more. Kapolski wasn't himself, not since his wife and son died three months earlier in a bus accident in Quebec. He still hadn't properly recovered from the traumatic experience.

Mary had been a pretty English woman, ten years younger than himself. He met her in England in 1940 and as quickly as he fell in love with her, so had she with him. She had been kind, good-natured and patient. She had possessed the kind of patience expected from a pilot's wife. The service had a lot to offer, but it also moved you around a lot. Mary had never complained, not even when her husband wanted to move to Canada at the war's end in order to transfer to the Royal Canadian Air Force. The Kapolskis had lived on bases in West Germany, England, North Africa, Quebec, and Ontario. *Where we hang our hats is home,* she would say.

But now she was gone forever, and how the pilot missed her. The air force thought that by stationing the pilot away from Quebec he might shake off this depression he was going through. But Kapolski could only blame himself for letting her and their only child, an eight-year-old-son named Robbie, take that bus trip from the base to Montreal. The weather had been terrible that day in January. The vehicle hit an icy patch of road and overturned, killing four people.

These last few months had been the worst time of his life, for not only did he miss his family, but he also missed his native Poland, where many of his relatives and former friends still were.

Born and raised in the central plains area, the agricultural region of Poland, Kapolski enjoyed farm life and thought of it often after he left to go to war. Farming was still in his blood. He recalled the bumper crops of potatoes and sugar beets that his father used to grow on the family farm east of the capital of Warsaw. Although the old days of prewar Poland still drew Kapolski like a magnet, he knew he could never go back, not with the Russians in control. They were the same Russians who had snatched his two brothers in 1946 and sent them off to the Siberian workcamps.

As Kapolski watched a CF-100 climb away from the

runway, he thought of his early days with the Polish Air Force prior to 1939. Life in general had seemed so serene, so uncomplicated. Adolph Hitler had come to power in Germany to the west, but nobody thought much of it.

Kapolski remembered the single-engined biplanes he had flown. He remembered the maneuvers: the slow rolls, the snap rolls, the barrel rolls, the split-S's. He felt so at home in an airplane, a natural flier. He recalled the day he'd received his wings. Standing in line with a half-dozen others, all proud as peacocks they were. Then, a little over a year later, September 1, 1939, Hitler attacked Poland. Only nineteen years ago, it seemed like a hundred. Within a few weeks his country had fallen, but he and many other pilots managed to escape to Britain before the Nazi net closed around them. Kapolski and his good friend, Andrzej Zebrowski, had jumped aboard a Danish merchant ship in the harbor at Danzig and weren't discovered until halfway to Copenhagen. When the ship docked in the Danish capital, the two Poles reported to the British embassy and offered their services to the Royal Air Force. After considerable interrogation they were finally accepted and placed on a boat to England.

Kapolski, like the other Polish pilots who had escaped to Britain, had to take orders from the Royal Air Force. That was a problem for many Polish pilots, and Kapolski was no exception. He was a lone wolf, the last of a dying breed of fighter pilots. On many occasions during the Battle of Britain he had broken formation to attack the Germans, *his* mortal enemy. He had such a burning hate for the Germans, he could almost taste it. He was warned about his flying attitude, but only to a point, because the British needed every pilot they could get their hands on during the Battle of Britain, especially ones who possessed the bravery, nerve, and flying skill of a Bogdan Kapolski. Besides, his presence on a squadron, then as now, could electrify the pilots into believing they were invincible, and that was good for morale. That one thing was certain: Kapolski was a wizard in the air, and one of the best pilots the RCAF ever had. Many young, inexperienced pilots had learned more about flying combat in one week from Kapolski than they had learned in their previous months of training from anyone else.

Kapolski had survived the war unscathed, with a total of twenty-four kills to his credit. During the Korean War he helped immensely in the training of young pilots while in the Far East. For some reason, he did not see active service. His knowledge of jet fighter techniques, however, was indispensable to the Allied nations. Not wanting to lose him in battle, they kept him on the ground, except for the occasional jaunt in the air as a flight instructor, to teach others. He studied the F-86 Sabre, their fighter, till he knew it inside out. His students adored him. In fact, two of them exceeded ten kills during the air battles against the North Koreans over the famous MiG Alley. Both pilots attributed their success to what Kapolski had taught them on the ground, and in the air during mock air battles.

His superiors knew Kapolski's record. He had been well decorated during the war, with a British DFC, a Bar, and a DSO. But despite the medals and the twenty-four kills he collected, he lacked the proper discipline to ascend the ladder of advancement in the RCAF. He often said he didn't want to progress any further than a flight lieutenant anyhow. "Once you're a squadron leader or wing commander or group captain, you aren't one of the boys anymore," said Kapolski to his friends in the RCAF. And a desk job was out; too stuffy, and that boring paperwork. He wanted to fly. The only way to go.

But now Kapolski was thinking seriously of quitting the air force and moving into civilian life. He felt he couldn't contribute to the service any longer. But what would he do in the mundane world out there? His C.O. at Dixon had advised him to stick it out for a few years because there were big things about to happen in the RCAF. A new supersonic fighter was just around the corner. A new toy. "Hang on just to see what this fighter is like, then pack it in if you want." Kapolski promised to think about it.

The pilot stood in the snow, shuffling his feet. He was doing a lot of thinking lately. He took one last look at the handful of aircraft in the circuit, then stepped inside the hangar out of the cold, crisp air.

Flying Officer James Scott steadily pushed the throttles forward on his Avro CF-100 Canuck Mark IVB. The G-forces were pushing him and his navigator, Flying Officer Jacques St. Pierre, firmly back in their seats. At the precise mechanical moment, once they reached a clump of trees a few hundred yards beyond the strip, Scott banked the aircraft to port to follow the other aircraft in the circuit.

Scott came from a service family rich in air force tradition. His father was one of the oldest pilots to serve on a fighter squadron in England during World War II, flying Spitfires with 401 Squadron of the RCAF out of Redhill. Scott's grandfather had also been a fighter pilot with the British in World War I.

Born in 1936 in Winnipeg, the blonde-haired, unmarried, ambitious, sometimes loud and cocky Scott was a stark contrast to his twenty-four-year-old navigator. St. Pierre was a mild, soft-spoken, dark-haired Frenchman from Montreal who never smoked, drank or cheated on his wife. Nevertheless, these two CF-100 officers worked as a well-coordinated twosome, for they

had been together on interceptor procedures for the past
year. Over two hundred hours together, and from the
looks of things they were going to stay together for a
while.

Leveling out, Scott and St. Pierre looked over the
port wing and saw the entire base; the runways, hangars, tower, parked CF-100's, one other Canuck about
to take off again, and one more about to land. It was a
never-ending circle of aerial activity. Scott banked again
to port to line up with the runway on final approach.
He hoped to make a smoother landing this time than
on the last one, where he had dropped down much too
roughly for his liking.


THE SOVIET EMBASSY, WASHINGTON, D.C.
1250 HOURS (EST)


Alexander Miskin had been inside the filing room for
much too long. He had every right to be in there, of
course, because of his line of work, but he wanted to
be above suspicion. If he was gone much longer, someone would come looking for him. They wouldn't be too
happy if they caught him stealing top secret Soviet Air
Force photos and telexes. It took Miskin several minutes to find the files he was looking for. They had been
moved from their usual spot in one of the cabinets.
Now they were at the back of the cabinet, instead of the
front. He opened the files and nervously stuffed various
telex messages and photos under his shirt. Then he fixed
his black tie and gray plaid sports jacket. He fought to
control the trembling of his hands.

Miskin walked to the door, his heart pounding like a
big bass drum. Even the sound of his heavy breathing
seemed to reverberate off the walls and ceiling. He had
been the only soul in the room, luckily. He looked back

at the several pictures on the wall, all of Soviet government dignitaries, all framed in what he always thought were grotesque, dull oak borders.

Opening the door seemed to make his heart pound louder and faster. He could feel cold perspiration dripping down from his armpits. Steadily, he walked down the long gray corridor that smelled of fresh latex. His shoes clomped loudly against the hardwood floors. When he turned right to walk down the flight of stairs leading to the lobby, a fellow desk clerk, coming briskly up the steps on his left, glanced at him casually. Miskin turned his head to smile, but could barely move his lips, except for a smirk. He had never been so terrified in his life.

Only a few more feet now. That last door, the giant oak one, seemed like a million miles away. His trembling hand reached out, grasped the solid brass doorknob and clumsily turned it. A rush of chilly outside air immediately cooled his sweaty face. Thank God for the cool spring air of Washington. He closed the door, took one quick look up and down the street, then walked down the concrete steps and past several bushes that lined the walkway. He turned right at the gate, trying to ignore the two guards as best he could.

Twenty-third Street, otherwise known as Embassy Row, was busy with the usual twelve o'clock rush hour traffic. The sun shone brightly through the pollution. The temperature, Miskin determined, had to be in the forty-five-degree range. Under similar circumstances he would've slipped on his overcoat, but not now. The coat would make him much too warm, and he'd sweat all the more. Besides, it might have aroused suspicion if he went back for his coat when many of his fellow embassy workers had already left for lunch at the nearby restaurants on K Street without their coats. So why couldn't he?

As he walked, the events of the past few years whirled through his head. He was actually turning on his own country, the country he once loved; Mother Russia, the Union of Soviet Socialist Republics.

Alexander Miskin first arrived in America as a Russian embassy official during World War II, and his gentle love affair with the United States had commenced almost immediately. He quickly found that the United States was a country to be reckoned with. Its industrial output and ingenuity in the heat of wartime had proved this time and time again. But more importantly this country also contained a people of such fine generosity and moral standards; no stabbing in the back, from what he could see. Sure, every American was out to make a buck, who wasn't? But there was none of the tension of home, where you didn't know if your next-door neighbor was an NKVD agent or not.

Miskin had hidden his feelings for America when he returned to Russia in the fall of 1945 to work as a cipher clerk at Moscow Center, the Communist intelligence headquarters. He didn't even tell his wife his true thoughts of America. It was a good thing they didn't have any children. Children might have sensed the love of America in their father's eyes and have turned him in to the authorities.

Then came another Washington embassy post position in 1957. He would be a communications aid to the Russian Air Force attaché, a man who had been sent to this position from his lofty post as chief of the Soviet Air Force, following a sex scandal with the daughter of a Politburo official.

Now, at the age of forty-seven, Miskin felt the physical and mental strain of Communism. In the past, a number of comrades couldn't take the pressure anymore, always being watched and no matter what they did for their superiors it never seemed to be good enough. Losing face, it was called. Some just cracked up, no more guts for the World Socialist movement. When this occurred, it was the end of the line; get out or get snuffed out. Miskin wanted to get even with the mean, degrading Russian political system that for years had been working towards an eventual takeover of the entire planet.

The majority of Western democracies believed that the Russians' ultimate goal was world Communism. The Russians implied they only wanted some breathing space following World War II, to push out from their own borders. If they were ever attacked again, the enemy would have a long way to march to Russian territory. Russian officials learned a hard lesson from World War II. In the latter part of 1939 Hitler took Poland without much of a fight. After that minor skirmish, he was that much closer to Russia, right next to them in fact. Then in June 1941 Hitler hit the Russians with everything he had. The German offensive wasn't finally halted until just outside Moscow. The Russian winter set in, and the ill-prepared German Army was doomed. It took four years to push the Germans off Russian soil.

Twenty million Russians died during the war. Russian dictator Joseph Stalin swore his country would never be caught off guard again. Therefore, as his Red Army pushed the German invaders west, Stalin seized the countries that his army liberated from Nazi aggression and quickly set up satellite nations, all answering to Moscow. These countries were Stalin's buffer zone.

Miskin, too, had believed that all his country wanted was breathing space. But that all changed two weeks ago when he had discovered, strictly by accident, a set of telexes in the embassy files. To his horror, Miskin learned through the embassy grapevine that the Russians were mass-producing a long-range fighter-bomber of extraordinary speed and armament capabilities, and that Moscow was putting on a push to get several hundred finished within the next twelve months. Were they planning to use them to attack some poor unsuspecting spot on the globe? Why the rush in production? This was the last straw as far as Miskin was concerned. The Soviet Union, he determined, had really turned on him, not the other way around. Miskin had quickly made arrangements to contact American intelligence sources with the startling information. The second meeting was about to take place, and Miskin would hand over photos and specs of this remarkable fighter.

Miskin had walked several hundred feet when he stopped suddenly in the midst of a crowd of window-shoppers. Then he quickly stepped into the walkway between two stores.

He waited, carefully eying the passersby. Convinced that he recognized no one from the embassy, he darted out from his hiding place and set out walking once again in the same direction as before. After five minutes Miskin stopped at a red traffic light. As he waited impatiently for the light to change, he spotted his contact's car in the alleyway to his right; it was a dark green, almost black, 1958 Cadillac with tinted windows and license plate W-164. Miskin's short, stocky legs wanted to make a run for it, but his busy mind telegraphed to his limbs to tread easy. The light changed and the car moved up the alley. Miskin followed.

Even before Miskin got alongside the Cadillac, the back passenger door silently swung open. He quickly climbed inside the vehicle and closed out the world with a hard thud.

Behind the wheel was a young man of about twenty-five, smart-looking in a light brown business suit. He glanced once at Miskin, then looked straight ahead toward the dead end of the alley. In the backseat, across from Miskin, sat an American intelligence agent the

Russian knew only by the code name of Magna-One. The man, in his late thirties, wore a dark green suit with a flowery tie that Miskin thought looked ridiculous. His neck was long and his skin was a red tone that nearly matched the color of his straight, greased-back hair.

Magna-One stared hard at the thin-lipped, round-faced, blue-eyed Russian, the man known in intelligence circles as the statistical genius of the Russian embassy.

"Were you followed?" Magna-One demanded.

"No," Miskin answered.

Although only five-foot-six Miskin did not feel intimidated in the presence of the six-foot agent, who at times in the past had tried to bully his associates. The American had quickly realized, after their first meeting two weeks ago, that the Russian was no easy mark.

"Good. What did you find out since our last meeting?" His voice was terse, articulate, his forehead wrinkled in concentration.

"I have the papers." Miskin took the crumpled telex messages from beneath his shirt. "I could only snatch them and run. They're in code of course, but I know what they say because I've studied them. I have copies of photos too. I know I shouldn't have . . ."

"Never mind that," the American said. "Let's have them." He paused. "Please."

"My country," Miskin started to speak while handing the agent the papers. He stopped to clear his throat. Sometimes his voice soared too high when he was edgy. "My country is going full-steam in building the long-range MiG-K Skyjacker fighter. The telexes reveal that," Miskin blurted, trying to keep his voice low. The American continued to stare at the papers, which would have to be decoded by American intelligence before they made proper sense, for they contained a series of

confusing numbers and letters. The photos caught his
fancy.

"What about these photos? Are they for real?"

"They are."

The American slowly crumpled the top telex sheet
with his fist. He stared hard out the windshield of the
Cadillac. He did not particularly like the short, nervous
Russian, but he needed him.

"Moscow has been putting on the pressure to build
at least three hundred by next summer," Miskin continued.

"Three hundred?" At first Magna-One couldn't believe it. "Do you think they can do it?"

Miskin frowned. "Maybe. Thousands are working
on the project. But they're encountering problems,
slowdowns. It's such a sophisticated aircraft, they need
to take their time on the new airborne radar and fire-
control system."

"Where's it being built?" the agent asked.

"Inside eastern Siberia, approximately five hundred
miles west of Sapporo, Japan."

The agent's first thought was a Russian attack on Japan.

"Look," Miskin pleaded, "feeding you with information is very risky. I've been gone too long already.
Do what you wish with the information. If anything else
comes up, I will be in touch."

The American nodded. "Are these the only copies?"

"No. They're a duplicate set that I made and stuffed
away."

Miskin felt relieved as soon as he moved his right
arm onto the door handle. "I must go. I'm supposed to
be out for lunch. After an hour someone might come
looking for me. Good-bye." Miskin stared into the
American's icy eyes.

The agent looked ahead, through the windshield, then

turned to the Russian. He held out his hand. "Thanks. Thanks for everything."

Miskin closed the door to the car. The ordeal was over. Could it really be true that the Russians were mass-producing such a fighter? Would Magna-One really report this latest intelligence information to his superiors, and would it end up in the hands of the president? What if the president didn't believe the story? What then? He might think it was all a hoax.

It was drizzling now, so Miskin decided to walk farther up the alley, another hundred feet or so, to the back of the Flamingo, a restaurant that served fresh vegetables, homemade pies and pastries for the bargain hunter. The waitresses knew him there, and he'd get fast service. He'd grab a quick corned beef sandwich, their specialty, and still be back at the embassy on time. Miskin took one look behind him and saw that the Caddy was still there. He walked through the steady, light rain towards the Flamingo.

# CHAPTER TWO

Ben spencer sat busily typing at his desk, oblivious to the noise around him in the newsroom. His recent European vacation had been a pleasant change of pace, but now he was back to the grind.

He recalled the tours of the sights of London and his visits to many World War II airfields in England that were now collecting weeds. Then his mind raced to Paris and the beautiful countryside of France. After a week in each of these two countries he moved on to Spain for three days and finally finished up in Germany. It was a few weeks off for him and his wife, Claire; a much-needed vacation. He had made sure he was back for the Arrow's maiden flight, which he had covered for his paper just two days earlier. Now he was moving on to other newsworthy matters.

Spencer was a nationalist; a firm believer in the Canadian democratic system, as well as a strong military presence against the Soviet threat. The thirty-four-year-old columnist had been deeply moved by his visit to Berlin, because to him it was the German capital that was the dividing line between East and West, Russia and the free world, right and wrong. To him things were only black or white, never gray.

Spencer stopped tapping the keys to loosen his tie and scratch his curly, red head, trying not to mess up his distinctive left-side part. He snatched the paper from the typewriter and leaned back into the hardwood swivel chair to scan the typed sheet. His face, pitted from acne in his teens, glistened with sweat. He grabbed a handkerchief from his trouser pocket and wiped his face.

In the last ten years Spencer's weight had ballooned steadily. Now well over two hundred pounds, he finally admitted he had a problem on his hands, a point his observant wife had been after him about for several years.

Following World War II, while employed in Vancouver by the *Vancouver Daily News*, Spencer had worked out daily. He lifted weights, jogged, played hockey in the winter and baseball in the summer. The exercise was an enormous release from the hectic pace of journalism. Claire, whom he met in 1946 in the accounting department of the newspaper, fell for the man of her dreams, tall and muscular. They were married two years later. Soon after their marriage, Spencer began to devote more and more time to freelance writing. His three favorite subjects were World War II, the military, and international politics. The extra money from these ventures came in handy, but his workout days fell to three times a week, to two, to one, then to none. Claire, who returned easily to her youthful slimness after the birth of their two children, tried unsuccessfully to get her husband back on track. Nothing worked until, a month ago, Spencer's doctor told him to lose forty pounds, or else! The doctor had worked out a diet and exercise program and it was beginning to work. In the last three weeks Spencer had lost ten pounds and was trying to quit smoking.

Probably the best-known reporter in Toronto, perhaps even in Canada, Spencer made his reputation during his years as a war correspondent for the *Daily News*. He had arrived in England in May, 1944, just a month before D-Day. In the following months, he thoroughly covered the Allied assault of Fortress Europe. The Pacific war was just starting to heat up at that time and in 1945 he arranged to fly on an American B-29 Superfortress bomber raid on Japan. The B-29 bomber was the most advanced aircraft of the war. His firsthand report from this raid made him an instant celebrity in the newspaper field. He followed the article with some superb on-the-spot reporting during the 1948 Berlin Air Lift and the Korean War in the 1950s, both for the *Daily News*.

In 1954 the *Daily News* experienced labor problems. The unions servicing the paper had started demanding higher wages. After two severe strikes the paper decided that it had no choice but to jack up the advertising rates when the clients felt the rates were reaching unacceptable levels, and they pulled out and went to other papers; the *Daily News's* circulation decreased. The writing was on the wall and some reporters started looking for jobs elsewhere before the roof caved in for good. The other two Vancouver dailies offered Spencer a job, but when the *Toronto Tribune* approached him with an excellent offer, he grabbed it. Spencer was born and raised in interior British Columbia and had spent ten years with the Vancouver paper. He wanted a change. Claire, a west coaster from Victoria, at first didn't want to go east, but quickly relented when she heard that the *Trib-*

*une* offer was nearly double what her husband had been making at the *Daily News*.

The four years in Toronto had been good for the Spencers. They settled into a large two-story home in the suburb of Mississauga, just west of Toronto. The twins, Brent and Albert, were now nine.

Spencer made three typing corrections, then looked over at the small, black-and-white photograph on his desk. It was a picture of himself with the Superfortress bomber crew aboard a U.S. Navy submarine in 1945. This famous wartime picture had been printed in many newspapers and magazines across Canada. Spencer had often wondered where the crew was now, for he had not kept in touch with them since the raid. He knew only that the commander of the B-29, Edmund Schult, was now the new supreme commander of North American Air Defense.

Spencer read the article in his typewriter one more time.

*CURRENTLY SPEAKING* with Ben Spencer

*On my recent visit to Berlin I've witnessed how Berliners have "escaped with their feet." They are fleeing like scared mice to the free confines of West Berlin.*

*The Russian sector, known as East Berlin, is losing as many as 1,000 people per day. I spoke to some of the escapees; factory workers, doctors, teachers, women and children. Already over 4,000 doctors have left since 1945, leaving behind only 90 doctors per 100,000 population. Even many members of the Vopos, or "Peoples' Police" have made the leap to freedom.*

*To Berliners, the Russians are a hated regime. Following the cease-fire in Europe in the spring of 1945, the Russians held the gutted, war-ravaged city for al-*

most ten weeks until the other Allied armies officially moved in. During that time the Russians looted the city of the little it had left and shipped everything back east. They took the entire Berlin telephone exchange, a complete power station, machinery in manufacturing plants, as well as every piece of indoor plumbing they could get their hands on. They even had the audacity to loot hospitals and nursing homes of all their medical supplies. Berliners suffered terribly through the Allied bombing raids, and now were left with virtually nothing!

A new Berlin rose from the heaps of rubble.

A modern city of nearly two million and increasing substantially every day (at the Russians' expense), West Berlin is a bustling showplace of ingenuity that shows few clear signs of war damage. The one exception is the Kaiser Wilhelm Memorial Church, which has been preserved as a reminder of the war. Throughout the city, wide new boulevards, towering skyscrapers and endless parks dot the landscape.

The West Berlin economy is on an upward spiral. It has created 360,000 new jobs in a decade, with many of these new positions directed at the manufacturing of electrical parts, a thriving business in West Berlin. And let's not forget why they have such a sound economy: the almighty Yankee dollar! I'm sure all West Berliners will be forever grateful to the Americans for engineering the Berlin Air Lift, a daring and remarkable feat of strength. Berliners are reaping the benefits today.

Communications in the Western sector include a TV station, two radio stations, and several newspapers. One radio station, in fact, directs most of its signals to the East. The Communists have retaliated by urging their people not to listen to or watch any Western *broadcasts for fear of poisoning their minds with Western Capitalism.*

*The Russian sector is a stark contrast to the West. Many buildings are still gutted from the war, there is rubble in empty lots, the "best" hotels are in shabby condition, and the streets are almost deserted, except for the Vopos who roam the thirty-mile-long East-West border. East Berliners, however, still manage to escape, leaving behind a further depressed Russian sector.*

*In time East Berlin will be totally deserted.*

"Looks good to me," whispered Spencer to himself. He quickly made his way through the large, busy room to the closed-in office of the news editor, Sammy Hughes. He wasn't in so Spencer left the manuscript on his messy desk. He was looking forward to getting home today. There was a hot shower, an early supper, and then the Stanley Cup playoffs on TV awaiting him. Spencer and his family were avid hockey fans.

Spencer lumbered over to the coatrack by the entrance to the newsroom. He lit a cigarette and was about to put on his coat, when Sammy Hughes walked in.

The news editor was smiling. A good omen, Spencer thought. Usually by this time of day he was in a bad mood; sometimes downright miserable.

"Sammy," Spencer said, puffing on his cigarette, "I left the new column in your office. You should be able to find it easily because it's right on top of that filthy, disgusting mess you have on your desk."

"Okay, you smart jerk. Hey, I thought you quit smoking?" His voice was squeaky, bird-like. His nickname around the office was "budgy," but only behind his back.

The reporter laughed. "I know, but it's too hard. I'm trying to cut down before I finally quit."

Hughes frowned. The news editor was not a handsome man, for he had a long hawk-like nose and a set of bushy, dark eyebrows that met in the middle. But he was slim, in good physical condition, and an avid tennis player. At fifty years of age, he could run circles around all the youngsters in the newsroom. "Yeah, sure, that's what they all say. Hey, you did a super job on the Arrow's maiden flight. Well done."

"Thanks, Sammy."

Hughes didn't often compliment a reporter directly, so Spencer knew Hughes must have been very pleased. "Hey, Sammy, tell me, who's going to win the hockey game tonight?"

"Montreal, who else?"

"Five bucks says Detroit does."

"You're on."

# CHAPTER THREE

IN THE OVAL OFFICE THE PRESIDENT OF THE United States was reading newspaper press clippings. It was an off day for world news events, except for a blockbuster in Canada. Only a few hours ago he'd received word that the Canadian prime minister had won the federal election with a solid majority. The news hit the Canadian people and him personally like a thunderclap. The prime minister was top billing.

Meanwhile, south of the border, the president's years in office were slipping by nearly unnoticed by the American and Canadian public. One Washington writer referred to the tall, slim, bald man as "the president no one really knows," which was an unfair assessment of the sixty-seven-year-old leader. The American public might not know him well, but other countries around the globe did. Just two weeks earlier, the Iraqi government of Nuri as Said was overthrown by an Egyptian-

43

backed coup supported by Gamal Abdel Nasser, who had been a two-year headache in the Middle East since the Suez Canal conflict in 1956. Since then, Nasser, in conjunction with his ally in Syria, was building up arms in an attempt to control the entire Mideast. When Iraq fell, Lebanon's president Chamoun asked the United States for immediate help. The same day the president received the request he issued orders to send four hundred planes, seventy ships and over fourteen thousand army and marine corps troops to the trouble spot. In addition, as a backup, marines stationed in Okinawa were transferred to the Persian Gulf, and an air force strike unit from Western Europe was transferred to Turkey. This entire lightning-fast orderly movement of U.S. armed forces was mobilized within one day and within a mere few hundred miles from Soviet borders!

North Koreans also found out what the current president was made of. When he was elected in 1953 in a landslide victory, the Korean War had been dragging on for three years, a matter that the president-elect found revolting. So, through underground channels he told the Russians, the Chinese and the North Koreans, plus all others fighting directly or indirectly against South Korea and the United Nations Allies, that he would have any enemy target bombed with any type of weapon he saw fit to use, including the atomic bomb. After that, negotiations moved along quickly until a truce was signed on July 27 of the same year.

When the president preferred not to take direct action himself, he went through the United Nations and advised other countries to do the same thing. During the Suez dispute of 1956, in particular, he called an emergency session of the General Assembly and within two days a cease-fire was called. By the end of the week, a U.N. force occupied the Gaza Strip. When the Soviet Union marched into Hungary in 1956, the president, through the United Nations, demanded the Soviets leave, but the USSR vetoed the bill.

In his own country the president was considered a weak politician. Some called him a Democratic Republican, but the opposite was a more apt description. The president started each day by arriving in the Oval Office by eight in the morning and worked straight through until late afternoon, the time of day where he actually accomplished more than in the morning. On rare occasions like today, he worked late at night.

He looked slim and fit, despite suffering a heart attack in late November 1957. Prior to his collapse he had planned to attend a December 13 NATO conference in Paris, France. His friends and doctors advised him not to go, but he went anyway. He spent six days delivering speeches and attending conferences. To the surprise of his associates he came back to Washington feeling better than he did before his heart attack.

The president was tired today, but pleased that he had accomplished a large amount of paperwork. He was going to turn in, much later than usual, after he absorbed Ben Spencer's *Toronto Tribune* column. The president admired this writer and read his articles thoroughly. He read the last three paragraphs of the column a second time.

*I believe the problems confronting this country are not going to go away overnight. My biggest concern is how the prime minister will treat the United States, our good neighbor to the south. He has said in the past that "we have the right to assert our rights and not have them determined by another country." Meaning the U.S., of course. Someone once accused the prime minister of being anti-American, but he insists he's pro-Canadian.*

*How can the U.S. be accused of determining our*

*rights? If it weren't for their military umbrella over us, where would we be now? Under the merciless, crunching fist of Communism for sure. Therefore Canada and the U.S. have to get together and support projects like ALCANUS, the DEW Line, NORAD, NATO and even the Arrow project, the latter being the only purely Canadian project of the group. It's quite a project, but we still need American support in defense matters. We can't do it alone.*

*The prime minister, now with his majority, is the key to good U.S.-Canadian relations. I have been accused in the past of having a one-track mind when it comes to defense, but as a European statesman once said, "Once a country cannot defend itself, it will soon cease to be a nation." History bears this out. Remember pre-1940 Europe! So I urge you, Mr. Prime Minister, to walk softly and carry a big stick. But please don't use it on the wrong people. Don't bite the hand that feeds you.*

The president smiled when he read the last paragraph. The prime minister has a majority now, he thought to himself, but for how long? Then the American leader's mind raced back to the Arrow. He'd been thinking about it all day, couldn't get it out of his mind. He breathed out heavily, easing back in his chair.

OTTAWA, ONTARIO, FRIDAY, MAY 23
1540 HOURS (EST)

The prime minister and his finance minister, Alex Kralick, were in the prime minister's office discussing the mounting financial woes of the Canadian economy. Everything seemed to be resting on the P.M.'s shoulders since his Conservative party had been elected to power with the greatest majority ever recorded in Canadian federal politics. But the honeymoon was over. Now it was down to the business of running a country that was growing more and more financially unstable.

Today, the tall Tory leader wore a newly-tailored, black, pin-striped suit with a white monogrammed shirt and red tie. He slouched behind his desk, peering through various financial reports. Seated to his left was Kralick in his shirtsleeves, his sports jacket resting on the arm of his chair.

"Alex, you realize of course that it doesn't look good for the economy right now."

Kralick took a sip of some strong coffee. "I know," he replied in his deep, clear voice. He nervously scratched his right temple. His hair was a strong black, with some gray around the temples and the back of his neck.

Before he could respond further, the prime minister cut in. "We've got to cut back in spending. Business is slumping. Car sales are down here and in the States. Construction of new homes is at a standstill. Interest rates are starting to climb. Our dollar is dropping. What did the Liberals leave us?"

"A bloody mess, that's what." Kralick tried again to squeeze a word in edgewise. As the youngest member of the Conservative cabinet, he hadn't established his presence yet. The prime minister nodded without looking up from his desk.

"We've got to cut back on hiring for any new federal government jobs, at least for the time being." After a few moments of staring hard at the ceiling, the leader picked up a manila file that had been placed on his desk earlier by a member of his inner staff. In the top right-hand corner in red letters were the words DEFENSE REPORT. He opened the file and skimmed through the pages inside. "Even the defense budget is getting out of line. I realize we have to defend ourselves, but at what cost? ALCANUS. Look at ALCANUS,'' said the prime minister, pointing to one of the pages. ''This Alaska-Canada-U.S. defense system is costing us nearly double what it was two years ago under the Liberals.''

''But sir,'' argued Kralick, finally able to speak, ''that's an important joint Canada-U.S. project. In fact, the States are paying for most of it. We need to protect our North. The Russians are a feasible threat to us over the Pole. They have bombers that can carry nuclear bombs at over five hundred miles per hour, at an altitude of more than forty thousand feet. And they're getting better equipped all the time. Sir, I read the report too. I don't pretend to be an expert on defense business, but if you ask me, what we can do without is—''

''Okay, let's skip defense for now,'' interrupted the prime minister as he glanced at his watch. The leader grabbed another file on his desk and opened it. When would it end? thought Kralick. How many files does he have? ''According to recent employment figures, there are 386,000 people out of work and that number is climbing. I'm sure it's not going to get any better, especially with the recession in the States. We're tied too closely to them. They take sixty percent of our exports. You know, I was reading in an auto magazine just yesterday that the Edsel, that car that Ford sunk all kinds of promotion money into, is a complete disaster. Nobody's buying the car, and one of the reasons has to be the recession. The public is not buying that car or any other new car when it comes right down to it. And when people don't buy cars it seems every other business is affected, either directly or indirectly.''

Kralick knew that his superior was, for some reason, avoiding the discussion of a certain federal government defense project that was on both their minds: the Arrow. For the time being the finance minister thought he might as well go along with the P.M. ''My brother-in-law bought an Edsel and he said it was the worst mistake of his life. He said the gas mileage is horrible. He's afraid to drive it around the block. And that toilet bowl grill is a scream.''

''Yeah, it is kind of ugly, isn't it?'' They both laughed. ''The Liberals knew the whole time about this mess and left us to hold the bag. They weren't so dumb losing the election. They got out at the right time.'' Then the leader leaned forward in his chair and picked up a pencil. He tapped it hard against the desktop several times. ''Well, Alex,'' he continued, ''What can we do to stop this horrendous slide?''

Kralick didn't like this kind of talk, as if the entire national debt was being passed onto his shoulders. However, he did have the ammo to fight with. ''We've already cut the excise tax on cars from ten percent down to seven and one-half. We've slashed personal income tax, as well as corporate taxes to small businessmen. We're looking at old age pensions now, pensions for war vets, the blind and the disabled. We'll increase the salaries of civil servants, the RCMP and the armed services.''

''It's a merry-go-round,'' grumbled the prime minister. ''These moves should encourage Canadians to spend their money and keep others employed. But you never know about Canadians. After the Great Depression, they prefer to hoard their money in savings accounts. Now, what about our record deficit in the trade world, especially to the United States? The cost of living is too high and our deficit is closely related to it. What if we lower interest rates?''

''We can, but if—''

Then there was a knock at the door.

''Oh, by the way, Alex, I've asked Dean Stedman to join us. There's a situation to discuss that involves both your departments. That's probably him right now. Yes!''

The prime minister's personal secretary announced

the arrival of the minister of defense. "Mr. Stedman is here."

"Send him in."

Since the Progressive Conservative party first came to power with a minority government in March 1957, Alex Kralick and Dean Stedman had been at odds with each other.

Though they disliked each other on a personal level, they managed to respect each other's working principles. But when it came to vital issues, such as the Arrow, that fine line of respect vanished. Although Kralick believed in the defense of the North and the ALCANUS plan, he did not feel that the Arrow project deserved all the attention it was getting. Financially, it was killing his budget. He knew better ways to spend these millions of dollars, ways that would stimulate the lagging economy.

The ministers came from totally different backgrounds. Kralick, a lawyer by profession, had been brought up in a well-to-do English-speaking section of Montreal, the third of four brothers in a Ukrainian family. He went to the "right" schools and associated with the "right" people. When World War II broke out, although he was of age to join up for active service, Kralick seemed to disappear. One story was that he was dodging overseas duty in the armed forces with the help of some of his father's political connections in Ottawa. In actual fact, he was employed in Canadian intelligence work in conjunction with Britain and the United States. Very few people knew what he really did during the war and he wanted it kept that way. Many of his missions were still classified. After the war he returned to Montreal and McGill University. In 1950 he joined an established Montreal-based law practice, then entered federal politics three years later as a Conservative representative in a Montreal riding.

Stedman, on the other hand, came from a family of

Alberta farmers near the town of Lloydminster, who had faced the Great Depression stubbornly, refusing to give up despite the hardships. When other prairie families in the vicinity moved out to escape the grasshoppers, dust and scorching heat, the Stedman family stayed and slugged it out. All the Stedman brothers and sisters, six boys and four girls, attended high school, quite an accomplishment on the isolated farm where extra money was in short supply. Dean went one step further and attended the University of Saskatchewan, but dropped out after one year due to lack of funds. The war had already been going strong for two years, so Stedman signed up with the Royal Canadian Air Force. After extensive training in Canada under the British Commonwealth Air Training Plan he was sent overseas. He flew twenty-four trips as a bomber pilot on Avro Lancasters. He was shot down over Germany and finished the war as a prisoner of war.

Stedman remained in the RCAF until 1954 and witnessed firsthand the coming of Canada's jet age: Canadian-built, Canadian-flown fighter aircraft. First the CF-100, Canada's first subsonic fighter aircraft, and now, the Arrow. He hadn't seen the air force this excited in years. The Arrow was something he believed in and defended at all costs, a matter that his constituents in Calgary supported him on. One of the Arrow's fiercest opponents, however, was Alex Kralick.

"Good afternoon, Mr. Prime Minister," said Stedman, as he entered the office. He held out his hand and the Tory leader shook it vigorously, almost to the point of embarrassment to Stedman.

Once the prime minister sat down, the defense minister turned to Kralick. "Good afternoon, Alex," he said, trying to be cordial to his archrival in the cabinet.

"Good afternoon," answered Kralick, extending his hand. They shook hands lightly.

Stedman took a seat facing the prime minister. He dug into his sports coat for his glasses. "Well, Mr. Prime Minister, what did you want to see me about?" Stedman gently placed the glasses on the bridge of his nose.

"I have a copy of your defense report here."

"I think I know what we're going to talk about." Stedman fussed a little in his chair before getting comfortable. He wanted to be ready for what was coming. He even undid his tie.

"To put it bluntly, Dean, we've got to cut back on our defense spending and I, we, in the party need your support."

Stedman flashed a set of cold, gray eyes at his superior, then at Kralick on his right. "It depends where you, or we, will have to cut back."

"The Arrow," the prime minister grunted.

"Let's not go through that again, sir. I realize it's over budget," protested Stedman, "but what can we do? We need it."

"We can do without it," snapped Kralick.

Stedman's could feel his blood boiling. "What do you know about defense, you—you draft dodger!"

"Okay, you two, knock it off," the prime minister intervened. "Take it easy."

Stedman had a short temper and often spoke carelessly or abruptly before properly gathering his thoughts. He had no patience with politicians and media personnel who were so-called military experts. These people did not think like military men, did not understand the defense needs of the future. As Stedman saw it, very few politicians could look beyond today. They couldn't comprehend that the Arrow was being built for the future, that money needed to be spent today so that Canada would be strong tomorrow. These men, men like Kralick, thought only of the enormous cost of the Arrow now.

The prime minister sighed. "Dean, I told you back in August last year that the Arrow would be under review by a government committee. Up to now, it's cost the taxpayers close to $400 million. That's nearly $300 million more than first projected. The army and navy are breathing down my neck. They're all wondering why the RCAF funding is almost fifty percent of the total defense budget."

"How did they ever find out it's fifty percent, if that is the right figure? I doubt that it is."

"It *is* nearly fifty percent," said Kralick.

The defense minister eyed the prime minister and shrugged. "Of course the arrow is over budget, how many government projects aren't nowadays?"

The finance minister folded his arms. "But nothing like this."

Stedman turned to his right. "It was the Liberal government that presented the original cost of $100 million and it was unrealistic. Mr. Prime Minister," he continued, shifting his body to the left, "we need the Arrow. This aircraft is shaping up to be the greatest fighter in history. More testing at Malton will prove my point ten times over. The Arrow is made by us, for us, made for our winters here in Canada. We didn't have to depend on anyone when we built the CF-100s, did we? They were built in Canada. But now they're outdated. The Arrow is twice the fighter and more. Believe me, both of you will find that out. Once the NATO countries find out what a great machine it is, they'll come knocking at our doors to buy the Arrow or the Iroquois engine, or both."

The prime minister gritted his teeth. "I disagree, Dean. There's a good chance we might have to scrap the whole project."

Stedman couldn't believe what he was hearing. "What! You're joking!"

"No, I'm not."

"It's being tested right now. If you scrap it, everything goes down the drain. What will we have to show for that $400 million? And look at all those jobs. There are fifteen thousand people at Orenda and Avro combined, and don't forget all those subcontractors who employ another fifteen thousand bodies. That's thirty thousand people, most of them skilled Canadian aeronautical technicians who will be out of work. You and Alex talk about cutting costs, but what's all that unemployment going to do for the Canadian economy? What are these people going to do? They'll eventually leave the country, that's what, and take all that technology with them, probably to the United States. What about votes, Mr. Prime Minister? You'll be finished in Ontario. All the families and friends of those workers wouldn't waste a ballot voting for you. They'll vote Liberal, sure as hell. Then look at the total picture. Who on earth will vote for a government that does away with a fighter aircraft that's going to break the speed record? According to A. V. Roe, the Arrow will easily exceed Mach two-point-five once it receives the Iroquois engines."

The mention of votes made the prime minister hesitate. As Stedman implied, he had to think of the future. "But it has limited range," he muttered, backing off slightly from his earlier stand.

"What limited range? A five-hundred-mile radius under normal conditions. Nothing wrong with that. Look, sir, if we go ahead with mass-producing the Arrow in Malton, we won't ever have to buy another fighter aircraft from the Americans. We'd be building our own for our own use, for our own needs. Tailor-made, you might say."

"Dean," Kralick muttered, "there's plenty of good aircraft built in the States and we won't have to spend millions in development and production costs. There's the F-104 . . ."

"Forget the Starfighter. It might be fast, but it's too

dangerous to fly. No wings. Besides, since when are you a defense specialist, Alex?''

Kralick stared hard at Stedman. ''Since when are you financial expert? We still have CF-100s, Sabres and . . .''

Stedman rolled his eyes. ''Look, the CF-100 was obsolete when it first came off the assembly line. As for the Sabre, it was a super fighter during the Korean War, but not now.''

The prime minister got back into the discussion. ''The Americans will have Voodoos available and we might eventually purchase those for our fighter units.''

''Don't do it. They're not as good as the Arrow.''

The prime minister looked down at the defense papers spread out on his desk. ''We'll have to make a decision soon. The army and navy people are after me, and they won't quit. They think they're being cheated, and maybe they are. There aren't many defense dollars left for them. What am I supposed to tell them?''

''Leave that to me. I'm supposed to be the minister of defense,'' Stedman answered, grinning. ''Our biggest threat right now is an enemy air strike, not a naval or land assault. The other branches of the service will have to understand that. I've already spoken to them about this issue. They've been down my neck too. Vice-admiral Kelly lets me have it real good every couple of weeks just so I won't forget him or the navy! He thinks the Arrow is overrated, but it's not. Look at how versatile it is!

''Its weapon bay can carry air-to-air missiles plus rockets. Or it can carry four 20mm cannons, two hundred rounds each. Or it can be a fighter-bomber when it's loaded up with four thousand-pound bombs. It can carry a camera pack and become a photo-reconner. It can take more fuel in the same bay and then become a long-range interceptor. There's the range you were talking about. Avro is even working on an operational trainer version that will carry a second pilot.''

When it came to military aircraft specifications, Stedman knew that Kralick and the prime minister could not really muster a proper rebuttal in their defense. Now Stedman went for the jugular. ''You think you have a lot of people breathing down your neck now; if you go ahead and scrap the Arrow, you're in for lots more trouble. The members of the Chiefs of Staff Committee are all for the Arrow project, except, of course, for Kelly. But what do you expect from a member of the senior service?'' he said with a deliberate sneer. ''They never liked us flyboys anyway. Kelly doesn't know that Avro is working on zero launch tests for the Arrow. You know what that means? Carrier launches. That sure would interest the navy.

''The minister of defense production and his deputy are both for it. The Americans are enthusiastic about it, especially about the new Iroquois engine, idle to thrust in two-point-eight seconds. That's incredible!''

''Dean,'' the Tory leader said, ''many of us just don't believe the Soviet bomber threat is there anymore. And if it's not there, then we don't need the Arrow. This is the missile age. Manned interceptors are falling by the wayside. The electronics is too much for pilots these days. There's too much to do, too much to watch out for, too much to listen for in the cockpit. Pilots can't successfully fly anymore because there's too much else to do.''

Stedman tried to smile. ''I know what you're trying to say. They call it 'information overload.' But you have to remember that the Arrow will have a two-man crew, pilot and navigator. It's not a one-man fighter. Manned interceptors will be around for decades yet.''

''The world is moving too fast for you. This isn't World War II anymore,'' Kralick interjected.

Stedman shook his head. ''Here it comes,'' he said,

throwing up his arms, "the Bomarc missile, the Yankee reject. Don't even consider buying it. It's a dud."

"But according to defense information . . ."

"Whose defense information? Ours or the States? Did it ever occur to you why the Americans are so eager to rid themselves of the Bomarc? Because it doesn't work and they know it. They poured millions into the program and it doesn't perform. It can't hit the target. Now they're trying to recover the money they spent on it. The age of the manned interceptor is *not* dead. Look, every so often Russian bombers come through the Canadian North and deliberately cross our airspace. Do we fire a missile at every Russian bomber over our territory? We're constantly picking up unidentified aircraft on our radar screens. To find out what each blip is, whether it's friend or foe, we deploy fighter-interceptors to identify it. When you identify it, you take the necessary action. Now, if we end up having missiles to perform the job that interceptors once did, you mean to tell me that as soon as we sight an unidentified aircraft we fire a missile at it?" Stedman shook his head. "Of course not. It could be one of ours."

"I don't think it's going to be quite like that."

"Really? That's what you're proposing. If you take away interceptors, how will we get proper identifications?"

Kralick scratched his ear. "But we still have our CF-100s and, in a few years, Voodoos to do some manned interceptor work."

Stedman shrugged again. "I don't understand the government's thinking on this issue. You tell me that manned interceptors are outdated and that this is the missile age. Then you tell me we're going to purchase Voodoos and we're still going with Canucks. Your idea is a Band-Aid solution. In the long run the Arrow will cost less and be more effective."

The prime minister ran his hand across his forehead. "I just don't know how all this will come out in the committee meetings."

"Well," Stedman said, pulling his chair away and standing up, "I'll have to go. I have to prepare for my tour of air bases in Western Canada. The flight leaves early tomorrow. I suggest you take into consideration what I've said and do what you can to influence the committee. Don't let the cost blind you. We'll get it all back in the end."

"I'll think about it," replied the prime minister, obviously exhausted by the conversation. "Have a good trip, Dean."

"Thank you sir." Stedman walked out quickly, without shaking hands with either man.

Kralick's eyes met his superior's. "It sounds like he has you convinced."

The leader didn't answer at first. He trusted Stedman more than any other minister. Maybe it had something to do with the Western Canadian upbringing that he and Stedman had in common. Or maybe he respected his wartime record. Stedman still suffered shell shock, which would erupt occasionally in the form of an uncontrollable shake that would come and go. He had nightmares of still being held in a POW camp. To top it off, Stedman suffered from migraine headaches (at times they were so bad he was forced to leave the Parliament chamber), which doctors attributed to the back injury he had received when he parachuted out of his burning Lancaster bomber over Nazi Germany.

The prime minister looked down at his desk again. "Don't worry about it, Alex," he said, not bothering to lift his head.

# CHAPTER FOUR

THE PRESIDENT OCCUPIED HIMSELF STUDY-
ing a Senate committee report on constitutional amend-
ments while waiting for the Soviet ambassador. He was
twenty minutes late, but the president had expected that.
He swung his chair around to face the White House
grounds through the large windows. As he dropped his
head down to read more of the report, the intercom
buzzed.

"Yes."

"Mr. President, the Soviet ambassador is here to see
you."

"Send him in."

"Yes, sir."

The Russian smiled when he met the president at the
door. Georgi Chenkovsky was a stout man in his forties, almost six feet tall, with dark eyes and complex-
ion. He had three long scars on his broad face, lasting

59

evidence of his partisan days on the Russian Front during World War II. The most prominent scar was imbedded deep into his scalp and was easily seen through his thinning brown hair.

"Thank you for coming, Ambassador Chenkovsky."

The Russian smiled again and looked around the room. "So this is where the president of the United States conducts his business," he said in a gravelly voice. Although his accent was plainly Russian, his English was perfect.

"Come and sit down."

The president had positioned two chairs so that they faced each other on the same side of the desk.

"Mr. Ambassador," the president began, "we have evidence that your country is building new, highly sophisticated, supersonic fighter-bombers at an alarming rate. Is that true?"

The Russian was as cool as a riverboat gambler with a straight flush in his hands.

"No, it is not true."

The president picked up a large envelope that lay on his desk. Chenkovsky stirred in his chair as the American leader pulled out several typed sheets and sat down on the edge of the desk. "According to our overseas intelligence reports," he said, putting his glasses in place, "over two hundred of these aircraft have been built since the beginning of the year. Do you deny that too?"

"Yes. We have no such aircraft."

"Really," the president muttered. There was a pause in the conversation as he appeared to study the pages, flipping them back and forth. "This new aircraft, whose existence you so adamantly deny, is completely computerized. It's a long-range, two-seater fighter-bomber armed with electronic detection and warning equipment, and a weapons package that includes cannon, heat-seeking and/or radar-homing missiles, in addition to carrying up to twelve thousand pounds of bombs. Its maximum speed is reported to be nearly Mach 3. I'll even tell you the code name, if you like." Chenkovsky didn't say a word. "The MiG-K Skyjacker."

"Where did you get this information?"

"You know I can't tell you that. We protect our sources, just as do you."

Then the president pulled out four photographs from the envelope and handed them to the Russian. "Now do you still deny the existence of this aircraft?"

Chenkovsky was shocked to find before him glossy black-and-white photos of the Russian aerial weapon. One picture showed a side view of a MiG-K on a take-off roll, afterburners blazing, drop tanks in sight. Another was taken when the fighter was being refueled under floodlights, another was an aerial shot. The last was an extreme nose view that exposed the radar equipment and showed clearly the thin delta-winged construction; a missile under each wing, and two large intakes. The cat was out of the bag.

In preparation for the United States possibly uncovering the Skyjacker's existence, the Soviet ambassador had been thoroughly briefed by Moscow on what steps to take in rebuttal.

"Yes, it's true, Mr. President."

The president stood up and put his hands into his jacket pockets. He appeared relieved. "What do you plan to do with it?"

"What do you plan to do with all your fighter aircraft?"

"What's that supposed to mean?"

"You're building fighters to protect yourself. We have to protect ourselves."

"You're mass-producing the MiG-K. We're not building at that rate. What's the rush? Your Skyjacker is designed as a strike aircraft, not a defensive one. The U.S. Air Force arsenal doesn't have a fighter like that in production. And certainly not one that has to meet such priority production schedules as yours."

"We know that, but the Canadians have a fighter in production right now that is the talk of NATO."

"The Arrow?"

"Yes, the Arrow. It has strike capabilities, too. What do you plan to use it for?"

"It's a defensive fighter," the president replied brusquely.

Chenkovsky shook his head. "It's not that much different from the Skyjacker. And I hear that A. V. Roe is expecting big things from the new Iroquois engine to be installed in the fighter." He rubbed the back of his neck. "Moscow feels the Arrow is a threat to world peace."

"We feel the Skyjacker is a threat to world peace," the president responded promptly.

"What we have then is a stalemate. Moscow has instructed me to present a compromise to your government. In simple terms, you destroy the Arrow, we destroy the Skyjacker."

The president took his hands out of his pockets and walked behind his desk. "The Arrow is a Canadian aircraft. We don't have the authority to destroy it."

The Russian stood up. "Meet with the Canadians and discuss it. From what I've heard, through rumors and the Canadian newspapers, the Canadian government might be on the verge of scrapping it anyway. It's costing them too much. And your government isn't going to pick up the tab because you'll have too many American aircraft builders screaming foul. You might be able to help, how do you say it? Drive the final nail into the Arrow coffin."

"I'll talk to them, but I want your word on one thing."

"What's that?"

"Halt production of the MiG-K."

The ambassador looked amused. "Moscow anticipated your reaction. As you wish, you have my word. I'm sure your intelligence sources will keep tabs on our production anyway." Chenkovsky bowed his head, in a type of respectful salute. "Your sources are very good and very thorough."

"It might take a few weeks to see the Canadian delegation on this, to arrange everything."

"One month?"

"I'll try for a month," the president snapped. "I'll let you know. In the meantime, your production must be at a standstill."

"Agreed," confirmed the ambassador. "We'll shake on it."

# CHAPTER FIVE

THE CANADIAN PRIME MINISTER, DEAN Stedman and Air Marshall Hugh Phillips, the deputy commander of the North American Air Defense, were aboard the luxury-modified presidential DC-8. All had been invited, in complete secrecy, to a meeting in Washington. In addition, there were three Secret Service bodyguards that the president had insisted on having aboard the aircraft. The prime minister very seldom had bodyguards with him when he traveled in Canada, but this was the president's plane, so the president called the shots.

The prime minister noticed that Stedman, in the seat next to him on the starboard side of the aircraft, was dozing off, his head weaving from side to side.

"You're going to give yourself whiplash, Dean," the prime minister said, giving his minister a slight nudge in the ribs.

Stedman mumbled, "Yeah, I guess so." Then he curled up against the window and fell asleep again.

On the ground the president greeted his visitors warmly. "Mr. Prime Minister," he said, "it's good to see you again. Thanks for coming on such short notice." They shook hands while standing under the port wing of the DC-8, shielded from prying eyes. There was no formal welcome and no press.

The two leaders were in high spirits after their last meeting in Ottawa only two months earlier. Their encounter had been a resounding success, as the men communicated with each other very well. The president knew Canadians and understood them better than any previous president had. As Supreme Commander of the Allied Forces in Europe during World War II, he had seen firsthand what Canadians were like. He respected their bravery, their loyalty to their country, and their broad knowledge of other countries, including the United States.

"Mr. Stedman, Air Marshall Phillips, welcome to Washington. I hope you enjoy your stay. I'm sorry I didn't get a chance to meet you when I was in Ottawa, Mr. Stedman. I heard you were in Europe on NATO business."

"Yes sir, that's right." Stedman shook the president's outstretched hand.

"We have some important business to discuss, but let's have dinner first. Come, I have my cars waiting." Although the limos were in plain view, the president pointed to four shiny black 1958 Lincolns on the airport tarmac. "Mr. Prime Minister, you and I will go in the first car, Air Marshall Phillips and Mr. Stedman will follow in the second, and the rest of the party can bring up the rear."

As the group were led to the cars, the prime minister couldn't help but notice all the Secret Service men surrounding the president, a good half-dozen. Far more security, he thought, than was really needed; certainly more than what he was used to in Canada. When the entire group had covered the short distance to the cars, the engines were fired up, and a convoy was formed.

The windows were up and the air-conditioning was on full, for it was a warm, humid day in the U.S. capital. The prime minister looked briefly behind him to see the trail of cars. "Just extra security," the president said to his guest. "So, how are things in Canada? How is the Arrow coming along?"

"I'd rather not say here." The prime minister seemed startled by the president's blunt question and he eyed the two Secret Service men in the front seat.

"Yes, of course. I hope you and your aides are hungry because we have a splendid dinner waiting for us. Later on in the afternoon we can get down to business. I'm sorry the wives couldn't get together again."

"Yes, my wife was disappointed that she couldn't make this trip. She's in western Canada visiting her relatives."

The leaders relaxed as they watched the Washington traffic flow into the airport in a steady stream while they were whisked through traffic in the opposite direction.

The White House, the home of the president of the United States, is situated at 1600 Pennsylvania Avenue in Washington, D.C. It covers an eighteen-acre plot, and could almost be classified as one of the wonders of the world. The beautiful South Lawn, often called the President's Park, contains many shrubs and trees planted by former presidents. One corner, in fact, has a gorgeous magnolia tree planted by Andrew Jackson.

The West Wing of the building contains the Cabinet Room and the offices of the president and his staff. The offices of the social secretary and the president's military aides are situated in the East Wing.

Near the center portion of the immense mansion, just west of the South Portico, on the first floor, stands the State Dining Room. Under special circumstances the room could accommodate nearly 150 people for dinner; but today, there were only the president and five guests. The high-ceilinged room, with its long table and numerous chairs, overwhelmed the six important government officials.

In addition to the president, the prime minister, Phillips and Stedman, two more men arrived soon after the convoy of limos pulled up from the airport. They were the American secretary of defense, Jeffrey Kolb, and the newly appointed supreme commander of NORAD, General Edmund Schult, who had already started to work closely with Air Marshall Phillips in conjunction with the aerial defense of the North American continent.

During the dinner Schult, Phillips and Stedman, all World War II air veterans, chatted easily, obviously enjoying each other's company. Schult and Stedman, former bomber pilots, seemed to have a particularly close rapport.

The forty-three-year-old Schult had ascended the military ladder in a very short time. He was genuine officer material, a natural leader. He had seen many changes in the air force since first joining up in early 1941. At that time the service was called the United States Army Air Corps, and was under the jurisdiction of the army. In May of that year the organization had formally changed its name to the United States Army Air Force. It was in this outfit that Schult completed his required thirty-five bomber missions aboard the famed B-29 Superfortress. In 1947 he saw the air force become its own separate and powerful entity, the United States Air Force. By the time of the Korean War in 1950, Schult was a lieutenant colonel, by war's end he jumped to brigadier general and was helping to plot bombing strategy against the North Koreans. He saw more combat action as commanding officer of a B-29 bomber squadron. Within eight years Schult had moved all the way up to a four-star general and was now the newly appointed supreme commander of the North American Air Defense, or simply NORAD.

Schult hadn't put on a pound in over ten years. He looked fit and youthful in his uniform, though his dark brown hair was starting to gray a bit. His high cheekbones and protruding chin were still as prominent as ever.

He was known to be stern but fair in dealing with subordinates. With friends he was self-effacing and cheery, often funny, a good storyteller. Today, Phillips and Stedman listened intently as Schult told them about the Tokyo mission in which he was shot down.

Phillips laughed out loud when Schult recited some of the comedies of errors that occurred when the B-29 crew were scrambling to get aboard the United States air-sea rescue submarine. Some men fell back into the sea and one of the gunners nearly drowned because the crew thought his cries for help were his versions of bawdy songs. Phillips especially enjoyed Schult's story of the radio operator, Owrie Bradley, who, on orders from Schult, stopped shaving twenty-four hours prior to every takeoff. During the first fifteen missions, whenever he did shave, the crew usually experienced a horrendous trip; when he didn't, it was a breeze. Bradley was clean-shaven for the trip on which they were shot down and just before they bailed out, Schult gave Bradley royal hell over the intercom. Phillips was a big man with a big belly, and when he laughed, he really enjoyed himself.

Kolb was in his fifties, a big man who often appeared overpowering because he liked to wear a black, pinstriped suit on his massive six-foot-three frame. His eyes were alert and piercing; gray, cold as ice.

The six government officials sat in elegant Queen

Anne–style chairs that had originally been ordered for the room in a 1902 renovation during the Teddy Roosevelt administration. The large chandelier glittering majestically above their heads and the three consoles were also part of the renovation. Above the white marble mantelpiece hung a portrait of Abraham Lincoln that had been painted by G. P. A. Healy in 1869. In this historical room the men ate a roast beef dinner so delicately prepared by the White House staff that the meat melted in the their mouths. The vegetables were slightly overdone, but the rich cheesecake was divine.

After lunch, the president showed his guests around the top floor of the house. By late afternoon they were all seated around the giant, highly polished mahogany table in the Treaty Room. Three American security agents were stationed outside the door.

The Treaty Room had formerly been the president's Cabinet Room until the major renovations of 1902, when it was transformed into a sitting area. Now it was a meeting room. The Victorian-style chamber included wallpaper that resembled the green velvet that had been noted in the room President Lincoln had been taken to following the Ford Theater assassination. Along with some of the original furniture that had been retained, it held the original table, swivel chair, sofa and clock from the Johnson era. A large painting depicting the the Civil War reception that Lincoln held for General Ulysses Grant hung above the mantle clock. Several rococo revival wine-red velvet armchairs were in the corners of the room, all facing towards the cabinet table.

The president sat at the head of the table, the furthest point from the door. To his right were Jeffrey Kolb and General Schult; to his left, the Canadian prime minister, Dean Stedman, and Air Marshall Phillips. "Gentlemen," the president rose from his chair, "I have called this meeting to discuss some very important defense matters which concern not only the United States of America, but also the Dominion of Canada.'' The president paused to further gather his thoughts. "Gentlemen, I won't beat around the bush, I'll give you all the facts straight. My government has obtained classified information regarding a fighter-bomber that the Soviet Union has been mass-producing for the past several months. It is known as the MiG-K, code-named the Skyjacker. We believe the Russians plan to use it in the near future, in an unprovoked strike. Where? We don't know yet.'' The president surveyed the faces around the table, then swallowed half the glass of water set before him.

Jeffrey Kolb opened his briefcase and pulled out a manila folder full of typed copy that he passed to the president. Everything related to the MiG-K had been typed on a series of eight-and-a-half-by-eleven sheets of paper. The president pulled out the sheets and set them down on the tabletop, while he took his reading glasses from the breast pocket of his suit. He glanced again at the faces in the room, then started reading the main points of the report.

"Gentlemen, the Russians have an all-weather, two-man fighter-bomber that can reach and exceed Mach two-point-five." The president flipped his glasses down to rest on the bridge of his nose. "Also," he said, speaking a little louder than before, "the surface ceiling is sixty-five thousand feet. Range: one thousand miles under normal circumstances, fifteen hundred with drop tanks. Engines: two Mikulin afterburning turbojets with twenty-two thousand pounds of base thrust each. The weapons package consists of six 20mm cannons in the nose, rockets, heat-seeking missiles, and carrying capacity up to twelve thousand pounds of bombs. In addition, it is armed with electronic detection and warning equipment."

Dropping the paper to the table, the president paused to let his news sink in. The silence was haunting. Stedman and the NORAD commanders were impressed by the statistics, a worthy foe. The president sat down and looked towards these three. "You must agree, this is a formidable weapon we're dealing with. I realize we are testing our own aircraft and they can match most of these specs, but right now they are only tests of prototypes. The Russians, on the other hand, are mass-producing an excellent machine. We have reason to believe that one hundred have already been manufactured at a secret base in Siberia."

Stedman glanced at the president. To his horror, he could see the American's lips moving but couldn't hear his distinctive voice, only a voice far off in the background that was gradually getting louder. Was Stedman dreaming? Was his shell shock erupting? No, this couldn't be shell shock, he thought. He rubbed his face. His forehead started to sweat, but he quickly wiped his skin with a handkerchief and regained his composure. Stedman realized he was getting another migraine. He grabbed for the bottle of aspirin that he kept in his jacket.

"I don't understand what we have to do with this," said the prime minister.

The president turned to the Canadian leader and touched his arm. "You'll see very shortly, Mr. Prime Minister."

Stedman understood exactly. "Our Arrow can nearly match the MiG-K right now with the Pratt & Whitney engine, and it will probably exceed those specs with the Iroquois engine."

The president smiled. "Quite right. Gentlemen, the Arrow is the reason why you are all here. Mr. Stedman, I understand you've copied a statistics report on the Arrow."

"Yes, Mr. President, I have."

"Let's have it then, if you don't mind."

Stedman handed out copies of the five-page report that included general data, specifications, and observations, as well as a complete cockpit layout and control column drawings. He spread several eight-by-ten glossy black-and-white photos of the Arrow on the shiny tabletop. He put his glasses on, then read the report out loud as the others followed.

### AVRO ARROW MARK I ALL-WEATHER FIGHTER-INTERCEPTOR

*1) General Data*
*Without the aid of a prototype, six Arrow Mark I's have been built and tested at A. V. Roe in Malton, Ontario. This aircraft, once mass-produced in Mark II and III models, will be the bulk of the Royal Canadian Air Force fighter squadrons by the year 1961. The Avro CF-100, now used extensively by the RCAF, will be phased out. The Arrow Mark I was designed in 1952 and first flown March 25, 1958.*

*2) Specifications*
*Wingspan: 50 feet.*
*Length: 80 feet, 10 inches.*
*Empty Weight: 49,050 pounds.*
*Maximum Loaded: 68,600 pounds.*
*Engines: Two Pratt & Whitney J-75s with 12,500 pounds of thrust each (18,500 pounds with afterburner).*
*Fuel Capacity: 2,897 gallons.*
*Maximum Speed: Mach 2 at 40,000 feet.*
*Combat Speed: Mach 1.5.*
*Cruise Speed: Mach 0.92.*
*Ceiling: 53,000 feet.*
*Climb Rate: 38,450 feet/minute from sea level; 16,500 feet/minute from 40,000 feet.*
*Combat Radius: (high speed) 250 miles.*
*Maximum Range: 450 miles.*

*Armament: Can be fitted for nose cannons (4), 20mm, 200 rounds; wing missiles and rockets/missiles in bomb bay.*
*Aircrew: Two, pilot and navigator.*

*3) Observations*
*a) The Arrow Mark II model will be a vast improvement on the above specifications, due to future installation of the Orenda PS-13 Iroquois 2 engine which is capable of 19,250 pounds of base thrust and 26,000 pounds with afterburner. Fuel capacity will increase to 3,297 gallons, and overall length will reach 85 feet, 6 inches. Speed is expected to reach Mach 2.5 plus.*

*b) The Arrow models can be adapted for a zero launch, a pure fighter, a fighter-interceptor, a fighter-bomber or for photo-reconnaissance.*

*c) Because of its onboard computers, in particular its AFCS (Automatic Flight Control System) which contains three modes (Normal, Automatic and Emergency), this aircraft is one of the most highly advanced fighter-interceptors in the world, with unlimited potential.*

*d) Estimated cost to build each Mark II is set at $5,750,000–$6,000,000.*

Stedman sighed, "Well, that's it."

"Five to six million each?" asked Schult, as he studied one of the eight-by-ten photos.

"It's worth it," said Stedman sternly, as he sat down. The president stood up again. "Now to the main point of this meeting. Three weeks ago I met with the Soviet ambassador to Washington. I told him the United States knows all about the MiG-K and its production schedules. At first he denied everything. Then I showed him these."

The president reached into another folder, this time pulling out the photos he had shown Chenkovsky, and spread them out on the table. Kolb, Stedman, the prime minister, and Schult each picked up a copy, while Phillips looked over Stedman's shoulder.

The supreme commander of NORAD whistled. "Then what?"

"I accused him of building an aircraft that was a threat to world peace, and he turned around and said the same thing to me."

Schult motioned with his hand. "How are we a threat to world peace?"

"The Arrow."

Stedman didn't see the connection. "The Arrow? It's an interceptor. The MiG-K is a strike weapon."

"We know that. Frankly, I think they're scared of the Arrow. It's too advanced. At any rate, Moscow has agreed to fully scrap the MiG-K, providing we do the same to the Arrow."

"Do you want us to scrap the Arrow?" Stedman grunted, staring at the prime minister in shock.

The president looked over at his defense secretary. "Tell them, Jeffrey."

"No," answered Kolb, facing the Canadians, "we want you to *pretend* to scrap it."

The prime minister raised his eyebrows. "How do we go about pretending?"

"Here's the plan," Kolb went on. "In the next few months you downgrade the Arrow. Call press conferences about the fighter. Tell the public that you're examining the importance of the costly, controversial fighter."

"Wait a minute," the prime minister interrupted, "we've been doing some of that already. I've been all for scrapping it."

Kolb shrugged. "Well, step it up. Let the public know that you're seriously considering the program's cancellation, then go ahead and announce the end of the Arrow. But before you pull the plug on it, we can pull out the operation and move it to the Northwest Territories. The aircraft will be built, tested and flown in complete secrecy.

"Why pretend?" the prime minister asked Kolb.

"To see if the Russians are true to their word. We don't know if they really will destroy their new fighter. If they don't, then we've still got the Arrow."

The prime minister's thoughts turned to money. "Who's going to pay for this? We're talking millions of dollars."

"The U.S. government will pick up the entire tab. We can work it into our military budget so that no one will see it. All we want is Canadian approval on this. Do we have it?"

Stedman eased back in his chair and breathed out like a whale coming to the water surface. "Are you guys serious?"

The president nodded at the Canadian defense minister.

Kolb sat forward. "This is no gag."

"Well then," said the prime minister, "go ahead. Get the wheels in motion. You got approval right here and now."

"Great!" said Kolb, "We plan for the official scrapping to take place sometime in February next year."

"That doesn't give us much time," the prime minister said.

"No, it doesn't, but we can do it," replied the president. "From here on in, the code name for this project is TUNDRA." Everyone nodded. "Okay, let's take a break. Open the window and bring in some refreshments before we get down to the nitty-gritty of all this."

* * *

Later that evening, the president, tired after a long day, reached the premier of the Soviet Union on the Washington-Moscow hotline. It was past midnight in the Russian capital, but the Russian leader had been anxiously waiting to hear from Washington.

The president was in his shirtsleeves, and his tie was dangling loose. He and his personal translator were in the Oval Office.

"Mr. Premier," the American leader began, speaking loudly into the receiver, "the Canadian government will agree to suspend production of the Avro Arrow in four months."

The president nodded and eyed his translator, a thin, short, curly-haired Italian-American named Alan Sicino. The young man spoke in Russian on his own set to the European leader.

"Four months is too long, Mr. President," said the premier, in his clear baritone voice. Sicino conveyed the message to the president.

"Mr. Premier, we have no choice. There are political complications."

"What kind of political complications?" the premier asked gruffly.

The president knew that in order to make the TUNDRA operation perform without a hitch, the Canadians and Americans needed time to pull all they could from Malton and set it up in northern Canada. This part of the strategy was vital. "The Canadian government has already signed numerous deals with various subcontractors attached to the Arrow project." The president paused as his translator quickly caught up. "They can't cancel these contracts immediately, but most of them lapse in February, anyway. There are too many men and women involved in the Arrow program. They would all be out of work. We need some breathing space to provide the workers with jobs elsewhere in the aircraft or space industry."

"Why are these political complications?"

"The backlash for the Conservative party in Canada would be devastating. They would be voted out of office."

"That is capitalism, I suppose. We do not have problems like that in the Soviet Union." The premier sounded perturbed. "We are the people. We know what is best for the people."

"I know, Mr. Premier, but you must understand this is our way. The Canadian public would not accept a cancellation right now. We need time to turn the public against the Arrow, to tell them about its deficiencies and its enormous cost."

"What if it's longer than four months?"

"It won't be, I promise you. We'll set the date for February 20."

There was a long silence on the other end. The president and Sicino eyed one another for what seemed like an eternity.

"Mr. President, we will agree to your proposal."

"On that date, then, you will terminate the Skyjacker. Is that correct, Mr. Premier?"

"That is correct. Mr. President. This is peace for our time."

"I hope so," the president sighed. It was easier then he'd imagined, too easy. He thought back to 1938 and the Munich Agreement. Britain's prime minister, Neville Chamberlain, had spoken those now famous words, "peace for our time," following that epic meeting with Adolf Hitler in Germany. Only time will tell, thought the president, if this latest development will really bring peace for our time.

# CHAPTER SIX

TUNDRA HEADQUARTERS, A COMBINED OPerational training center for pilots and ground crew of the Royal Canadian Air Force and the United States Air Force, was 170 miles north of Yellowknife.

The giant complex, hidden inside the tree line of the Northwest Territories, was a city in the middle of nowhere. It contained multiple runways varying from eight thousand feet to eleven thousand feet; an extra large control tower with the latest in electronic and radar equipment; numerous hangars, garages, armament and machine shops; two-story houses for the officers and barracks for the ranks; two large mess halls; and, in the center of the complex, a three-story building looking much like a schoolhouse that was called the administration building.

On the first floor of this solid wooden administration building was a spacious auditorium, painted pale blue

78

and dominated by enormous Canadian and American flags hanging from the ceiling. A meeting was about to begin. Nearly 220 Canadian and American fighter pilots were sitting in front of a long stage on which the commanding officer of the base, Group Captain Ronald Aberhardt of the RCAF, stood erect, all spit and polish. His shoes shone like a showroom car. Off to his right, but still on the stage, was an RCAF officer and between the two was a large, mobile movie screen.

"Ten-shun!" the officer shouted.

Bogdan Kapolski and the other officers rose in unison. Kapolski glanced again about the massive room. Everything on the base was big: the shops, the runways, the rooms, the mess halls, the meals; and everything was first class, something the pilot wasn't used to in the air force. There were big bucks here all right. But he still hadn't seen a single fighter aircraft since he'd arrived on the base in a DC-3 twelve hours ago. What gives? he thought. What are they flying here?

"At ease, men, and take your seats." The C.O. spoke deliberately over the P.A. system. "Welcome to TUNDRA headquarters. All of you are part of a very important and very secret joint U.S.-Canadian military project. So secret, in fact, that you are advised, no, commanded, to keep your mouths shut!" The C.O.'s voice rang in the auditorium. "Total secrecy is vital to the air forces of our two countries. I repeat, vital. Now, I have a letter in my hand from General Edmund Schult, the supreme commander of NORAD." Aberhardt unfolded the letter. "It reads: *Gentlemen. Please be advised that all you see, hear and do in connection with the TUNDRA project is to be kept top secret. As far as outsiders are concerned, this entire base does not even exist. For the next few months you will all be involved in the training and flying of an advanced fighter aircraft. This machine will place us far ahead of the So-*

*viets for many years to come. It will be armed with a new and highly effective air-to-air missile.*

*"You have been handpicked to perform your duty, therefore I expect only the best, a top-notch performance from each and every one of you. You will have to learn all aspects of the aircraft in a matter of five months. You will eat, sleep and breathe this aircraft. All of you have had fighter training, with some of you experiencing combat in either World War II or the Korean conflict. We do not have any doubts concerning your ability to learn."*

The C.O. strolled a few paces to his left, his steps echoing through the silent auditorium. *"The work is intense and painstaking. Many of the methods used will be very new to you. You will be introduced to new forms of combat formation flying, a high standard of air weapons training with missiles and 20mm cannons, night flying, bomber interception, high-speed combat, and so on, all with a fighter that can reach speeds in excess of Mach two-point-five."* The auditorium broke into pandemonium: whistles and chatter like a noisy pub on a Saturday night.

Kapolski only smiled and wondered what the aircraft was.

Aberhardt hadn't expected a reaction like this. He held the letter with both hands and let the noise die down before continuing. "Your enthusiasm is electrifying. I like that. Now I want you to watch a film of the new fighter. Roll it." Aberhardt walked down the three stairs that led off the stage and down the center aisle. He stopped halfway down the aisle, where another officer was winding a 16mm camera. The lights went out.

The pilots waited anxiously. There was the typical countdown: 10–9–8–7–6–5–4–3–2–1. The first image on the black-and-white film was a bright light, the sun.

They were looking at a nose view from an aircraft skimming over a heavy cloud layer. The nose dropped, the aircraft gained speed and cut through the clouds. Then it came above the cloud layer. It banked severely to starboard, then leveled off. In the distance they could pick out the rear of a four-engined, prop-driven bomber from World War II, a B-29 Superfortress, more than likely remote-controlled. The distance between the planes was perhaps five hundred yards. Missiles fired from underneath the nose of the fighter and they headed straight for the bomber. The bomber banked to port. The missiles followed. The bomber banked some more. The missiles still followed, right on course. Then, a horrifying explosion and the bomber fell apart into thousands of pieces. The fighter pulled to starboard, away from the debris.

The screen went blank for a few seconds; then came another piece of film that had been spliced into the first. However, this one had sound and was in color. It showed a ground view of a delta-winged fighter about to take off, probably about three hundred yards from the zoom lens camera which was parallel with the runway. The fighter started to roll. Gaining speed quickly, very quickly, the officers saw its nose-wheel gear lift off. Then it was gone and their last view was the glowing afterburners soaring into the sky until the plane was a mere speck.

The noise and speed of the fighter sent a chill up Kapolski's spine, as he sat wide-eyed, gaping at the screen. He noticed the plane had U.S. Air Force markings on the fuselage and a long horizontal stripe on the peak of the tail section. Kapolski was stunned by it all, unable to really believe it. That this was an advanced fighter aircraft was an understatement. It was far superior to anything he had ever flown. It was the Avro

Arrow. Was it ready for combat already? he wondered. Wasn't it still undergoing tests at Malton?

The lights were turned on and the C.O. moved briskly back to the stage, amid more pandemonium. "Pilots of the Royal Canadian Air Force and the United States Air Force." The crowd quickly quieted down. "This is your new fighter and your new weapon. Training will begin at 1200 hours in the simulator rooms for those of you stationed at TUNDRA. The rest will be ready for transfer to other bases. You have all been given prior instructions and know which group you have been assigned to. That's all."

"Ten-shun!" the stage officer bellowed. The pilots jumped to their feet.

Aberhardt stared at a few of the faces in the front row, most of them Americans, all in elaborate new uniforms. The C.O. was glad the Americans were on his side. He liked Americans and their fighting spirit. He took in the other faces in the room and spotted Kapolski near the back. The Pole could sense the C.O. was looking right at him.

Aberhardt let them stand at attention for several seconds. "Dismissed!" he finally bellowed.


OTTAWA, ONTARIO, FRIDAY, FEBRUARY 20, 1959
1055 HOURS (EST)

Dean Stedman squeezed into his front-row seat on the Conservative side of the House of Commons, five seats to the right of the prime minister. Stedman squirmed a little in his chair, for his back had been bothering him lately. He tugged at his collar, fixed his tie, and brushed away some lint from his new blue suit.

Stedman's wardrobe included many blue outfits, air

force blue like the RCAF uniform he'd worn during the war. His suits, socks, slacks and ties were all blue. The color seemed particularly appropriate today.

Stedman leaned over to Kralick, on his immediate left, and gently dropped his left hand on the finance minister's desk, disturbing a few papers.

"Well, Alex, this is it."

Kralick looked surprised. He had no time to respond before the prime minister rose to address the House. Stedman positioned himself back in his own chair to listen to the prime minister's morning address. He knew exactly what his boss was going to say because he had helped him write the speech.

The prime minister appeared calm, in complete control. He glanced down at several typed sheets in his hand, then turned to face the speaker of the House on his right.

"Mr. Speaker," he began confidently, "with the leave of the House I should like to make a somewhat lengthy statement on the subject of one facet of the national defense of Canada. After all, the effectiveness of the measures taken for our national defense constitutes the passport either to survival or destruction. The announcement I wish to make has to do with the decision regarding our air defense which was foreshadowed in the statement made by me to the press on September twenty-third last.

"The government has carefully examined and reexamined the probable need for the Arrow aircraft and Iroquois engine, known as the CF-105, the development of which has been continued pending a final decision. We have made a thorough examination in the light of all the information available concerning the probable nature of the threats to North America in future years, the alternative means of defense against such threats, and the estimated costs thereof. The conclusion arrived at is that the development of the Arrow aircraft and Iroquois engine should be terminated now.

"Formal notice of termination is now being given to the contractors. All outstanding commitments will of course be settled equitably.

"In reaching this decision . . ."

Stedman eyed the opposition members for their reactions to the bombshell. The Liberal leader swung back in his chair, his hands dropping to his sides. He remained transfixed in that position for several seconds before sitting up and whispering to the M.P. next to him. The opposition defense critic, a Liberal member for a Toronto riding, stared at the prime minister in utter disbelief, but maintained his composure. Up in the press gallery, behind the House speaker, the reporters scribbled madly on their notepads, while a handful immediately flew from the chamber to relay the shocking news to their editors.

The prime minister was steady, solid as the Rock of Gibraltar, as he continued to read his carefully prepared speech. He was still the master of the House, the same as he had been the master of the courtroom during his criminal lawyer days in Saskatchewan.

"Work on the original concept of the CF-105 commenced in the air force in 1952," the leader went on, "and the first government decision to proceed with the development and production of two prototypes was taken late in 1953. The plane was designed to meet RCAF requirements for a successor to the CF-100, to be used in the defense of Canada. At that time it was thought some five or six hundred aircraft would be needed, and their cost was forecast at about one and a half to two million dollars each. From the beginning, however, it was recognized by the previous government, and subsequently by this government, that the development of an advanced supersonic aircraft such as the 105, with its complicated engine and weapons system, was highly hazardous, and therefore all decisions to proceed with it were tentative and subject to change in the light of experience. This was known to the contractors undertaking the development, to the air force, and to Parliament.

"The development of the Arrow aircraft and Iroquois engine has been a success, although for various reasons it has proceeded far behind the original schedule. The plane and its engine have shown promise of achieving the high standard of technical performance intended and are a credit to those who conceived and designed them, and translated the plans into reality.

"Unfortunately, these outstanding achievements have been overtaken by current events. In recent months, the bomber threat, which the CF-105 was intended to avert, has diminished. Alternative means of meeting our defense needs have been developed much earlier than was expected. The first long-range . . ."

## MALTON, ONTARIO, 1121 HOURS (EST)

Rumors had been afloat for months concerning a pending cancellation of the Arrow; so many rumors, in fact, that the Avro technicians at Malton chose to simply ignore all grapevine talk or gossip. They had a hectic round of daily duties to perform to meet the production schedule of new Arrows. These Arrow Mark IIs were advancing steadily down the assembly line, ready for outfitting with the highly acclaimed Iroquois engine. The Iroquois technicians were promising that the first Mark II, RL-206, was only a week or two away from a test flight, providing all went well with the installation. The engine cavities for it had been fitted with the engines only a few days earlier. There was great excitement throughout the Avro factory. They all sensed that history was in the making.

The assembly line was busy at this time of day, as usual. Then, suddenly, a loud voice crackled over the P.A. system:

"MAY I HAVE YOUR ATTENTION PLEASE. THE RADIO NEWS HAS JUST REPORTED THAT THE PRIME MINISTER STATED IN THE HOUSE OF COMMONS THIS MORNING THAT THE AVRO ARROW AND IROQUOIS PROGRAMS HAVE BEEN TERMINATED. THE MANAGEMENT OF THIS COMPANY HAS RECEIVED NO OFFICIAL WORD."

Terry Robertson, one of the oldest technicians on the line and the head of his section, looked up towards the nearest loudspeaker, just a few feet away, in total disbelief. He, of course, had been hearing the nagging rumors since last year, but had pushed them aside. He stood there with his tray of tools in his hands, coveralls open to the waist, staring at the speaker, trying to concentrate on the rest of the announcement.

"IT IS IMPOSSIBLE AT THIS STAGE TO GIVE YOU ANY FURTHER DETAILS UNTIL SUCH TIME AS WE RECEIVE AN OFFICIAL ANNOUNCEMENT FROM OTTAWA. IN THE MEANTIME, I WOULD ASK YOU TO CONTINUE WITH YOUR WORK. WE WILL KEEP YOU INFORMED."

What? Continue? Robertson thought. Who are they trying to kid? What do they mean, continue with our work? How are we supposed to continue our work if the Arrow's been canceled? They finally did it. The prime minister, that old horned-tooth loudmouth, I'd like to take that waving finger of his . . . What does he know about defense matters? It can't be true. It's a joke, or a mistake. The party won't let him do it. They can't!

Robertson decided to continue his work on the initial stages of the final assembly of RL-209, three aircraft behind the first Mark II. His work involved riveting the skins onto the center section, as well as installing the inner wings. His fellow crew members continued working at the station as if the announcement hadn't happened. Were they disappointed? Were they angry? Either they hid their feelings well or were too stunned to react.

Robertson's group was a cheerful, hard-working crew who were devoted to the Arrow. Robertson knew that his workers, all much younger than he, were deeply affected by the announcement, but he appreciated their professional attitude and loyalty. So he too went right back to the workload at hand, as did the crew directly in front and behind his aircraft, those working on RL-208 and RL-210.

Robertson and his crew toiled away at their routine functions for another hour before heading off to the cafeteria for lunch. They arrived back in time to see company officials handing out papers to several workers on the floor. Robertson ran between two Arrows to one of the men distributing the literature and demanded to know what was happening. "See for yourself." He handed Robertson one of the papers. Jason Williams, a baby-faced technician from another station, leaned over Robertson's shoulder as he read:

*"To all employees. Following the prime minister's statement we have received wires from the government instructing us to immediately cease all work on the Arrow and Iroquois programs at Malton, and by all suppliers and subcontractors."*

"Damn it!" screamed Robertson, stamping his foot on the concrete floor. "It really is true! Why?"

As Robertson read the rest of the notice, Williams turned and leaned on the fuselage of RL-208, his hand gently grazing the skin of the aircraft.

"Wait, Jason," Robertson said, turning to Williams. "There's more. We're out of a job too. Listen to this: *As a result, notice of termination of employment is*

*being given to all employees of Avro Aircraft and Or-
enda engines, pending a full assessment of the impact
of the prime minister's statement on our aeronautical
operations.''*

Robertson paused. *''All monthly, weekly, and hourly
paid employees are hereby given notice of layoff as of
this date. Your separation pay, separation notice, vacation pay books, et cetera, will be mailed as soon as
possible.''*

In a state of shock, Robertson turned and lumbered
down the line of Arrows to his own. He wanted one
last look at the fighter before he left. He ignored the
uproar around him, the noise like the steady droning of
bees in a hive. The entire plant was reacting to the news
now and the workers' attitudes ranged from disbelief
and shock to anger and defiance.

Robertson noticed some blueprints of the wings and
fuselage on one of the nearby toolboxes. While the com-
motion went on, he picked up the papers and stuffed them
into a large pocket in the front of his coveralls. Then he
climbed the scaffolding to get onto the starboard inner
wing of RL-208. Once there he grabbed more blueprints
and this time stuffed them inside his shirt. Then he bolted
down the scaffolding. When his boots touched the floor,
he met Williams face to face.

''What are you doing?'' Williams asked.

''Never mind what I'm doing.''

''You're swiping the blueprints!''

''Shut up! Not so loud. Just mind your own business.
If this project is over and done with, then I want to
have something to show for it. Just a souvenir.''

Put like that, Williams reasoned that what Robertson
was doing wasn't so bad after all. So he turned around
and strolled up the assembly line to speak to the technicians on RL-206.

''What a shame, eh?'' the man said to Williams.

"Here's 206 all ready to blast the world speed record to smithereens! I'd like to grab the prime minister and twist his son-of-a-bitchin' neck off!"

## OAKVILLE, ONTARIO, 1314 HOURS (EST)

Lance Tiemans was suffering from a head cold and had decided to take the day off work. He lived alone in an apartment on Kerr Street in Oakville and had woken up at eight that morning, called work, had a bowl of cereal, then fallen back into bed. A few hours later, the phone rang.

Tiemans sniffed, then picked up the receiver. "Hello," he muttered gruffly, stretching across his bed.

"Hey, Lance, you've been sleeping?"

"Not anymore. Who is this?"

"Barrie."

"Barrie? What are you calling for?"

"Gee, you sound awful. I heard you phoned in sick today."

"That's right," said Tiemans, still half asleep. "And I feel worse than I sound." Tiemans swallowed, feeling a pain in his throat.

"Well, if you've been sleeping, then you probably didn't hear the news."

"What news?" Tiemans asked, looking at his alarm clock to check the time. He detected anger in his friend's voice.

"The prime minister finally went and did it. This whole place is in a flap."

"Did what?"

"He terminated the Arrow and Iroquois programs. They're history. The greatest fighter plane in the world obliterated, shot down by our own government!"

Tiemans sat up in bed. "You're putting me on!"

"Oh, no I'm not. Turn the radio on!" Barrie shouted over the voice on the hangar's P.A. system.

"When did you hear all this?"

"Hold on a sec, the P.A.'s still blaring in my ear." The caller paused for a short while, giving Tiemans time to reach for his radio. "There, that's better. I couldn't hear myself think. I was on the tarmac with some of the crew when one of the ground support trucks pulled up and out jumped Billy, saying that all hell had broken loose at the plant. They announced over the P.A. that the P.M. got up in the House of Commons and declared the Arrow was officially scrapped. He supposedly had a bunch of crap figures to support his plan. How he ever arrived at those figures, I'll never know, then he scrapped it."

"Oh, great. Now I really feel sick, and just with the weekend coming up."

"There's something else."

"What is it?"

"We're out of work. All of us. We got termination notices. They're going to send us our separation pay, vacation pay book and all that in the mail."

"Oh, damn. I've got debts to pay."

"Like that '57 T-Bird."

"Yeah, like the T-Bird. How's our chief test pilot taking it?"

"He just walked away, didn't say a word. He was going to retire soon anyway. But what about the rest of us, we're still young."

Tiemans sighed. "Well, thanks for calling, Barrie. I better go, I've got a splitting headache."

"So do I, old man. So do I."

RCAF Station Fort Franklin, NWT, Saturday
February 21, 1136 Hours (1336 est)

"At least this place is a lot nicer than Dixon."

"You're right," replied Flying Officer James Scott, in agreement with his navigator, Flying Officer Jacques St. Pierre. "But what are we doing up here in no-man's-land?"

The chatter was soft in the briefing room where over forty CF-100 aircrew were sitting, all wondering what they were doing so close to the Arctic Circle.

Scott could hear loud footsteps out in the hall. He turned to St. Pierre. "I think we're going to find out. Here comes the C.O."

Group Captain Edwin Fisher, the commanding officer at Fort Franklin base, and his adjutant burst into the room and stopped only a few feet from the door.

"Ten-shun!" shouted the adjutant.

"At ease, men," declared Fisher in a clear voice. "Take your seats." The C.O. was a huge man, over six-foot-three, with some gray around the temples, dark eyes, and a permanent five o'clock shadow. "Welcome to our new facilities at RCAF Station Fort Franklin. I will make this as brief as possible. You will be stationed here for the next six months or so, on special assignment. Never before has an operational air base of this size been situated this far north in our NORAD airspace. The reason, gentlemen, is this."

Fisher walked towards the center of the room. He took up a pointer and tapped a large map of the Northwest Territories on the wall behind him. "To the east of here, perhaps twenty minutes away by air, is a top secret air force project. It is in a restricted area two hundred miles square," he said, turning to the map. "We are not to go anywhere near it under any circumstances. Our job is to keep unauthorized aircraft from approaching it. That includes civilian as well as enemy aircraft. We all know the Soviets have been sending heavy bombers into our airspace further north to test our fighter reaction times. For any type of aircraft that we might intercept, even our own military aircraft, take the necessary steps to send them back where they came from.'' Fisher smiled dryly, turning his body completely around to glare at the fliers. ''Questions?''

Scott raised his hand. ''Sir?''

''Yes.''

Scott stood. ''What if they refuse to turn back?''

''I rather doubt that we'll have any trouble.''

''What if it's a Russian bomber?''

Fisher looked annoyed. ''As I said before, the Soviets are only checking our reaction times. Once you come along on the port side, the pilot will break off. If he doesn't, fire warning shots. All communication will be conducted by voice, not in code. The restricted area will take over radio transmission once you've left our base.''

Scott sat down and glanced over at his navigator. St. Pierre was looking straight ahead.

''Any more questions?'' Fisher looked the room over. ''Okay, take down the position of the restricted area, then you're dismissed.''


TORONTO, ONTARIO, MONDAY, FEBRUARY 23
1231 HOURS (EST)


In the corner of a bar in Toronto's west end, Lance Tiemans was waiting for his friend and former ground crew technician of the Arrow project, Barrie Johnson. Tiemans had arrived an hour before his friend and was drinking heavily.

"Stupid idiot," Tiemans moaned. He slammed his fist down on the table just as Johnson came in.

"Who?"

"You know who. Our great, illustrious prime minister."

Johnson merely took off his coat and shrugged. "Been here long?"

Tiemans stared at his friend. "Don't you care?"

"Sure I care," Johnson replied as he rolled up the sleeves of his shirt. "But what can we do about it? The Arrow's dead."

"No," Tiemans declared, "he didn't really do it. He couldn't have." He grabbed Johnson by his muscular shoulders. "We're out of work." Johnson noticed his friend's speech was starting to slur badly.

Johnson hung his head, unable to console his friend. Then he noticed that Tiemans had been reading the newspaper. "What does the paper say?"

"That Spencer is right on the mark." Tiemans grabbed the paper with both hands.

"Just listen to this." He cleared his throat. *"We should have known something was in the wind when the prime minister sent out a press release back in September 1958. It stated that 'The government has concluded that missiles should be introduced into the Canadian air defense system and that the number of supersonic interceptor aircraft required for the RCAF air defense command will be substantially less than could have been foreseen a few years ago. The CF-105 will not be available for effective use in squadrons until late 1961. Revolutionary changes have taken place since the project began, which have made necessary a review of the program. The preponderance of expert opinion is that by the 1960s manned aircraft, however outstanding, will be less effective in meeting the enemy threat than pre-*

*viously expected.'* " Tiemans lowered the paper for a moment. "What a bunch of bull."

"You're right about that."

Tiemans continued reading. *"What about the cost? The original estimate of $100 million, predicted by the past Liberal administration, has now grown to over $300 million, according to the present Tory government. The figures are probably accurate, but so what? In my opinion, when it comes to defense, you can never spend enough. But our government is in deep financial trouble, and they can only see dollars and cents. This is only the beginning of rash government spending cuts. During their first year in power the Conservatives predicted a surplus of over $150 million, with the end result being instead a $39 million deficit. Then came Alex Kralick's 1958 budget on June 17. By this time, the Tories had finally come to grips with reality and projected a deficit of $648 million, the largest national deficit in over twelve years."* Tiemans stopped reading.

"For somebody who's drunk, that was great reading. You didn't slur once."

Tiemans smirked. "I like this guy Spencer. He's got spunk. I hope I meet him again someday."

Two young couples at the table nearest to the former Arrow workers were listening to the conversation. One of the men leaned over. "Excuse me, but I couldn't help hearing you read that column about the Arrow." Tiemans and Johnson just looked at the man as he went on. "It's really too bad, but we couldn't afford it. We couldn't. The Tories had no choice but to get rid of it."

"Who asked you?" snorted Tiemans.

"Cool it, buddy," the other man said, holding up his hand.

Tiemans looked at the four faces around the next table. "I worked two years on the Arrow. Two years! Now it's all gone." His speech was slurred now. Then he stood up and stared at the first man who'd spoken. Tiemans took one step towards him and fell flat on his face.

MISSISSAUGA, ONTARIO, 1714 HOURS (EST)

The temperature was near freezing and large snow-flakes were falling. Snow, snow and more snow. Didn't they have enough already?

Ben Spencer was exhausted after a hectic day at the *Tribune*. Sammy Hughes had told him to head home early, and Spencer had taken advantage of his offer. But the snow tied up the traffic for miles, and he still wouldn't arrive home much earlier than usual.

Driving down the street in his red 1958 Chevy, Spencer thought once again of the government decision to terminate the Arrow and Iroquois programs. The writer had received a deluge of phone calls that day regarding the epic and abrupt ending to the massive projects. Maybe, he thought, if enough public reaction against the scrapping could be mustered, the government would change its mind. Maybe. Some of the calls were from angry Arrow workers who were now out of work. One call was from a government cabinet minister from Toronto who defended the decision. He rambled on and on and Spencer finally hung up on him.

Spencer steered the car into his driveway. He shut the motor off, grabbed the day's *Tribune* and his briefcase from the front seat, and stepped out, only to slip on a fresh patch of wet snow. Luckily he landed in a nearby soft snowbank instead of on the concrete driveway.

It seemed to be a perfect ending to the day he'd had. "Well," he thought to himself, "I needed that."

"Hi Dad, what are you doing in the snowbank?"

Spencer propped himself up on his elbow and saw

his son Brent in a dark green snowsuit, standing near the gate that lead to the backyard.

"I'm playing baseball," Spencer snorted.

Brent ran up, a grin on his red-flushed face, grabbed some snow from the driveway's edge and threw the powder into his father's face. Then he ran through the gate.

Spencer knew his son wanted to play so he rolled up a large snowball in his bare hands and started to run for the gate, but he lost his footing and fell down again, this time barely missing the car. "Stupid loafers, they're not meant for this!"

Spencer pulled himself up slowly and walked towards the front door of his home. He steadied himself with his right hand against the house as he walked up the steps. When he looked towards the large bay window, he saw his wife, Claire, and their other son, Albert, laughing at him. He must've been quite a sight, snow clinging to his coat, slacks and face, his hair messed up, holding onto the rail for dear life.

Claire tapped on the window and pointed to the patch of snow where Spencer first fell down. He'd left his briefcase and newspaper on the ground. Shaking his head, he backed carefully down the steps to retrieve his belongings. Inside the house, Claire helped her husband remove his coat. "Did you have a rough day or something?" she asked, with a smile. Claire was always in a good mood and always looked smashing. She wore her blonde hair pulled back neatly in a ponytail and dressed in casual clothes. Today she had on the tight-fitting black slacks that he liked and a baggy white shirt unbuttoned down the front to show off a vivid red tank top. She was a knockout, all right. Spencer often thought she looked like Betty Grable. "You want me to make some coffee before supper?"

"Sure."

"Why don't you take a hot bath while I perk some."

Spencer took off his shoes and brushed the snow off his slacks. "What's for dinner tonight?" he asked, as he sniffed slowly. The smell of something delicious cooking filled the house.

"Your favorite, spaghetti. But none for you because you're . . ."

"I know, I know. On a diet."

"That's right. You get a nice, juicy, sink-your-teeth-into . . ."

Spencer eyes grew wide to mock her. "What?"

"Green salad!"

Whoopee, thought Spencer.

OAKVILLE, ONTARIO, 2105 HOURS (EST)

Two men in dark overcoats pounded at the door until it opened. One man was tall and skinny, the other of medium height and weight.

"Lance Tiemans?" asked the taller one, as both flashed RCMP intelligence identification for Tiemans to see.

"Yeah, that's me," answered Tiemans, as he finished the glass of orange juice he was holding. He looked awful and he knew it. He'd just gotten out of bed; his T-shirt and slacks were wrinkled, and his hair was pasted to his head.

"May we come in?"

"I guess I can't say no, now can I? Yeah, sure, come on in." Tiemans opened the door to his Oakville apartment and motioned the men to have a seat on the couch. He sat on the rocker a few feet away and faced them.

Tiemans must have been quite a sight. After collapsing in the bar earlier that day, his friend Barrie Johnson had dragged him out to the street and called a cab to take him home. The cab driver told Johnson that it would cost him plenty because Oakville was a good distance away, but Johnson paid his buddy's tab by slipping the driver a twenty-dollar bill. When he got home, Tiemans stumbled up the stairs to his place, fell down on the couch, and went to sleep. He had only been awake for ten minutes when the men knocked. He'd drunk two glasses of juice but was still thirsty.

"What can I do for you?" Tiemans asked, as he plunked the empty glass down on the shag carpet by his feet.

"I take it you're the Lance Tiemans who worked on the Arrow?" asked the tall agent.

"That's me, all right. I was ground crew. But I'm out of a job now. And very hung over too."

The agent smirked. "We have a job for you. A job of national importance."

Tiemans raised his eyebrows in disgust. "Sure you do. The Arrow was of national importance too, but where did it get me? Son-of-a-bitch Tories!" He belched.

"This is different."

"Yeah, how different?" Tiemans leaned on the right arm of the rocker and stared hard at the agent.

"We need people with your experience to go up to our fighter bases in the Northwest Territories."

Tiemans shrugged. "I don't know. I have a chance to work at Lockheed in the States for pretty good money. I'm just waiting to hear from them." Tiemans could tell the agents didn't believe him. They must've known he had no leads at all. "I don't want to work up north, it's too damn cold up there."

The shorter agent got up from the couch and walked over to the window that overlooked Lake Ontario to the south. He played with his tie, then turned to face Tiemans. "You will be paid two thousand dollars a month, and your accommodation and clothing will be provided."

"You're kidding?" Tiemans' mouth hung open.

"No, we're not," said the taller one.

"Why didn't you say so earlier? Sure, I'll go!"

"Excellent," said the agent. "You're to be at Malton Airport on Friday at 1:00 P.M. with only your basic personal belongings; you're to travel light. Go to the number four hangar and ask for Smitty."

"That's just a few days away. I've got a lease on this apartment and I'll never get out of it that soon." Tiemans stood up, slowly, awkwardly.

"Don't worry about it, we'll look after everything. Just be at Malton in plenty of time."

Tiemans put his hands in his pockets. "Okay, you're the boss."

"One more thing. This meeting never happened. If anyone asks you where you're going, you got a job with the RCAF up north. That's all anyone needs to know. Is that understood?"

"Understood."

The agents let themselves out, leaving a startled Tiemans shaking his head.

"My employment problems are over," he whispered to himself. Then he smiled widely and got himself another glass of juice.

# CHAPTER SEVEN

RCAF STATION COLLINS, NWT, TUESDAY, APRIL 14
0858 HOURS (1058 EST)

BOGDAN KAPOLSKI WALKED DOWN THE
long hall and opened the door to the crew room.

As usual at this time of day the room was stirring
with activity. A-, B- and C-Flights had been coming
and going since 6:00 A.M. Most of the C-Flight crew,
who had practiced circuits and bumps earlier, were still
in the long, dull-green rectangular room. B-Flight had
left ten minutes before and were now in the process of
receiving their instructions for fighter-interceptor maneuvers one hundred miles to the west. Only a handful
of A-Flight pilots, the group Kapolski belonged to, had
arrived. The rest would be there shortly.

Everyone was in his flying gear and waiting. Most
seemed very relaxed. At the end of one wall was a
counter stacked with sandwiches, cookies, and hot and
cold drinks. Three young officers were seated inside the
door sipping coffee and discussing fighter strategy.

Other aircrew were either relaxing in chairs, standing near the counter, or sitting at the small circular tables in the center of the room.

Kapolski sauntered over to the counter, grabbed a ham and cheese sandwich, then poured himself a coffee. Just before he turned around someone tapped him gently on the shoulder.

"Hey, Danny, where you sitting?"

Kapolski looked behind him and saw the round, smiling face of a chunky Canadian pilot from C-Flight, Jimmy Doraty. Jimmy was one of the few men that Kapolski had a close relationship with. Though he'd lived in Canada for many years and his accent was slowly disappearing, the Pole still felt out of place. He felt especially alien here at Collins Air Base, where all the pilots were younger than himself.

They sat down in the middle of the room and ate quietly until Kapolski asked how the morning circuits and bumps went.

"No problem. Piece of cake. I'm finally getting used to that over-the-nose view. The first time I ever did a touch-and-go in that thing I came down too hard and almost broke the landing gear off. Wilkinson really chewed me out for that one. I think we all had a little trouble at first. They sure don't land like Canucks."

Kapolski nodded as Doraty finished his sandwich in a hurry, then lit a cigarette. Kapolski ate calmly and watched Jimmy blow perfect smoke rings. Suddenly the room shook slightly, and the cups and plates rattled.

"B-Flight's taking off, Danny, so I guess your group will be up soon." Kapolski looked unconcerned as he sipped his coffee. "The Ops board shows you're on with Wilkinson. How do you like him?"

Kapolski shrugged. "He's okay as far as higher-ups go."

"Well, I don't like him," Doraty whispered. "He's always getting on my tail."

Kapolski only shrugged. From what he'd heard about Doraty's first circuit-and-bump, Wilkinson had every right to chew the bugger out; his first one had been atrocious. This was a multimillion-dollar machine he was playing with.

The loudspeakers outside the hangar echoed a clear voice: "SCRAMBLE FIRST PAIR! SCRAMBLE FIRST PAIR!"

Kapolski closed the canopy to the Arrow, glad to cut out the below-zero weather. He flicked two switches and the Iroquois engines quickly came to life with a roar of raw, thunderous power, twenty thousand pounds of earth-shattering thrust. He glanced at the instrument lights that were flashing a kaleidoscope of glistening color. Outside, he could see his ground crew silhouetted against the hangar lights. One of the men yanked the ladder away; the other viewed the aircraft's surfaces as Kapolski ran through the routine checks: *speed brakes open, speed brakes closed, left aileron, right aileron, left rudder, right rudder.* The crewman raised his thumbs upwards to signal that everything was okay.

Radio communication aboard the fighter crackled to life as Kapolski taxied down the perimeter track. In front of him was Group Captain Wilkinson in his own fighter. The wing lights of both machines illuminated a path in the darkness as they lined up side by side and gave left rudder onto Runway 27.

Kapolski checked to make sure the canopy was locked, the harness was closed and his chin strap was on. When the fighters obtained clearance for takeoff, Kapolski pushed forward on the throttle levers with his left hand to full military thrust. He watched the RPM indicators, at the five o'clock position, as they rose quickly.

Kapolski looked to his right at Wilkinson, who would now take over the radio communication for the takeoff.

"BRAKES OFF," the C.O.'s voice crackled over the R/T. He paused. "NOW." They both started rolling. "AFTERBURNERS, AFTERBURNERS." He paused again. "GO!"

Kapolski pushed the throttles forward from the 100 percent military position. The afterburners kicked in with a jolt. The airspeed rose; fifty knots . . . seventy . . . one hundred. . . . The tower on his right disappeared. He felt the air under the wings. Halfway down the eleven-thousand-foot runway he lifted the nose section skyward and the front wheels gently lifted off. The cool, dry northern climate could shoot any aircraft into the air quickly and effortlessly. A few hundred feet further, at a speed of 170 knots, the fighter was in the air. By the time Kapolski was soaring over the end of the runway, he had pressed the landing gear lever to the UP position. The landing gear position indicator displayed to the pilot that the gear was safely in the wings. Outside, the red lights to either side of the runway raced by, forming two flaming darts running side by side. He watched his instruments. Revs and pipe temperatures were normal.

"MIKE-DELTA-ZERO-TWO, GO CHANNEL TEN."

"ROGER, MIKE-DELTA-ZERO-ONE, SWITCHING TO TEN." Kapolski moved the R/T through the frequencies. "MIKE-DELTA-ZERO-TWO ON TEN."

An overall gray bleakness surrounded the aircraft, stretching out to the horizon line in every direction. The well-lit base was far behind them. This was Canada's North in the dead of winter; total darkness nearly every day. Below the two machines were trees and snow, trees and snow; above, only the moon and stars. Kapolski glanced out his cockpit to see his C.O. spreading the gap between them.

At twenty-four thousand feet they came off the afterburners. It had taken only a minute and twenty seconds to get to this height from brake release. They climbed higher, this time on full military power. Kapolski had already been fed the information he needed for his interception via the Data Link antenna on the bottom of the aircraft. He had already received voiceless high-frequency signals from TUNDRA ground control for his attack vector and target information, altitude, heading, range and speed. In this case his target was at thirty-five thousand feet, on a heading of zero-four-zero degrees, at a speed of 450 knots, and thirty miles away.

Then Kapolski picked up a bogie, a large blip, in the nine o'clock range; a bomber, more than likely. Their paths would cross in mere minutes. Wilkinson broke down and away as Kapolski continued on at a speed of Mach 1.1 and an altitude of thirty-five thousand feet. The blip was now in the ten o'clock range. Kapolski locked onto it by engaging the Phase I display of the Lead Collision Course. A wide circle burned on his radarscope and read twenty seconds till contact. Modern military technology left nothing to chance; it was a far cry from World War II, where it was merely hit or miss. *Phase two, ten seconds to go.* Ten seconds till the bogie was done for. There was no escape now, not with a radar lock-on. According to the scope the bomber was slipping sideways towards Kapolski and would soon cross left to right. *Four-point-five seconds to go.* The circle was getting smaller on the radar screen. *Three seconds, two, one . . .*

Kapolski squeezed the firing button on the control column. An X blinked on the radar scope. The Fire Control Coupler took over and avoided the intended explosion. The Arrow pulled hard to the left and a new course was set, all automatically. The interception from beginning to end was over in a few minutes, but to Kapolski it seemed even quicker; a mere handful of seconds.

"MIKE-DELTA-ZERO-ONE, THIS IS MIKE-DELTA-ZERO-TWO. DO YOU READ?" he said into his R/T.

"I READ YOU, MIKE-DELTA-ZERO-ONE."

"ONE B-52 STRATOFORTRESS SPLASHED."

Kapolski had successfully "shot down" a Strategic Air Command B-52 bomber that had been sent up from a base in North Dakota. Although it was only a practice operation, Kapolski felt the old familiar thrill.

"GOOD WORK."

With the excitement of the interception over, Kapolski leveled off and set course for the base. He relaxed in his seat and watched the full moon through the cockpit perspex. His body felt tired, he could smell the rubber mask in his nostrils and his lips were cracked. He hated the cold, dry northern air. If he didn't like flying so much he'd never be up in these boondocks, practically at the North Pole. If a man ever got lost up here, he was finished.

Just last week he and a dozen other pilots had been sent on an outdoor survival test for three days. They ate nothing but prepackaged northern delicacies like lichens and mussels. Kapolski told the others that if he had to eat that stuff to stay alive in an emergency, he'd rather be dead. The other pilots weren't sure he was kidding.

Kapolski loved this new, highly secretive aircraft. He loved the maneuverability, the all-out speed, the lightness of the controls, and the weapons system. He had beamed when the powers-that-be turned the fighter into a one-man aircraft. He did not like flying with a navigator, as he had in the CF-100. He realized that in the years to come a two-man crew would be a must for any fighter, but by that time he would be long gone from the air force.

Soon he spotted Wilkinson off starboard, at a distance of several hundred yards, his strobe lights glowing red in the darkness.

Kapolski recalled the first time he had met Wilkinson. The crew met their new C.O. in the briefing room at Collins. He was about thirty-five years old, short, and average in build except for large shoulders. He had a high forehead, dark brown hair, and sad eyes. His uniform fit him well and it was pressed very neatly. Kapolski's first impression was that Wilkinson was a wimp, but he quickly informed the pilots that he expected 100 percent and then some from everybody. He forewarned his men that he would work them hard; they would practice, practice, practice until they could fly this new fighter in their sleep. His favorite expression was "Hack it or pack it!"

On one occasion, while coming in for a landing, Kapolski did a victory roll about a hundred feet off the runway. Wilkinson canned him for two days before allowing him any more flying time. "You remind me of me," Wilkinson told the pilot. The C.O. had flown Spitfires on the same base as Kapolski's Polish Air Force squadron during the latter part of the Second World War. "I used to do those kinds of stunts during the war, and I got canned for them. Do a victory roll again on my base and I'll kick your ass back to Warsaw!"

On the ground, a tired and hungry Lance Tiemans had been walking through a hangar door in the direction of a parked interceptor about fifty feet away, when two twisting contrails set against the dark sky high above caught his eye. He had seen contrails from Canadian and American fighter aircraft before, but none like these. Then the hangar door, as if by magic, started to shake, and the large window rattled violently.

"Man, are those guys moving!" he muttered to himself. He noticed that the aircraft were now flying in a straight line, side by side. Then one broke off, followed by the other. He had no doubt that they were exceeding Mach 1.

Kapolski started his initial approach to Collins, a series of left-handed turns. At fifteen hundred feet he throttled back to 280 knots, then called the tower. "ICECAP. MIKE-DELTA-ZERO-TWO APPROACHING DOWNWIND LEG."

"ROGER, MIKE-DELTA-ZERO-TWO, THERE IS NO OTHER REPORTED TRAFFIC. WIND AT TWELVE KNOTS, TWO-SIX-ZERO DEGREES."

Kapolski's mind slipped back for a moment to the Battle of Britain, nineteen years earlier. England, 1940; grass airstrips and prop-driven fighters. How crude those Hurricanes were in comparison to this roomy, fully computerized piece of machinery that was comfortably wrapped around his body, ready and willing to receive his every command. The Hurricane cockpit resembled a metal shoebox compared to this advanced piece of technology.

Once on the downwind leg, Kapolski cut back the speed and dropped the speed brakes and tricycle landing gear. He noticed the one-thousand-foot point, which was a red-roofed shack with two yellow fog lights on top. He checked his altimeter and found he was right on. Next he double-checked the hydraulic pressures, made sure his harness was good and tight, and increased the RPM about ten percent to offset the drag produced when the speed brakes and wheels were dropped. Kapolski made sure the emergency fuel switch was off before turning the control column to the left in order to line up with the base leg.

Then he turned ninety degrees in a wide turn for the final approach. Now he saw the three-hundred-foot mark, a multicolored series of lights forming a small square and overlooking a man-made trench, and a well-lit safety truck where a sergeant always checked to see if the landing gear of incoming aircraft was down. If not, he would fire a red Very pistol to signify an emergency. Kapolski saw that the flare was green. As he approached the brightly lit runway, he noticed the windsock at a slight angle and knew therefore that he had a slight crosswind to play with.

"MIKE-DELTA-ZERO-TWO ON FINAL. OVER."

"MIKE-DELTA-ZERO-TWO CLEARED TO LAND."

At 180 knots Kapolski centered ten degrees to the left on Runway 27. Dropping the speed to 160 and holding, he chopped the throttles. The main gear met the pavement with a cushioned, controlled thud; the piercing, thunderous sound of the engines slowed to a gentle, easy moan. The fighter gobbled up another two thousand feet of runway before Kapolski dropped the nose gear. Finally, at 100 knots he pulled the drag chute, and the fighter slowed down to a crawl within seventy-five hundred feet of runway.

Kapolski thought back to his crash landing at Dunsbridge, England in 1940, at the very height of the Battle of Britain. His Hurricane was in flames and he was unable to escape from the cockpit. He had somehow manuevered the craft in for a wheels-up landing. On the ground, Kapolski pulled at the jammed latch with superhuman strength, broke it loose and stumbled free from the fighter just before it exploded, not fifty feet from his escape path. He had stood looking back at the burning Hurricane and felt his face, for the heat inside the cockpit had been like a furnace.

When he gave left rudder at the end of the runway,

Kapolski felt annoyingly hot. He always sweated terribly inside the G-suits. He couldn't wait to take off his helmet and breathe some fresh unpolluted air. He steered the fighter-interceptor off the runway and taxied it to one of the dispersal points, off to the right and in front of a set of large hangars.

A bundled up Lance Tiemans, his hand wands glowing red, waved Kapolski down a row of camouflaged interceptors and into position between two of them. Kapolski glanced around the cockpit, letting the engines idle momentarily before shutting down the thundering giants.

Kapolski was tired. He disconnected his G-suit and oxygen hoses, pulled off his helmet, and slid open the canopy. For a few seconds the cold air was a welcome relief. Then the warm cockpit air dispersed into the cold outside air and he felt chilled to the bone. His teeth started to chatter. He rubbed his face several times while Tiemans put the ladder in place and climbed up.

"Was that you pouring it on up there? Thanks to the moon I could see it all. It was you, wasn't it?"

Kapolski nodded and grinned. "Me and Wilky," he said, breathing steam into the air.

Tiemans looked back in the direction of the group captain's fighter, which had touched down only minutes before Kapolski's. "Wilkinson?" He seemed surprised, for the C.O. usually left the dogfights to his flight instructors. "You and Wilkinson were having a dogfight?"

"You bet we were. Help me out will you, I'm stiffer than a board. I must be getting old, and get that parka on me. It's cold out here."

Tiemans helped the pilot into his parka. Once they were both down the ladder, Tiemans leaned over to Kapolski and asked in a whisper, "What did she do?"

"Mach two-point-three, no sweat, and it handled like

a dream. And still wanted to go some more," Kapolski whispered back. He jumped to the pavement to meet Wilkinson, who was about fifty feet away and walking towards them.

Then a strange feeling hit Kapolski like a sledgehammer. He felt like he was going to faint, something he hadn't experienced in a long while. He leaned against the ladder for support.

Only minutes earlier he and Wilkinson had flown several tight turns that reached high G-forces. Their G-suits, which were made up of an intricate system of air tunnels that blew up and pressed against the stomach and legs as the turn pressure increased, helped to a certain degree—1 G. But even with these suits on, one could "gray out" at 7 Gs. At one point in the dogfight Kapolski did "take a nap," as some pilots called it.

It often happens that there is tremendous strain on a pilot in the period after jet combat, whether real or practice, is over. His body sweats so badly, and he's so exhausted that he can't fly for at least twenty-four hours. Usually, the pilot doesn't feel anything until after touchdown, when he steps out onto solid ground. He is hit by a drunken sensation that lasts for several hours. Kapolski felt this and was ashamed that it had happened to him.

Following the debriefing, Kapolski crossed over to the hangar. Under the bright lights inside, two Arrows were undergoing a fifty-hour inspection. Ground crew were on top of, inside, and underneath the fighters. The ground crew chief stood under the nose of one, signing numerous reports and papers attached to his clipboard. Kapolski walked around the aircraft and slowly up a flight of stairs.

He clumped down the hallway and turned in at the

freshly painted white door with PILOTS ONLY marked on it in large black letters. There was no one in the lounge, and Kapolski wasn't interested in the mess of magazines and pocketbooks scattered on tables and chairs. He walked into the locker room where he peeled off his parka, G-suit, shirt, boots and undergarments. He started the shower and let it run as he stared at his naked body in the thirty-foot-long mirror attached to one side of the wall.

Kapolski frowned. He was thirty-nine and no spring chicken anymore, but he still looked pretty good. He had lost some hair around the temples, but his crew cut was a deep brown, no grey showing yet, and his skin was clear and healthy-looking, except for some stress lines. His husky six-foot build was powerful and natural; he'd never had to lift weights or play sports to keep fit.

The new fighter had given Kapolski a real shot in the arm. He didn't want to retire now. For the first time in the year and several months since his wife's death he finally felt he was valuable again. Wilkinson obviously thought so too. Big things were happening in the air force, but he didn't understand all the secrecy. Why was the Arrow being kept hidden? Why the fake scrapping? What were they being trained for?

Kapolski sighed and stepped into the shower. He let the hot spray pierce his body until his skin tingled and the stream of rushing water dulled his senses.

# CHAPTER EIGHT

"THAT WAS CHUCK BERRY SINGING HIS NEW SMASH HIT 'ALMOST GROWN' AND IT'S GOING RIGHT TO THE TOP OF THE CHARTS HERE AT WBDD TORONTO, 1415 ON YOUR DIAL," declared the disk jockey from his radio studio. "AND REMEMBER, YOU TEENS, CHUCK BERRY IS COMING TO MAPLE LEAF GARDENS NEXT SATURDAY NIGHT. YES, NEXT SATURDAY NIGHT AT SEVEN-THIRTY. RIGHT AFTER THE SHOW, LISTEN FOR OUR LIVE INTERVIEW WITH CHUCK, HIMSELF, BACKSTAGE. I'LL BE THERE, BUDDY DIAMOND, WITH THE ONE, THE ONLY CHUCK BERRY. HE'LL TALK ABOUT HIS NEW WAX 'ALMOST GROWN' AND SOME OF HIS PAST HITS, AND WE'LL TALK ABOUT THE FUTURE. ALL THAT AT NINE-FORTY NEXT SATURDAY NIGHT. SO DON'T MISS IT. AND FOR THOSE WHO DON'T HAVE TICKETS—TOO BAD. ALL THE TICKETS HAVE BEEN SOLD. IT'S A SELLOUT. THE GARDENS IS GOING TO ROCK AND ROLL THIS SATURDAY

NIGHT, AND DON'T FORGET TO LISTEN TO THE CHUCK
BERRY INTERVIEW AT TWENTY MINUTES TO TEN, ALL
HERE AT WBDD TORONTO, THE MUSIC STATION THAT
ROCKS AROUND THE CLOCK. WE'LL HAVE MORE ROCK
AND ROLL RIGHT AFTER THE NEWS."

Then, from another part of the studio, "THE TIME IS
NOW 1:00 P.M., AND I'M LARRY STEPHENSON. THIS IS
THE ONE O'CLOCK NEWS." A short pause. "AT THIS
VERY MOMENT AT MALTON AIRPORT, SEVERAL AVRO AR-
ROW FIGHTER-INTERCEPTORS ARE BEING TORN APART ON
THE TARMAC, AND THE ARROWS INSIDE THE PLANT ARE
BEING TORCHED. ALL NEWSMEN AND JOURNALISTS HAVE
BEEN BANNED FROM THE AREA. MEANWHILE, IN OT-
TAWA, DEFENSE MINISTER DEAN STEDMAN HOLDING A
NEWS CONFERENCE TO DEFEND THE GOVERNMENT'S DE-
CISION TO SCRAP THE AIRCRAFT . . ."

"Ben!" shouted Sammy Hughes, waving a pad of
paper. "Ben, get over here, pronto!" Hughes' voice
rang through the newsroom of the *Toronto Tribune* like
the piercing shriek of a five o'clock whistle.

Spencer sprang up from his typewriter and strode
quickly over to the glass-enclosed office of the news
editor.

"Ben, I just heard a strange report on the radio."

"Yeah?" Spencer closed the door behind him.

"All those Arrows at Malton are being torched to
bits, so WBDD says, and the media has been banned
from the site. I guess Ottawa is all in a sweat. We have
to move on this. I'm going to take a chance but I think
it'll work." Hughes stretched his arms over his head
and groaned. "I should have gotten more sleep last
night. Anyway, I've arranged a pilot for you at the Island Airport. Get over there and ask for, let's see . . ."
He rummaged through the messy stack of papers on his
desk. "Where is it?"

Spencer shook his head. "Your desk's a dog's breakfast!"

"I just had it here. There, the name is on here," he said, handing a sheet to Spencer. "McCarthy. He flies choppers. He'll fly you right over the Avro plant so you can snap some pictures. We want lots of pictures. Then we'll find out for sure what's going on over there. If they really are torching the Arrow, then we've scooped the other papers.

"One more thing. Tell McCarthy that once he's approaching the Malton Airport control zone he's to tell the tower he's covering an accident at Derry and Airport Road. They get awfully touchy around Malton, and we've got to be careful."

"Are we likely to run into trouble?"

"I don't know. The copter has to get clearance from the tower before it can fly any further. You might have to fake it."

"Got it."

"Good. Now get going before the chopper pilot chickens out. He knows all about it, by the way."

"I'm out of here, Sam."


"You don't really think they're torching those beauties, do you?" asked the chopper pilot over the noise of his droning engine. He was wearing a grubby Detroit Tigers baseball cap and an equally dirty pair of coveralls that reeked of grease. Spencer hoped he took better care of his chopper than he did of himself.

"I don't know," Spencer shouted back, as he adjusted the camera that was slung over his neck. "I guess that's what we're going to find out."

"Not so loud," said the pilot. "I can hear you in my headphones without you having to shout."

"Oh yeah, sorry." The writer moved the small mike

in his headset farther from his mouth. The headgear reminded him of the Tokyo raid he'd been on during the war.

He checked the sliding window twice, to make sure it worked. Then he left the window open, placed his reflex camera lens through it, and positioned his right eye at the viewfinder. Perfect, he thought. He quickly closed the window to keep the cold air out.

It was a bright, sun-filled day. A thousand feet below them, in the city of Etobicoke, cars and trucks moved almost bumper to bumper on the expressways. Malton Airport was a few miles further on, on their left, and busy metropolitan Toronto, with over a million people, was off to the chopper's starboard.

"They probably think we're a traffic copter," the pilot muttered, scratching his two-day-old growth of whiskers.

"Who?" asked Spencer, his mind elsewhere.

"Those poor slobs down there," replied McCarthy, pointing to Highway 27. "The city's supposed to make the road into a six lane highway because there's always such a traffic snarl. But who knows when they'll get it done?" The pilot looked over at Spencer. "I wonder what it's going to look like over at Avro."

"According to the radio, the Arrows are being dismantled on the tarmac. The ones inside are getting the torch. But I don't believe it. It's bad enough the Conservatives stopped production a few months back, but to destroy the planes is insane, especially after some of the offers they've gotten."

The pilot's eyes grew wide. "What offers?"

"I've heard, through a source in Ottawa, that the British were ready to pay the federal government a substantial sum for three of the Arrows. They want them for supersonic test flights over in Britain. The British and the French are supposed to be in the preliminary stages of designing a supersonic jet airliner together, and they want the Arrows for testing.''

The pilot leaned over to Spencer. ''Only testing?''

''That's right.'' Spencer shrugged. ''The British have lots of fighters of their own and the Arrow doesn't fit into the RAF's plans. Their fighter strips are closer together than ours in Canada. Also, they're a smaller country and don't need a long-range aircraft like we do. We don't have a lot of strips, and the ones we have are far apart. Also, our fighter requirements are geared towards a fast twin-engine machine in case one engine fails.''

''You sure know your work.''

''I make it my business to find out about things, that's my job. I'll tell you something else.''

''I'm all ears.''

''General Electric was prepared to buy all the Arrows for spare parts, but the Tories turned them down cold.''

''That's hard to believe. What happened to the British deal?''

''I haven't heard anything more. But if the Arrows are being dismantled, then I guess it's off.''

''There they are!'' shouted McCarthy.

The helicopter was still a mile away, but McCarthy and Spencer couldn't miss the unmistakable design of four sleek Arrows glistening in the sun.

McCarthy radioed the tower for clearance. ''Okay, we're cleared.''

''Let's go around that way,'' Spencer said, pointing towards the southern part of the airport. ''Then just fly back and forth while I fire away.'' The pilot nodded. Spencer checked the light meter, shutter speed and aperture setting on his new Pentax single-lens reflex camera.

McCarthy flew the helicopter close to the airport, dropped the machine down to just under a hundred feet, then banked slightly to the left. Four Arrows and two

CF-100s outside the hangar were now in plain view. They could also make out four men in coveralls with tools in their hands.

"They've already started the torching, Spencer. Look, there's pieces of some of the aircraft on the ground. My God, there's only the fuselage left on that one. Looks like number two-zero-five."

"I don't believe it! I just don't believe it!" Spencer's heart was beating so hard and fast that he could almost hear it over the helicopter's propeller.

"Hey, don't forget, you came here to take pictures. Quit gawking and start snapping."

"Yeah, okay, I know, I know." Spencer slid open the window and peered through the camera lens as the cold air hit his face. "Okay, I'm ready. Hold her steady." Spencer shot a few frames as McCarthy flew north over the compound. The Arrows were below and to the right. "Great. That's it. I've got them. Now go right."

"What?"

"Go that way," Spencer blurted, pointing to the right. "I want to get right over top of them. This time can you bank the chopper more?"

"Sure. Oh, no."

"What's the matter?"

"The tower's calling us. They want to know what we're doing."

"Ignore them!"

On the tarmac, the torchers were watching the helicopter. "Hey, Spencer, one of the torchers is waving at us." Spencer kept snapping more pictures as the pilot flew across the compound. "He's waving us to go away."

Spencer took another half-dozen shots. "Okay, let's head back. I've got enough pictures of this funeral."

"Good thing. We better get out of here before we're in deep trouble, if we aren't already. Hang on, I'm going to bank it."

WASHINGTON, D.C., FRIDAY, MAY 1, 1321 HOURS (EST)

The American president and his defense secretary were strolling past a White House flower garden, both deep in thought. The two were surrounded by budding roses that were not yet in full bloom. Several White House gardeners were busy trimming and weeding on the grounds.

The president was wearing golf shoes, a stylish sport shirt, and straight-legged slacks. He was firmly clutching an April 30 edition of the *Toronto Tribune* in his left hand and a two-iron golf club in his right. The day was sunny, not a cloud in the sky, and the air was unseasonably cool. Spring was late this year.

"Mr. President?" Jeffrey Kolb spoke first, tugging at the collar of his white monogrammed shirt as if his tie were too tight. "Do you really think this whole thing will work?"

The leader stopped and smiled. "You mean the Arrow scrapping?"

"Yes."

"I do," the president answered calmly. "It's got to. Besides, it's too late now to stop it, isn't it?"

"There are so many people involved. Thousands of them, and all it takes is one to spill the beans."

The president walked across the grass, toward the walkway, leaving Kolb standing by himself in the garden. "Come on out to the tee," he called back to his secretary. "It's quite nice out this afternoon, what with the sun shining. Just a little cool. We'll have some coffee sent out to us, so we can warm up."

The president had erected a golf tee in the Presidential Garden behind the White House Oval Office, where he could shoot the occasional two- or three-iron swings in the direction of the White House Fountain. He usually waited till the leaves were full, so he could be hidden from any prying eyes along East and South Executive Avenues. But this year he couldn't wait a few more days to hit some balls down the "fairway." In his spare time during the winter he hit golf balls into a specially made fixed net in the White House gymnasium.

The defense secretary sat on a lawn chair and watched the president shoot a bucket of balls. "You know, this guy Spencer at the *Toronto Tribune* has been carping at the Canadian government for canceling the Arrow." Kolb had the paper open at Spencer's column. "Reporters like him are dangerous, and snoopy too. He might uncover something."

The president shrugged, then shot a ball into the trees to the right. "Doesn't that tick you off?" he said. "That's three in a row into the trees. What do you think I'm doing wrong, Jeffrey?"

Kolb dumped the newspaper onto the grass. He was annoyed that the president was so relaxed. "If you're slicing, sir, then you're probably not holding the club properly," he grunted. "Maybe your thumb is dropping off, and you don't know it." Kolb was an expert golfer and often shot a few rounds with the president when he got the chance. On a par-72 course he often slipped inside the 80 range.

"Do you think so?" The president turned to Kolb. "Maybe you're right," he said, winking. The president knew Kolb was getting irritated.

The president placed another ball on the tee, then studied his fairway carefully. He dropped the club from his shoulder, gripped it with both hands, making sure the thumbs did not drag, and looked up at the fountain a few hundred yards away. "Fore!" he yelled. This time the ball took off straight as an arrow, in a high arc down the center of the grass fairway. A perfect shot.

Kolb knew the president needed this time to relax and get away from the pressures of his job. It was no use discussing politics until he'd finished his round. "Great shot, Mr. President," Kolb spoke sincerely. "That's the best one yet."

The president was obviously pleased with himself. "You must have been right about the thumbs. Maybe I better stop while I'm ahead. How's your coffee?"

"Fine, sir." Kolb swallowed another mouthful. The president walked over to the table and drank from his full cup.

"Now, about the Arrow," the president said. "This whole thing is looking better all the time. That paper," he pointed to the *Tribune* on the ground, "is full of Arrow articles, pro and con. Thanks to Spencer, everyone believes the planes have been scrapped. His photos from the helicopter were the clincher."

"Mr. President," said a young voice behind the leader. "I have a telex from American Air Force Intelligence in Japan that you might be interested in." A short, lean United States Air Force officer in dress uniform stood to the left of the president.

"Thank you." The president scanned the telex quickly. "You may go," he said to the officer, "and please let me know immediately if anything else comes through."

"Yes sir, Mr. President."

The President handed the sheet to Kolb. "Jeffrey, have a look at this and tell me what you make of it."

Kolb spent a few seconds studying the message. "Hmmm, the Russians are practising light naval maneuvers off their coastline in the North Pacific for the next three days."

"Now read the next few lines below it."

"Let's see. An unidentified twin-engine delta-winged fighter is mentioned. You don't suppose it's the Skyjacker?"

"Would it surprise you?"

"No," Kolb replied, shaking his head. "When it comes to the Russians, nothing surprises me. They must still be building it."

"We expected it, didn't we? I contacted the Soviet premier on February 20 to let him know that we had suspended the Arrow's production. He informed me that the Skyjacker was also history."

"What about the American air force delegation that was invited to Russia to witness the dismantling?"

"The Russians were probably just as good at disguising the MiG-K scrapping as we were the Arrow's," the president said.

"That's true. What do we do now?"

"I think Schult would be interested in this. Send him a message at Colorado Springs right away. Magna-One has to make contact with his Russian source. I want some answers. And I want a meeting set up with the air staff for tomorrow. See to it."

TORONTO, ONTARIO, THURSDAY, MAY 14
1145 HOURS (EST)

Ben Spencer pushed back his chair and reached for his cup of coffee. "Aw, who made this sludge? I could use it in my car," he said to another writer in the newsroom.

Sammy Hughes, sleeves rolled up, tie undone, was walking across the office and stopped at Spencer's desk. "I made it, do you mind?"

"You made it? What's the matter, don't you like us around here?" Spencer asked sarcastically. "And if you made it, how come you're not drinking it?"

"Because I already had two cups this morning."

"Two?"

"Yes, two."

"Of this?" Spencer pointed at his cup.

"Yes, of this."

"Take my advice, just . . ."

"I don't want your advice. Last time I took your advice I bought a Mercury."

Spencer laughed. "Let's not talk about that lemon again."

Hughes pretended to be angry. "Well, you told me to buy that lemon because a good friend of yours owned it."

"Sorry, I have to be wrong sometimes. It's a writer's prerogative."

Hughes groaned. He looked down at Spencer's typewriter. "What's in the column tomorrow?"

"Our illustrious prime minister."

"Again?"

"Yes, again." Spencer went back to his typing.

"The Arrow?"

"Not this time. I've written so many articles on the Arrow that I'm even dreaming about it. No, this time it's about the P.M. himself."

"Mind if I read it?"

"What's the matter, got nothing else to do?"

Hughes smiled. "I'm on a break," he said, reaching for his glasses in his shirt pocket.

"You're not in the union. You're not supposed to get a break."

"Shhh." Hughes motioned with his forefinger to his lips.

"Sure, go ahead. The other pages are over there."

Hughes picked up the typed pages on the right-hand side of the desk and started reading.

### CURRENTLY SPEAKING with BEN SPENCER
*When our prime minister first gained power in 1957, we were led to believe that the illustrious member from Prince Albert was a true, card-carrying Tory, who would support big business and create the*

*kind of atmosphere where the big empires on Bay
Street would flourish like never before. No welfare
state. No government handouts. No leeching of the
public purse. Well, we were all steered wrong.*

*Since coming to power, the prime minister has put
a damper on big business (completely ignored it is
more like it) by concentrating on social and liberal
policies. The individual now means everything. The
family, the community, and small business are the
elite. Free enterprise has been stonewalled in the last
two years, a complete reversal of the policies of the
last Tory federal government under R. B. Bennett.*

*It's really all a game. Believe it or not, the prime
minister is attempting to squash the Liberals by draw-
ing them in to oppose his left-wing proposals, and so
leave them dangling on the right. The CCF and Social
Credit parties, the two dead-end parties (at least fed-
erally), are too small to mount any reasonable opposition. The prime minister's only enemy, besides
the news media who like to call a spade a spade, is
the Liberal party. The Tories are trying to turn the
Liberals into a disorganized movement devoid of any
rational policies.*

*Handouts are being poured into veterans' pen-
sions, family allowances, unemployment insurance,
compensation for the sick, the injured. . . . On and
on it goes. Soon, we will surpass the United Kingdom
as the welfare state of the Western world.*

*We should have known back in 1948 that something
was in the wind. At that time the prime minister, who
was the opposition foreign affairs critic, almost single-
handedly halted a proposal to outlaw the Communist
party of Canada. He believed that if the movement
were outlawed, these people would only go underground. It was better to leave them be, he said. The*

*other Tories eventually agreed with him, but later branded him a Commie.*

*In addition, during the mammoth 1958 election campaign, the prime minister did not give one shred of evidence that he was a friend of big business. He sided with his friends, the Western farmers, a maneuver that, I believe, is dividing this country, East and West.*

*Under the present Conservative government the Agricultural Department's budget has been nearly doubled. Farmers' incomes are rising at a much faster rate than inflation, triple to be exact, thanks to federal incentives.*

*Alvin Sampson, the Minister of Northern Affairs and National Resources, who was instrumental in creating the Vision theme savagely used by the prime minister in the 1958 election campaign, has helped to virtually lock up Tory votes on the prairies for years to come. Sampson, a farmer himself, from Delisle, Saskatchewan, and the prime minister seem to be the only friends of the "underprivileged" farmer.*

*While our prime minister is devising more ways to build up his welfare state, to help out the "average Canadian," unemployment has risen steadily and now sits at 8 percent. How high will it go this winter when the seasonal trades are laid off?*

*Where is all this going to lead? Unless there are some gutsy individuals in the Tory machine who have the courage to stand up to the prime minister and shake up the government, our economy is going to take a nosedive. We need to get back on the "right" track before it's too late.*

Hughes finished the pages and read the remainder on the typewriter as Spencer finished up.

"There we go," Spencer snapped, pulling the last

sheet from the machine. He dropped it on top of the others and turned off the typewriter. "I'm going to Louie's."

"Some of that good old-fashioned Italian cooking."

"You got it."

"Louie, how are you doing?"

"Ben! Hey, it's good to see you. Where have you been lately?"

"Oh, I took two weeks off to go to Vancouver, then the last while I've been bagging my lunch to work."

"Spent too much on the coast and can't afford my prices?"

Spencer laughed. "That's part of it. I also can't afford your calories."

Spencer often ate at Fortino's restaurant on Yonge Street, three blocks from the *Tribune*. He had known the owner, Louie Fortino, since he had arrived in Toronto to take up his new job with the *Tribune*. Fortino and Spencer hit it off right away, probably due to their mutual love of professional sports, mainly hockey and baseball.

The cozy restaurant was a popular eating spot in Toronto. The pale blue walls were hung with pictures of great National Hockey League players and New York Yankee baseball players. The prices were competitive, the service friendly, and the atmosphere nostalgic for sports fans. The food consisted of a fine mixture of Italian and Canadian cuisine.

Fortino usually stood behind the counter to the left of the entrance door. On the right, all along the wall, were a dozen separate booths that could seat four persons. Every booth had a jukebox that contained the latest rock and roll records. In front of Fortino, along the counter, were several swivel stools. At this time of day the place was packed, but Spencer had called ahead and asked Fortino to keep a booth free.

"Is that my table in the back, Louie?"

"Sure, your favorite spot. Go have a seat, and I'll be right with you." Fortino signaled another waiter to take his place behind the counter while he waited on Spencer.

"What do you feel like eating today, Ben?"

"What's the soup of the day?"

"French onion."

"Great. I'll have a bowl of that, and a dish of your great lasagna, with some coleslaw on the side. To hell with my diet for today. And coffee to drink. Oh, by the way, someone's meeting me here later."

"No problem, my friend." Fortino went directly to the kitchen to relay the food order.

Spencer watched three teenagers, two guys and a girl, in the booth next to him plugging dimes into their table jukebox. Soon they were softly singing along with the Everly Brothers' "Bye, Bye Love." The girl, a blonde, was very pretty, with her hair up in a ponytail, and the guys both had their hair slicked back with grease. They seemed to be nice kids, not bothering anyone.

In record time Louie brought Spencer's steaming hot soup out to him. "I'm supposed to be on a diet, but I haven't been doing so well lately. I just couldn't resist your onion soup. By the way, I've been eyeing that poster of Satchell Paige behind the counter. Where on earth did you get it?"

Fortino smiled broadly. "That's my latest addition. My sister out in Manitoba picked it up at an auction sale near the Minnesota border. It's supposed to be authentic, from the 1930s when Paige pitched for an all-white semipro team in Bismarck, North Dakota, and the team barnstormed in western Canada. Great, isn't it. Everybody comments on it."

"I'd love to have it in my rec room."

"Sorry, it's not for sale."

"Can't fault a guy for trying," Spencer chuckled, breathing in the delightful aroma of the soup.

"Remember, Ben," Fortino whispered, leaning towards Spencer, "don't dip your tie into the soup."

About a year ago, Spencer had accidentally dragged a new tie through his soup one lunch hour, and the good-natured Fortino had never let him forget it.

Spencer smirked, opening his suit jacket. "I won't. See, I tucked it into my shirt."

Louie laughed out loud. "You got me this time!"

Spencer ate his lunch quickly, and was soon relaxing over his coffee. He saw a tall man in his fifties enter the restaurant and approach the counter. Louie met him and pointed towards Spencer.

"Hi, I'm Terry Robertson."

Spencer stood to shake his hand. "Pleased to meet you. Have a seat. Can I get you anything?"

"No thanks," Robertson answered. "I ate before I came."

Spencer took a sip of his coffee. "So what's on your mind, Mr. Robertson?"

Robertson looked worried as he unbuttoned his jacket. He was a good-looking man with curly, brown hair, smooth skin, and white even teeth. He spoke in a slow, almost drawling manner that began to annoy Spencer, as he explained his position with A. V. Roe's Arrow project.

"I couldn't tell you this over the phone, but I stole some of the wing and fuselage blueprints before I left Avro. I'll show them to you, but don't spread them out over the table." Robertson reached for an envelope in the inside pocket of his jacket. He pulled out some papers and set them down on the table. Spencer opened them only partway but he could see that they were from the Arrow all right.

Spencer didn't show any emotion. "You're not the only one who stole blueprints when the Arrow went under."

"I'm not?"

"No, you're not. Someone else lifted the nose gear blueprints. I know, I've seen them."

"Well," Robertson whispered. "Why didn't you write the story?"

Spencer was getting bored. "What story? You stole some blueprints, so what?" He looked at his watch and drank his last few drops of coffee. "I've got to go. Is there anything else?"

"Well, you could say that RCMP intelligence has questioned me about the missing blueprints."

"What?"

"The RCMP wanted them. Now what do you think?"

"Now I'm interested. If the Arrow was terminated, why would they want the blueprints? Are you sure it was the RCMP?"

"I saw their badges. I told them I didn't have anything. I hid the prints in the attic after that, just in case. And it's a good thing too because they came back a second time and searched the house, but they never found them."

"Really?"

"What do you think now?"

"I don't know. It doesn't make sense."

"Funny thing, too," Robertson pondered, looking down at the table, "I haven't seen them in about two months now."

"You mean all this happened two months ago and you haven't seen the RCMP since?"

"That's right. It's almost as if they don't need the blueprints anymore."

"Why did you wait so long to come to me?"

"I don't know, scared I guess."

"By the way, where are you working now?"

"I'm not, I'm unemployed. I'm hoping to land a job soon, on the assembly line at de Havilland. Are you going to do anything, Mr. Spencer?"

"I don't know what I can do." Spencer thought for a moment. "Why would the RCMP want this stuff?"

"It doesn't figure, does it?"

TORONTO, ONTARIO, MONDAY, MAY 18
0904 HOURS (EST)

Spencer was trying to work on his next column, but he couldn't get the conversation with Robertson four days earlier out of his mind. Were the RCMP really after him? Why? It just didn't make sense, unless the Tory government wanted everything to do with the Arrow totally destroyed. What was happening to this country?

Then the desk phone rang. He let it ring twice while he finished a sentence.

"Ben Spencer," he said, hunching over the typewriter to correct an error.

"Mr. Spencer," the voice spoke formally, "I'm calling on behalf of the prime minister."

Spencer sat up straight in his chair. "Yes, what can I do for you?"

"It seems you've done enough already."

"Sorry, I must be missing something here."

"The prime minister takes offense to an article you wrote stating that he was a Communist." The voice remained calm.

"Sir," Spencer spoke loudly enough for his area of the busy newsroom to hear, "I did not say that the prime minister was a Communist. I said that his party branded him a Commie after he blocked . . .''

''I'll have you know that most of his colleagues congratulated him on the stand that he took. You also implied that the prime minister concentrates too much on the little guy, the farmer, the average Canadian. Well, if it weren't for the average Canadian there would be no Canada. The farming industry, not the big corporations, is the backbone of this nation, and we need to support it.''

A crowd of fellow workers was beginning to gather around Spencer's desk. ''Please inform the prime minister for me that I know quite a bit about the average Canadian, myself. I saw the average Canadian die on the beaches on D-Day. I saw the average Canadian being pulled out of bomber turrets, minus an arm or leg. I saw the average Canadian fight for this country with everything he had and then some. They are the people that made this country what it is; they are the backbone of this country. And they're from all walks of life, not just farmers.''

''The prime minister feels you have no business saying the things you do.''

''Why not?'' Spencer said, his voice getting louder. ''I saw combat right up front, something that the prime minister never did. All your prime minister can do is ruin our economy, and destroy the best fighter in the world at the same time.''

''I see you still haven't gotten that plane out of your system.''

''No, I haven't, and I never will.''

''The Arrow was good, but it couldn't fly. It's dead, just forget it.''

''What do you mean, it couldn't fly? What do you or the prime minister know about military matters? The prime minister only got as far as boot camp during World War I. Then he picked up a bout of measles and got sent home." Many in the newsroom snickered. Spencer leaned forward in his chair.

"You haven't heard the end of this. Your editor might receive a call some day."

"That won't change anything. The owners of the *Tribune* dislike your government's policies as much as I do. You forget that this is not Ottawa. I've heard through the grapevine that any time the prime minister reads a column he disagrees with he rants and raves about it. I know of one right-leaning reporter who was demoted for daring to disagree with our illustrious leader. You just sit tight and listen to me. This is not Ottawa, it's the Big T.O. The *Tribune* doesn't owe the prime minister anything. If he wants good press, then he should start doing something right for this country and get the economy going, because if he doesn't the *average* Canadian will throw him out on his ass in the next election. The Conservative party was very lucky to get 208 seats last year, sir. In fact, you got in on a fraud, just like I said in my column. The people won't fall for it a second time. They are on to your boss. Now, I'm a busy man and I'm sure you are too, so I must say good-bye."

Spencer hung up the phone. "What's everybody looking at?"

"Who was that?" an older reporter in the crowd asked.

Spencer yawned, pretending to be unconcerned.

"Oh, it was someone in the P.M.'s office," he shrugged. "I never did get his name." Then he went back to his typewriter, not bothering to glance at the keyboard.

"Ben?" one of the onlookers interrupted.

Spencer stopped to look up at the crowd of people still milling around his desk. Some were laughing. "Yeah?"

"Your tie is stuck in the typewriter."

# CHAPTER NINE

IT WAS A WARM SUMMER EVENING IN THE CAnadian capital. The air was calm, the sky partially overcast in the west. The sun was about to set and overhead, vapor trails of a jetliner could be seen through a large gap in the clouds, over thirty thousand feet up, coming out of, perhaps, Toronto or Chicago, and heading east to Europe. A motor boat roared through the water towards Hull on the Quebec side of the Ottawa River.

The prime minister and his wife were entertaining the Kralicks at 24 Sussex Drive, an impressive three-story, gray stone mansion situated on a bluff above the Ottawa River. The women sat and chatted on the couch, while the prime minister and his finance minister stood at the other end of the room, near the piano. The two men engaged in small talk as they looked at the prime minister's autographed photos of world politicians and Royal Family photos.

Kralick stirred his tea nervously, wishing the spoon was a swizzle stick and the liquid a good stiff drink. The Tory prime minister and his wife were both teetotalers and never served liquor at their dinners and receptions.

"How did you like the dinner? Did you have enough?" the prime minister asked.

Kralick appeared to be daydreaming. "Huh? Oh, fine sir. Very good. I'm stuffed."

"Let's go to the study. I've never showed you my book collection."

"Good," said Kralick. "I want to talk to you about a particular matter."

Downstairs, in the prime minister's study they talked on as the Tory leader pointed to his collection of hardcover books spread along a long wall.

"I have nearly every work of Sir Winston Churchill, and autographed too. Here," he declared, pointing at the middle of three shelves.

"He's quite a politician."

The prime minister's face grew taut. "That's for sure. You have to hand it to him, he was still Britain's prime minister at eighty years of age. That's amazing. I wish I could . . ." He stopped short, possibly embarrassed about what he was thinking. "Over here is my ten-volume edition of the works of Molière. It once belonged to Sir John A. Macdonald. Henri Laurier, Sir Wilfrid's great-nephew, presented the volume to me last year."

"I'm impressed." Kralick had never expected such a valuable collection.

"I'm rather proud of it," the prime minister beamed. For several more minutes he showed more of his books.

"Now, what did you want to talk to me about?"

"I don't know if it's anything," Kralick eyed his superior, "but I wanted to wait until we were clear of the women to tell you. When I left your office yesterday, I found this piece of paper on the floor just outside your telex room.'' He took a folded sheet out of the back pocket of his trousers. ''Here it is.''

''Let's see it.'' The prime minister snatched the paper, leaving Kralick with a startled look on his face. He didn't know what to think. ''Why did you do that? It's only . . .''

''You found it outside my office?''

''Yes.''

''Were there any more?''

''No, just that one. Tell me, what does TUNDRA mean?''

''Never mind!'' said the prime minister, still gawking at the paper in utter disbelief. ''This is a military top secret!''

''But sir, what's going on? Shouldn't I know? A mass-produced fighter is mentioned. It says thirty-five will be transferred . . .''

''I know what it says. Just forget you ever saw this paper. As far as you're concerned, it never existed. You got that? Just put it out of your mind.'' The prime minister waved the paper so close to Kralick's face that he was forced to take a step backwards. ''Forget you ever laid eyes on this. Do you understand me, Alex?''

''Sure, but . . .''

''No buts! Just forget it!''

The prime minister's wife came into the study just then. She was appropriately dressed in a fashionable evening gown made of powder-blue silk. ''What are you waving at Alex, dear? You look angry. You're not campaigning anymore, you know.'' She laughed.

''Oh, it's nothing, dear. Right Alex?'' The prime minister patted his minister on the shoulder and smiled mechanically. ''Come on, let's go back to the living room. It's getting too warm down here.''

What an understatement, thought Kralick. The prime minister's arm felt heavy on his shoulders as they walked upstairs.

"Remember," the prime minister stopped abruptly in the hallway, "not a word to anyone."

OTTAWA, ONTARIO, WEDNESDAY, JUNE 24
0550 HOURS (EST)

"Corporal Salisbury, Sergeant Cratton, I want to talk to you both," Defense Minister Stedman said sternly, as he closed the door to the prime minister's communications room. He carefully placed the key to the door in his wallet, then returned it to the breast pocket of his suit jacket. With him was a tough-looking young man in a brown double-breasted suit.

In the middle of the fifteen-by-twenty-foot room opposite the prime minister's office in the Parliament Buildings were two long tables. Five telex machines were perched on one table; three of the latest IBM electronic typewriters were on the other. On the wall to the right, just in front of the EXIT ONLY door, hung a large four-by-six-foot map of the Northwest Territories, and two other maps of the same size showing the east and west sections of the Canadian Dominion. Spread throughout the room was assorted office equipment; telephones, desks, file cabinets, swivel chairs, and bookshelves, all neatly arranged in military fashion. Two out-of-uniform Royal Canadian Air Force noncommissioned officers were busying themselves in the room. Both were in their shirtsleeves, for the room was warm. One of the men, Corporal Salisbury, had been typing when Stedman demanded his attention. Sergeant Cratton, the slightly taller one, was reading some data coming through on one of the telexes. When the thin and prematurely balding Salisbury looked at Stedman's face, he knew right away that something was wrong. Cratton, about twenty-five, dark-haired and husky, continued studying the pounding telex machine. "I'll be right with you, sir, as soon as I . . ."

"I want to talk to you NOW!" said Stedman, trying to contain his anger.

Both men were startled by the demanding, crackling voice of Stedman and they bolted upright. "Yes sir," they answered, almost in unison.

"I have something to show you."

Stedman reached into the inside pocket of his jacket and pulled out a piece of paper, a telex flimsy, slightly crumpled and well creased into four equal parts. He unfolded it and pushed it almost into the faces of the officers. He demanded to know who had received the telex, an important message concerning the transfer of TUNDRA aircraft to an operational base.

Cratton swallowed hard. "We were on duty then, sir. I took the message myself two days ago and sent it through the usual channels."

Stedman waved the telex through the air. "Then what did you do with it?"

"I received it back. Then I filed . . ."

"Stop right there. You did not file it because it is here in my hand."

"I was supposed to file it, sir."

" 'Supposed to file it' is not good enough." Cratton felt stupid and looked straight forward, avoiding the defense minister's icy stare. "Cratton, let me tell you where it ended up. A member of Parliament, a Conservative, thank God, found the telex on the floor outside this very room. It was on the floor, just lying there for everyone and his donkey to see and read. Now, how in blazes did it ever get there?" No answer. "You dropped it, that's how!"

"I'm sorry, sir."

Stedman turned to his assistant. "Take him out of here."

Cratton tried to protest. "But sir . . ."

"No buts, you're through. Get him out of here!" The husky man grabbed Cratton by the arm. "You jeopardized the entire TUNDRA project. If these messages get into the hands of the wrong people we're screwed. If a Liberal or CCF M.P. had picked up that telex, our cover would be blown for sure and we'd have us a scandal on our hands."

Stedman waited for the two to leave. Then he looked at Salisbury. "And another thing, while we're at it, some M.P.s have tried to find out what's going on in here, why the secrecy and so forth. I know you've been briefed on this before, but make sure you stick to the story because things may get hot. Word is out on Parliament Hill, although I'm sure it won't reach the House of Commons floor. At least, it better not. You are simply involved in international communications, that's all. You are not air force noncommissioned officers; you are factfinders for the prime minister. You're civilians, remember? Civilians!"

"Sir," said Salisbury, in command of himself, "there will be no more slip-ups."

"There better not be." Stedman gazed at the noncommissioned officer long and hard. He decided he had made his point, and it was time to ease up. He sighed. "You'll be given some help within the hour. Meantime, you'll have to go it alone. Anything new?"

"Yes, there is," murmured Salisbury. "A northern air base has picked up a large target on its sets. A CF-100 from a base east of the MacKenzie River was alerted just minutes before you came in. That's the last message we heard. As you know, there have been a significant number of Russian aircraft sightings in the North lately, but none this deep into the interior. According to the telex, NORAD headquarters has been notified.''

''Just how deep into the interior is this target?''

''Here sir,'' answered Salisbury, as he and Stedman walked over to the map of the Northwest Territories. Salisbury pointed to a spot on the eastern waters of Great Bear Lake. ''That's the last position, five minutes ago, and the target is still moving east at high speed.''

''East? Further into the interior?'' Stedman's eyes grew larger.

''It appears so.''

Stedman rubbed his chin. ''You're right, they've never been that far east before. I don't like this. What base did the CF-100 take off from?''

Salisbury ripped the telex flimsy from the third machine on the left and brought it over to the defense minister. ''The target is on a heading of zero-six-eight, northeast of Fort Franklin.''

''Where's that?''

The corporal touched a red pin on the map that represented a CF-100 fighter-interceptor squadron in the western section of the Northwest Territories. Under the pin, in black block letters was the base name, Fort Franklin. ''Here it is.''

''Good heavens, the base is two hundred miles west of the target sighting, and the CF-100 is playing catch-up. That target should have been detected long before this. Obviously, it flew under our radar.''

Stedman's eyes shot over to the yellow pins, TUN-DRA squadrons, spread out to the right, in the interior. The closest yellow pin was only 175 miles away from the target's last position. Stedman pointed to it.

''Corporal, don't you think it's strange that only one interceptor was alerted?''

''Yes, I do.''

"If that's a Russian plane, we have to stop it fast, before it reaches TUNDRA!"

NEAR FORT FRANKLIN, NWT, 0350 HOURS (0550 EST)

As the twin-engined fighter climbed steeply through a thin, uneven stratus cloud layer, the two-man combat team of Flying Officers James Scott and Jacques St. Pierre was in an uneasy but ready state of mind. A large unidentified target had appeared on the ground radar screens in the area. No NORAD exercises had been reported in the vicinity, therefore the target couldn't be a NORAD or Strategic Air Command "faker" such as the B-52 or the B-47 bombers used for fighter-interceptor practice.

Teamwork in dual-manned interceptor work was of vital importance. Scott and St. Pierre excelled at precise, articulate teamwork, and they had the aircraft to work with. Their CF-100 Canuck Mark IVB was well prepared for an interceptor role. It was outfitted with a set of eight Browning .50-calibre machine guns totaling 1600 rounds, all contained in a one-piece unit below the pilot on the belly of the fuselage.

In addition, the fighter was carrying the new and highly secretive Sparrow 3D heat-seeking missiles, two under each wing. This deadly missile, the latest in sophisticated weaponry, had seen active service for only three weeks. It had a weight of 450 pounds, a length of forty-four inches, a span of forty inches, and a long-burning aero jet engine that reached speeds of Mach 3.5. The 3D could hit a target with an eighty-pound high-explosive warhead at a range of several miles.

Pressed well back in his seat, St. Pierre peered over the starboard side of the fuselage as the Orenda 11 engines pushed the Canadian-built fighter-interceptor through the cool northern air at a climbing rate of seven thousand feet per minute. The stinging rays of the midnight sun penetrated through the perspex of the canopy. The navigator could see only the endless landscape of thick forest and countless lakes below him.

Scott pressed the UHF transmitter. "PINETREE, WHISKEY-MIKE-ZERO-ONE ON TWO-TWO, HEADING ZERO-THREE-ZERO, CLIMBING TO ANGELS THREE-FIVE."

"ROGER, WHISKEY-MIKE-ZERO-ONE. I READ YOU FIVE SQUARE. HOW ME?"

"PINETREE, WHISKEY-MIKE-ZERO-ONE, FIVE BY FIVE. ARE WE PLAYING TONIGHT OR WORKING?"

"WORKING, I'M SORRY TO SAY. TURN RIGHT TO ZERO-SIX-EIGHT. BUSTER, ANGELS THREE-FIVE."

"ROGER, TURN RIGHT TO ZERO-SIX-EIGHT. BUSTER, ANGELS THREE-FIVE."

"WHISKEY-MIKE-ZERO-ONE. WE HAVE A BOGIE BEARING ZERO-SIX-EIGHT, AT FIFTY MILES, ANGELS THREE-FIVE. SPEED THREE-EIGHT-ZERO-PLUS."

"ROGER."

Scott banked right. As the ground-to-air communication continued, St. Pierre switched on his radar set and waited for it to time in. He bent over the scope and adjusted the visor on his helmet.

"ANYTHING ON THE SCOPE YET, JACQUES?" asked Scott, after a short while.

"NOTHING YET," replied the Frenchman.

Scott leveled off the fighter at thirty-five thousand feet.

"SCOTTY, IT'S ON THE SCREEN AND DEAD AHEAD. RANGE IS TWENTY MILES. IT'S A BIG ONE. IT'S EITHER A BOMBER OR AN AIRLINER OFF COURSE."

"WHISKEY-MIKE-ZERO-ONE, THIS IS PINETREE. GO TO CHANNEL EIGHT AND REPORT BACK."

"ROGER, PINETREE, SWITCHING TO EIGHT."

Scott's left hand went for the UHF channel selector,

the selector snapping as he ran through the frequencies. Then he pressed the transmitter button.

"PINETREE, THIS IS WHISKEY-MIKE-ZERO-ONE ON EIGHT. WE HAVE THE TARGET ON OUR SCREEN, BUT CAN'T MAKE A VISUAL BECAUSE OF HEAVY CLOUD. RANGE IS FIFTEEN MILES AND CLOSING. DEAD AHEAD. OUR AIRSPEED IN EXCESS OF FIVE HUNDRED KNOTS."

"ROGER, WHISKEY-MIKE-ZERO-ONE. TARGET HAS DROPPED SLIGHTLY. NOW AT ANGELS THREE-THREE AND ON STARBOARD. DO YOU READ?"

"ROGER, PINETREE. DROPPING TO THREE-THREE."

Scott eased the stick forward, and when he reached the required altitude level he hit the transmitter. "PINETREE, THIS IS WHISKEY-MIKE-ZERO-ONE. AM LEVEL AT ANGELS THREE-THREE. STILL IN HEAVY CLOUD AND CAN'T MAKE A VISUAL."

"STAY WITH HIM, WHISKEY-MIKE-ZERO-ONE."

"SCOTTY, RANGE IS FIVE MILES AND CLOSING FAST. WE SHOULD BE ON HIS ASS SOON."

St. Pierre had no sooner finished speaking, when the heavy cloud dispersed to reveal a Russian Tu-95 four-engined bomber straight ahead.

For the past six years the Russians had been sending long-range bombers into Canadian and American airspace to test North America's air defense; its reaction times and radar defenses. In 1958 alone, there were 205 Tu-95 sightings at the edge of or inside NORAD territory, mostly near Alaska and Iceland, and sometimes right over the Northwest Territories. But none had ever ventured as deep into Canada as this Tu-95, now only three thousand feet away from the CF-100 interceptor in hot pursuit. Why hadn't the bogie been detected earlier on the ground-based radar? How did it get this far?

The Tupolev Tu-95 Bear was an indirect descendant of the Boeing B-29 Superfortress, a model of which was impounded and copied by the Russians during World

War II, following an American bomber crew landing in Russia after a raid on Japan. The Russians, allies then, eventually sent back the crew, minus the aircraft.

The Bear's four large, durable turboprop engines were capable of a cruising speed of 400 knots, a maximum speed of 480 knots, a ceiling of forty-one thousand feet, and an unbelievable maximum range of ten thousand nautical miles. The long-distance Bear was not considered a practical weapon because the recent NORAD fighters, which were equipped with airborne radar and new heat-seeking missiles, were more than a match for the bombers. In fact, American and Canadian interceptor aircrew were well trained in fighting the mighty Bear. Nevertheless, the range of the bomber made it a worthy foe.

"WELL, JACQUES, THERE SHE IS IN ALL HER GLORY, ANOTHER BEAR."

"BUT WE'VE NEVER TRACKED ONE OUT HERE BEFORE."

"PINETREE, THIS IS WHISKEY-MIKE-ZERO-ONE. WE'VE IDENTIFIED THE BOGIE. IT'S A TANGO-UNIFORM-NINER-FIVE."

"ROGER, WHISKEY-MIKE-ZERO-ONE. ESCORT HIM OUT. REMEMBER TO KEEP CLEAR OF THE WASH FROM THOSE TURBOS."

"ROGER, PINETREE, WE WILL ESCORT HIM OUT. AND ROGER ON THE WASH." Only five weeks earlier an Alaskan-based F-102 from an American fighter-interceptor unit had almost crashed after getting too close behind the propwash of a Tu-95 Bear. The incident was still fresh in Scott's mind.

"LET'S GO GET HIM, SCOTTY," said St. Pierre, his voice crackling in his mask.

Scott pressed lightly on the throttles until his Canuck was above and behind the Bear's port side, the side required under international law for interceptors. Then he gently eased off the throttles. The Canadian team closed in and both men glared to the right as they slowly passed the Bear's enormous tail section with the Russian red star painted partway up the vertical stabilizer. What a monster! Their eyes ran along the long pencil-like fuselage and the swept-back wings containing the four powerful engines. The entire length of the bomber was over 150 feet, the wingspan nearly 170 feet. Scott and St. Pierre quickly noticed several belly windows that were probably being used right now for aerial photography. Scott touched the throttles again until he and his navigator were right alongside the Bear's cockpit. The Russian pilot looked straight ahead, arrogantly pretending to be unaware of the fighter. Finally he glanced over once, but continued on his level course. Scott then tried creeping closer to edge the bomber off-track, a signal for the pilot to turn back. The Russian ignored him.

Scott asked the aircraft's occupants several times to turn back, but to no avail. There was no answer on the universal emergency channel. Scott thought that they didn't want to answer, or didn't know English.

Still on the bomber's left and above, Scott pressed on the throttles to pull ahead and rock his wings. Normally, with this procedure, the intercepted aircraft would acknowledge by rocking its own wings. The interceptor would go into a slow, level turn and the other aircraft would follow. Once again, however, the bomber refused to acknowledge the CF-100 in any way.

"WE GOT A STUBBORN ONE," St. Pierre joked calmly with Scott. "THEY USUALLY GET THE PICTURE BY NOW. WHAT GIVES?"

Scott was starting to get worried. "PINETREE, THIS IS WHISKEY-MIKE-ZERO-ONE. WE GOT A BEAR THAT'S STUBBORN AND DOESN'T WANT TO GO HOME TO ITS OWN WOODS."

"WHISKEY-MIKE-ZERO-ONE, THIS IS PINETREE. HANG ON AND SHADOW."

"ROGER, PINETREE."

"SCOTTY, WE'RE GETTING TOO CLOSE TO THE YOU-KNOW-WHAT-AREA. THEY BETTER DECIDE SOMETHING IN A HURRY."

Scott was thinking the same thing. "YOU'RE RIGHT, JACQUES. HOW FAR ARE WE?"

St. Pierre glanced down at the airspeed indicator on his navigator panel, then took a look at his maps. "AT OUR PRESENT SPEED, FIFTEEN MINUTES, TOPS."

"THIS IS CRAZY. PINETREE BETTER DECIDE SOMETHING FAST.

"DAMN RIGHT."

A new voice came over the R/T.

"WHISKEY-MIKE-ZERO-ONE, THIS IS PINETREE. FIFTH WHEEL TALKING. PLEASE ACKNOWLEDGE."

"I READ YOU, FIFTH WHEEL."

"I HAVE BEEN INFORMED OF YOUR INTERCEPT. ARE YOU STILL WITH THE BEAR AND WHAT'S YOUR PRESENT SPEED? OVER."

"WE ARE STILL WITH HIM. SPEED IS FOUR HUNDRED TEN KNOTS. WE ARE MAINTAINING AS SHADOW AND AWAITING YOUR INSTRUCTIONS."

"DID YOU ATTEMPT RADIO CONTACT ON THE EMERGENCY CHANNEL?"

"AFFIRMATIVE, FIFTH WHEEL. NO RESPONSE."

"DID YOU APPROACH ON PORT SIDE AND TRY TO EDGE HIM OUT?"

"AFFIRMATIVE, FIFTH WHEEL. HE HASN'T BUDGED."

"DROP BACK. ENGAGE GUN CAMERA. WE WANT PICTURES. THEN FIRE ACROSS HIS NOSE. REPEAT, DROP BACK, ENGAGE GUN CAMERA, FIRE ACROSS HIS NOSE. DO YOU COPY, WHISKEY-MIKE-ZERO-ONE?"

"I COPY, FIFTH WHEEL."

Scott dropped back a hundred yards, activated the gun

camera, and gripped the top portion of the stick solidly. He aimed through the gunsight, then fired a few short bursts just over the Bear's nose, every fourth .50-calibre being a tracer. The Canuck's airspeed dropped slightly from the recoil, and the cockpit shook as all eight Brownings blasted through the thin, high-altitude air.

"FIFTH WHEEL, THIS IS WHISKEY-MIKE-ZERO-ONE."

"I READ YOU, WHISKEY-MIKE-ZERO-ONE."

"I FIRED SEVERAL ROUNDS, BUT BEAR IS STILL ON EASTERLY COURSE."

"FIRE SOME MORE, WHISKEY-MIKE-ZERO-ONE. GET CLOSER THIS TIME."

"I READ YOU, FIFTH WHEEL."

Scott fired more sporadic bursts, then watched and waited. When the Bear still refused to change course, he fired a few more rounds over the bomber's nose, getting closer each time. Undaunted, the Russian pilot and his crew flew on, seemingly unconcerned about the Canuck's scare tactics. Then the Bear dropped altitude again.

The guy's crazy, thought Scott. He's on a bloody suicide mission.

"LESS THAN FIVE MINUTES TO GO, SCOTTY."

"FIFTH WHEEL, THIS IS WHISKEY-MIKE-ZERO-ONE. HAVE FIRED SEVERAL SHORT BURSTS OVER BEAR'S NOSE. TRACERS PLAINLY VISIBLE, BUT HE'S STILL ON EASTERLY COURSE. DO YOU READ, FIFTH WHEEL?"

There was no answer on the R/T.

"SCOTTY, WHY AREN'T THEY ANSWERING?"

"I DON'T KNOW. I THOUGHT OUR RADIO WAS FIXED."

St. Pierre detected the panic in his mate's voice. "IT WAS. THE LAST TIME OUT IT WORKED FINE. TRY AGAIN. WE'VE ONLY GOT A COUPLE OF MINUTES TO GO."

"FIFTH WHEEL, DO YOU READ? FIFTH WHEEL, DO YOU READ?"

"TRY ANOTHER CHANNEL!"

Scott played with the selector. "FIFTH WHEEL, THIS

IS WHISKEY-MIKE-ZERO-ONE. DO YOU READ? FIFTH WHEEL, THIS IS WHISKEY-MIKE-ZERO-ONE. DO YOU READ?''

''DAMN, IT'S DEAD. THE STUPID THING IS DEAD. THE SAME TROUBLE WE HAD A FEW DAYS AGO.''

No Soviet bomber had ever penetrated this far into Canadian airspace before. However, no Soviet bomber had ever been shot down over its airspace, either, and the Russians knew it. If a Soviet bomber were shot down over Canada's North it would create an international incident. That's what the Russians were banking on, and Scott and St. Pierre knew it.

''SCOTTY, THERE'S A CLOUDBANK COMING UP AHEAD. WE'VE GOT TO ACT NOW OR WE LOSE HIM.''

''WE BOTH KNOW WHAT HE'S OUT TO PHOTOGRAPH. BUT IF HE'S GOING THROUGH CLOUDS, THEN MAYBE HE WON'T FIND HIS TARGET EITHER.''

''WE CAN'T TAKE THAT CHANCE, DAMN IT!''

''WHAT DO YOU WANT ME TO DO, SHOOT HIM DOWN?''

''YEAH, SHOOT HIM DOWN!'' St. Pierre yelled.

Scott knew his navigator was right. They had to do it even without confirmation from Pinetree. No one was to go near the restricted area. They would have to shoot and face the consequences later. Scott swallowed hard and tugged at his oxygen mask, which suddenly felt very uncomfortable. Sweat trickled down his forehead.

''ALL RIGHT, JACQUES, WE'LL DO IT.''

Why us? thought Scott. Why didn't Franklin send up two fighters? Then we wouldn't have to make this decision on our own.

Scott throttled back and applied the speed brakes, quickly giving the Bear a lead of nearly eighteen hundred yards. Then he grazed the throttles to stay at an even and safe distance away from the propwash. Both planes were now at approximately twenty-five thousand feet. The Bear was on the Canuck's starboard and still dropping its nose gradually. There was no time to lose.

"COME ON, SCOTTY," St. Pierre pleaded, "LAUNCH THE MISSILES BEFORE HE GOES THROUGH THE CLOUDS. WE'RE OVER THE RESTRICTED AREA RIGHT NOW. DO IT, SCOTTY! DO IT!"

Scott no longer felt human. Mechanically, he hit the missile arm switch on the armament control box to his right. He selected two missiles, one from each wing. He could almost feel St. Pierre breathing down his neck. Then he pressed hard on the firing button on the column.

For a brief instant time stood still. The sky was a rich, postcard blue, with thick cumulus clouds rising well past thirty thousand feet. Below were the thick, murky greenish-pastel tones of the Northwest forest called the taiga. The scenery was breathtaking and uncluttered.

Inside the Tu-95 Bear's pressurized cabin the Russian pilot and copilot were confident that they were just about to accomplish their mission. At their briefing in Siberia only a few hours earlier, they were given a heading in northern Canada in which to photograph, and were told not to steer off course under any circumstance. They were to fly low as far as they could when approaching the continent from the north to avoid the DEW Line radar, and continue to stay low unless spotted. They flew near a fighter base just inside their western turning point. Once they were spotted, they had risen to high altitude to make it look as though they were on another catch-me-if-you-can, I'll-turn-back-once-you-intercept-me game.

The Bear was at the outer reaches of the photo area, with only minutes to go till the target. There were clouds ahead, the fighter somewhere behind, probably wondering what to do. The navigator announced four min-

utes to go till the main target. The mighty plane dropped
again for the final stage of the target run.

Suddenly the Bear was rocked by two explosions off
the starboard wing. The cockpit windows were blasted
into tiny pieces. High-octane fuel and bits of molten
metal were scattered throughout the cockpit. Due to the
rapid decompression, every loose piece of paper and
equipment was sucked through the ragged openings.
The cockpit was full of flames, melting everything. The
men inside didn't stand a chance.

The very instant the missiles were launched Scott saw
the X on his radarscope, his signal to break away. He
pulled the aircraft down and away to avoid the debris.
Even at a range of one mile he and St. Pierre witnessed
an explosion of such magnitude that for a brief second
it seemed to outshine the sun. The two missiles punc-
tured both of the Bear's starboard engines. The outer
wing turboprop went first, followed by the inner wing,
with one of the latter's props tearing loose and dropping
like an anvil through the frigid air. Soon, the last remains of the Tu-95 Bear were on fire and heading downwards in a slow, steady spiral.

OTTAWA, ONTARIO, 0621 HOURS (EST)

Corporal Salisbury stood hunched over a telex machine that was pounding away like a jackhammer on
asphalt. He and Dean Stedman were waiting anxiously
for word on the unidentified target that had been tracked
by NORAD radar. Not a word had come through in the
last fifteen minutes.

When the machine stopped, Salisbury ripped the long
message off and trotted over to Stedman, who waited
by the Northern map. ''It looks bad, sir.''

Stedman read the message and rolled his eyes. "Oh, no, it was a Bear," he said, flopping down into a nearby chair, "and they shot it down. That's all we need."

"I'm sure they had no choice, sir." Salisbury said. "According to the latitude and longitude readings on the telex, it was almost right over one of the TUNDRA bases when they shot it down." Salisbury confirmed his statement by pointing to the intersection point of the latitude and longitude readings on the wall map.

Stedman sighed. He realized that the CF-100 probably didn't have much choice. But why did it have to happen? Why now?

OTTAWA, ONTARIO 0630, HOURS (EST)

Alex Kralick and the prime minister were taking an early morning stroll down Sussex Drive. Instead of his usual route east towards Rockcliffe Park, the prime minister had decided to walk southeast today, down MacKay and Alexander Streets, where many fine stone houses from the Confederation period stood.

"I think it's going to be hot today. It's quite warm already. I don't know what's hotter, this morning or the flak I've been getting from the Liberal opposition. The backlash over the Arrow is still haunting us."

"Have you heard the latest rumor?"

The prime minister shook his head. "What rumor?"

"The Arrow still lives."

The Tory leader grinned nervously. "I haven't heard that one."

Their conversation the day before at Sussex Drive was still fresh enough in Kralick's mind that he knew it would be unwise to question the prime minister any further about fighter aircraft.

"Let's walk across the park today, Alex." The prime

minister peeled off the light sweater he usually wore on his morning walks and folded it over his shoulder.

"How's your Bill of Rights doing?" Kralick decided to change the subject.

"Great!" The prime minister seemed to perk up. "I want to present it to Parliament by late summer or early fall. I hope the hoopla over it will help to take everyone's mind off the Arrow. The Bill of Rights might be my lifesaver, the government's lifesaver."

"You first presented it to the House in 1947. What happened then?"

The prime minister stopped beside a flowerbed on his right. He shrugged. "What can you do as a backbencher in the opposition? The MacKenzie government was in power." His face took on a dreamy expression. "I rose from my bench and said, 'A Bill of Rights must deny the right of government to interfere with my right to serve my maker as my conscience demands . . .'" Kralick smiled as the prime minister, who had already gained a reputation as quite an orator, pointed his finger at no one in particular and chanted the speech he had made to the House of Commons twelve years earlier. When he finished, he turned to Kralick, looking somewhat embarrassed. "I memorized it."

The conversation about the Bill of Rights continued for another twenty minutes, then the Tory leader looked at his watch.

"It's a quarter after seven. We'd better get back. I promised my wife I'd have breakfast with her before she leaves for Prince Albert."

The two leaders strolled briskly back to Sussex Drive. Just as they turned down the street, Stedman drove up in his 1959 DeSoto and stopped the two strollers right across from the French embassy.

RCAF Station Fort Franklin,
NWT 0454 Hours (0654 est)

"Didn't you receive the orders to break off?" Group Captain Fisher was furious.

"No sir, we did not. The radio failed." James Scott stood erect, in full flying gear, answering his superior firmly. St. Pierre stood at attention to Scott's right.

"So I hear. I have an electrical crew checking it out now." The C.O. shook his head. He sat down behind his desk, barely able to contain his temper. "Do you two realize what you've done? Do you?" he yelled. "You have shot down a Russian bomber, that's what! Without authorization!"

St. Pierre glanced over at his pilot. Aren't you going to say anything? he thought to himself. Then he turned to his superior. "What would you have done in our situation, sir?" he asked calmly.

Scott couldn't believe his ears. The C.O. was so stunned he couldn't answer.

St. Pierre took a deep breath. "Sir, we were put in a terrible predicament. We were told that no unauthorized aircraft was to fly over the restricted area, and certainly no Russian aircraft. Then, at a crucial time, our radio malfunctioned. We were the only interceptor sent up."

"We couldn't get another one off the ground." Fisher had found his voice.

"That's not our problem. It seems we're being made the scapegoats for this incident. We were the last line of defense against a bomber that refused to turn back. We had to decide on our own to do what we thought was right."

Fisher rose so abruptly from his chair that it banged against the wall of his office. "I could have you two court-martialed!"

St. Pierre's face was starting to redden.

The phone rang on Fisher's desk. The C.O. let it ring twice as he stared hard at St. Pierre. "Yes, Fisher here," he finally said, reaching back behind him.

"Sir, I have the electrician on the line."

"Put him on," Fisher answered, still staring at the officers.

Scott and St. Pierre eyed each other quickly, as Fisher asked the electrician several questions regarding the crew's radio.

"Okay, thanks." The C.O. hung up and walked over to the two. "There was a short in it, all right. But there was still no excuse for what you did. And I'll tell you why. Two fighters from the restricted area were scrambled and lining up for a head-on attack at the same moment you fired your missiles at the bomber. The debris from the explosion almost blew one of our own fighters right out of the sky. That's why you were instructed to break off."

"St. Pierre," the flying officer looked straight ahead, "didn't you see the fighters on your radarscope?"

St. Pierre didn't answer. He couldn't. In the excitement of the radio trouble he hadn't noticed the fighters. This entire alert was turning into a fiasco.

Then the phone rang again. When Fisher answered the phone this time he seemed startled. He explained the radio incident and the trouble with the second CF-100. Whoever was on the other end of the phone appeared to be shouting at the Fort Franklin C.O. Fisher attempted to speak several times, but couldn't get a word in edgewise. "Yes, sir," he said finally, "right away, sir." The now deflated commanding officer motioned for Scott to take the phone.

"At ease, you guys," he said, his head held high.

Scott stepped forward. "Flying Officer James Scott here."

"Scott, this is General Schult, calling from Colorado."

Scott's mouth dropped. The supreme commander of NORAD was on the other end.

"Yes, sir!"

"We're in a little hot water, aren't we?"

"Yes, sir, it seems we are."

"Let me assure you and your navigator that you did the right thing. Under the circumstances, any one of us would have done the same thing. You had no choice but to shoot down that bomber. The Soviets had no business being out there. Did you get any pictures?"

"Yes, sir, we did," replied Scott. "They're being developed in the lab right now."

"Good. That's our evidence for the media. Now, what about our new missile? How was it in combat?"

"In my opinion," Scott spoke thoughtfully, "it worked beyond our expectations. I was down and to the starboard side, and the Bear dipped its nose just before I fired. Two missiles followed the bomber's heat to catch the two starboard engines."

"You fired two?"

"Yes, sir," Scott shot back, looking at a cutaway poster of the Sparrow 3D on the wall in front of him. Fisher glanced over at St. Pierre, who refused to look away.

"What was left of your target?"

"Not much, sir. The engines exploded and the fuselage broke almost in half from the impact."

"Any survivors?"

"I circled the area for a short time, but we saw no chutes."

"Good. I'm anxious to see the film. In addition, I want a full operational report from you, on telex, by 1000 hours. Is that clear?"

"Yes, sir."

"Good. And remember this, Flying Officer Scott.

You conducted yourself professionally out there, you did what needed to be done. There should have been two interceptors alerted. According to your commanding officer, the other crew had to turn back because of engine trouble shortly after leaving the base. They were late getting off to begin with and then had to turn back only a few miles out. You had no support and were right to shoot when you did. One more thing."

"Yes, sir."

"Let Group Captain Fisher handle the publicity over this affair. He's already been briefed on what's expected if the media picks this up. Do you understand?"

"Yes, sir, I do."

Inside of thirty seconds Scott and St. Pierre were out in the hall and walking away from the door marked DEBRIEFING. Scott stopped and told St. Pierre what the supreme commander had said.

"You know what, Jacques?" Scott added.

"What?"

"The second voice from Pinetree, Fifth Wheel, sounded a bit like . . ." He stopped short.

"Who?" St. Pierre asked, tucking his helmet under his arm.

"Naw, it couldn't be. Forget it."

OTTAWA, ONTARIO, 1418 HOURS (EST)

"Mr. Prime Minister, the Russian ambassador and his aide are here."

"Thank you, send them in."

The sixty-year-old Russian ambassador to Canada, Sergo Kabovok, was a husky, white-haired man of Eastern European stock. His personal secretary, Leon Bailov, was a balding man with a huge stomach that stuck out far in front of him. His shape made him look older than the forty-six he really was. The Tory leader shook their hands and asked them to have a seat in front of his desk. Bailov pulled out a notepad and pen from the briefcase he was carrying. His bushy eyebrows flickered as he started writing, almost as if to telegraph each letter he scribbled.

The ambassador and the prime minister had met once before, shortly after Kabovok became the ambassador to Canada in November 1957. The setting was a cocktail party in Ottawa for the then-new prime minister. The two did not hit it off and had kept their distance ever since. Now, however, they had no choice but to meet head on.

A Communist loyal to whoever was in power at the Kremlin, Kabovok had survived the Stalin purges of the 1930s, where several million Russian citizens, many of them high-ranking officials and their families, were liquidated. During World War II Stalin had selected Kabovok overseer of the immense and highly successful aircraft production in the Ural Mountains factories, deep in Russia. It was here that Yak and MiG fighters, unharassed by German bombs, were manufactured at a remarkable rate. Following Stalin's death in 1953, the new premier of the Soviet Union, Nikita Khrushchev, upon urging by the Kremlin Politburo, chose Kabovok to serve as an air force advisor for two years and then as ambassador to Canada. However, in the past few months American intelligence had revealed to Canadian authorities that Kabovok had solid links to the Russian secret police, the NKVD.

The two Russians shook hands with Dean Stedman, who was already in the prime minister's office discussing the unfortunate incident concerning the Tu-95 Bear. Following a brief telephone conversation earlier, the prime minister and the American president had decided that a press conference should be called. The journalists, photographers, and sound crew had left the office an hour ago. The prime minister had been calm and alert as he reported to the North American audience the details of the Tu-95 Bear episode. He expressed regret over the deaths of the Soviet airmen, he said there was nothing to fear, that the rumors of a coming war with the Soviet Union were false.

The prime minister was concerned, however, following a telex from the president which stated that America's Russian source in Washington, Miskin, had vanished. American intelligence hadn't been able to contact him in nearly two months and he was badly needed to verify Russian activity concerning the Skyjacker. The rumor was that he was back in Russia. Had the Russians found him out?

Kabovok folded his hands in his lap. "Mr. Prime Minister," he said, shaking his head, "Moscow is very unhappy about this unfortunate incident. We want an explanation for it."

The prime minister glanced at Stedman seated on his right, then rose from his oak swivel chair and leaned over his desk. If looks could kill, the two Russians were dead. "I explained everything at the press conference. I'm sure you saw it."

"Yes, we did. Moscow feels that we should have been contacted before you went public with this."

"We didn't have much choice. Word leaked out, and we had to do something. But I did leave out an important piece of information. Our fighter-interceptor fired warning shots over your bomber's nose. We have it on film and the tracers are plainly visible. You will see that on our news report tomorrow."

"My superiors are not happy with how this . . ."

"I don't think you were listening to what I said. Your superiors sent your plane into our airspace." The prime minister's voice was starting to rise. "Your air force deliberately sent a bomber over our territory and it refused to turn back even after our escort caught up with it and fired several warning shots."

The ambassador only smiled. "Does your country have something to hide in the North?"

"Look," the prime minister said sternly, pointing his finger at the ambassador, "there's no way your aircraft are going to take pictures of our northern bases. You seem to think you can send your bombers anywhere, anytime, and take pictures of whatever you like. For the past two years NORAD and NATO have caught up with a good number of your aircraft in western territory, and most of these have been reconnaissance aircraft, just like the Tu-95. What if we sent that many of our planes over your territory? You would have shot them down, as sure as I'm standing here. Yes, we have something to hide. We have something to hide the same way you have something to hide in your country. Nobody gets near our military installations."

"There will be retaliatory action taken, I assure you, Mr. Prime Minister." The ambassador stood up to face the prime minister.

"Retaliatory action? For what? What can you do? You wouldn't dare start a war over this, would you? Your bomber was caught photographing our northern bases and refused to turn back. Our fighter had no choice but to shoot him down. If one of our bombers flew over Russia on a reconnaissance mission, your fighter defenses would do the same thing with absolutely no regret."

"Are you implying that we don't play by the rules?"

"You better believe it!"

Stedman squirmed in his chair. He hadn't expected the conversation to turn this ugly.

"Our premier will not . . ."

"You tell your premier we've got you by the neck." The prime minister sat down hard in his chair. "Go ahead, start something," he said, waving his arms furiously. "You're in the wrong, and you know it. Our film tomorrow will prove it. No country in the world will support you. And I'll tell you something else; the next time a Soviet bomber is caught in our territory and refuses to turn back, we'll shoot it down too." The prime minister slammed his fist down so hard on the desk that a clock on his left nearly fell off. "Now, good day gentlemen. I'm busy and there is nothing more to say."

"I beg your pardon, Mr. Prime Minister."

"There is nothing more to say. That's it!"

Bailov's eyes grew large.

"You haven't heard the last of this," the ambassador said, pointing his finger. He nodded at his assistant and the two men turned on their heels and left.

Stedman chuckled at the prime minister, who was stomping around the office.

"Who do those people think they are? What are you snickering about, Dean?"

"You."

"Me?"

"Yes, you. I'm envious. You stood up to Kabovok and you beat me to it. I think you tore a strip off his hide."

The prime minister was calming down. "You really think so? I just hope that I didn't start something."

"Don't worry, it won't. There are two things the Russians respect; a strong defense and . . ." He stopped deliberately.

"And what?"

"A loudmouth who means what he says."

"Thanks."

WASHINGTON, D.C., TUESDAY, JUNE 30
2147 HOURS (EST)

Magna-One always enjoyed relaxing in his study with one of the many history books from his huge collection. He'd set aside tonight for some quiet reading and he was trying to take full advantage of it.

The large room was pleasantly decorated with aircraft photos on the walls and long bookshelves stocked with history publications. Salmon-colored wallpaper gave the room a cozy feeling. The agent was reading a book on the famous World War II general, George Patton, a military man he deeply admired. The phone rang. Oh, no, he thought as he set his scotch and soda down on the table and reached for the receiver.

"Hello." The agent continued reading as he answered the phone. "Hello," he said again, speaking more loudly when no one answered the first time.

"This is . . ."

"Yes, I know." The agent recognized the soft voice immediately.

"I have something important for you. Where can we meet? It's very important."

"I'll pick you up at the usual place in," the agent paused to look at his watch, "thirty minutes. Are you near there now?"

"Very near. Good-bye."

The agent hung up the phone just as his wife, a good-looking, tall woman in her forties, walked into the room.

"You look worried. Is everything all right?"

"Everything's fine, dear. I have to go out though. I'll be back in an hour or so."

"Oh, not again. I thought this was your reading night." She walked over to her husband and hugged him.

He kissed her lightly on the lips. "I'll be back as soon as I can."

It was a hot summer evening. Alexander Miskin, back from Moscow only two days earlier, waited behind the telephone booth at the corner of a park in the residential area north of Washington. He and the American agent, Magna-One, had met there several times before. The agent would pull up in front of the booth, and Miskin would hop into his car. Behind the tinted windows of the agent's new Chrysler Imperial they would talk, sometimes while driving around the area, sometimes while parked.

Miskin couldn't wait to tell Magna-One the latest Soviet military proceedings. He had telexes, photos and hand-drawn pictures he'd grabbed from the embassy only an hour earlier. It was time for him to call it quits. Things were getting too risky and tonight he would give Magna-One a list of demands: a new identity, new residence for him and his wife somewhere in the United States, or else no information.

Miskin thought briefly of the Tu-95 Bear that had been shot down in the Canadian North just three days earlier. The reaction around the world had been thunderous. Left-wing peaceniks were marching on right-wing newspapers that supported the CF-100's retaliatory action and setting up vigils at federal government offices. According to news reports and the film footage taken from the nose of the fighter, the Russians were clearly in the wrong. However, many naive Canadians and Americans believed that the planet was on the brink of a third world war. Miskin knew that the bomber was on a spy mission, and he had a fairly good idea what it was out to photograph.

Miskin looked at his watch. Twenty-five minutes had passed since his call to Magna-One. The Russian looked towards the west, down the wide, well-lit, six-lane street that was separated by a lush green boulevard where a row of young maple trees had been recently planted. The wind blew lightly, just enough to cool the hot, steamy air. People were out for a summer evening walk or drive, and he fit in casually with the surroundings.

One car slowed down and pulled onto the shoulder. Miskin immediately recognized the outline of the agent's Imperial. The passenger door swung open, and the Russian darted for the vehicle.

"Where the hell have you been?" asked Magna-One.

"Moscow," Miskin said, slamming the door hard.

"Moscow?"

"Yes. The Kremlin suspected a security leak at our Washington embassy. All officials were recalled at intervals and screened thoroughly by the secret police. They had nothing on me. When I returned to Washington, though, I shook them by planting phony information on another embassy employee and he was caught with the goods before he got out the main door. I made it look like he was ready to defect with important military secrets."

"Good thinking. You covered your tracks well. What's the latest?"

Miskin pulled out the package, but held onto it. "It's all here. They're still building the MiG-K; fifty in the month of June."

"Fifty?"

"And here's the location. I took the site information off the telexes and drew it out for you. It's inside Siberia, off the coast of Japan." Miskin placed the drawings on top of the sheets.

"But that's right near the previous site."

"They scrapped the old site for the benefit of the American observers. Then they moved the production elsewhere. Now the clincher. My country plans an air strike on your country, through northern Canada, by August 1. Our embassy has been ordered to clear out completely by July 31.''

Magna-One was shocked. ''So that's why the mass-producing of the Skyjacker!''

Miskin nodded.

''They're going to use it on us?''

''That's correct.''

Magna-One slumped in his seat.

''I want out,'' Miskin said firmly.

''Out?''

''Yes. I want a new identity, new residence for my wife and me, or no papers. I don't want my neck slit open. It's getting too dangerous. I got away with it for now; I can't get away with this forever.''

''You can't get out now. Your superiors will suspect something if they find you missing a month before the proposed attack. Go back. We'll contact you the day before you leave the States. I'll pull you free then.''

''That's too late. If something goes wrong, I'd be caught for sure.''

''All right. Three days before then, but that's the best I can do.''

Miskin sighed. ''Okay, I'll wait. Your idea better work.''

Magna-One didn't really know how he was going to get Miskin out. ''It'll work,'' he said.

''By the way,'' Miskin asked, ''if there is a fight, do you plan to use the Arrow against the MiG-K?''

''What are you talking about? The Arrow was scrapped months ago.''

''Don't play games with me. I know why that Tu-95 bomber was sent over the Canadian Northwest Territories. I think the Canadians are still secretly building the

Arrow. The Kremlin sent a reconnaissance bomber for proof, but didn't get it.''

''This is news to me. If it's true they're still building the Arrow, who else in the embassy knows?''

''I don't think anybody really knows; they only suspect. First off, we do know of excessive fighter-training activity in the far north. Secondly, there have been rumors that the Arrow lives. Thirdly, there have been too many articles written in the States and Canada about the Arrow since the February termination. The two governments are trying awfully hard to convince the public that it's really gone. I just put two and two together.''

''I don't know a thing about it.''

''Probably because too many people already know. The fewer the better,'' Miskin smiled. ''I find it amusing that both our countries are building an advanced, computerized fighter and trying to hide it from each other. I don't know what to think.''

''Whose side are you on?'' Magna-One asked bluntly.

''The right side.''

''Which side is that?''

Miskin's grin faded. ''Right now, I don't know.''

## WASHINGTON, D.C., 2258 HOURS (EST)

The White House bomb shelter, below the great presidental mansion, was almost a city in itself. It housed communication rooms, offices, computers, consoles, a central area with projection screens of North America, and employees to man the machinery around the clock.

The president sat behind his desk in a closed-in, dimly lit room, off to the side of the central area. After receiving the startling news that their Russian informant at the Soviet embassy in Washington had uncovered the plans for a Russian air attack on North America, the president had gone straight to the basement of his mansion by way of a special elevator.

Now, things would have to be speeded up. Luckily, one month before, General Schult had convinced the president that an alternative plan should be implemented in case their informant failed to produce the much-needed files on the Skyjacker program. That plan included the training of three pilots to engage in a long-range photo-reconnaissance mission to the Soviet Union, where they thought the MiG-K was being built. Thanks to Miskin's directions, the training base inside Siberia had been pinpointed.

The president picked up the phone that linked him directly to NORAD Headquarters in Colorado Springs. It was used only in emergencies. When he picked up the receiver, a small rectangular box attached to the phone flashed red.

The phone rang only once on the other end. Deputy Commander Hugh Phillips answered, "Yes sir, Mr. President."

"Deputy Commander, our source in Washington has given us the location. OPERATION KLICK is now in place. We want pictures of the Skyjacker, if it still exists. We plan to expose the Russians and their strike aircraft to the international news agencies. I understand three pilots have been in training for the mission."

"Yes, that's right, sir," came the answer.

"Have you picked one above the others?"

"Yes, we have." The president could hear papers rustling as Phillips leafed through a file. "Flight Lieutenant Bogdan Kapolski of the Royal Canadian Air Force," the assistant NORAD commander said. "Serial number J23198. Thirty-nine years old."

"What's his background?"

"He received his wings in Poland. He was a Battle

of Britain hero; twenty-four kills in total during World War II, ten during the Battle of Britain. Decorated with a British DFC and Bar plus DSO. Flew Hurricanes and Typhoons. Trained jet fighter pilots during the Korean conflict. He's flown CF-100s and the TUNDRA fighter, both extensively and both very well. In my opinion, sir, he's the best we've got in the entire TUNDRA operation. Commander Schult agrees with me.''

"His credentials speak for themselves."

Having spent several months in England during World War II, the president and Phillips knew what Polish pilots were capable of.

"How soon will the aircraft be ready for liftoff?"

"We'll start the final modifications immediately and be ready by early Friday morning."

"Very good. Now, give it to me straight, Commander. What are our chances of completing this successfully?"

"Well, sir, if Kapolski can't do it, nobody can."

"That's not what I asked you," the president spoke sharply.

"Mr. President, a mission of this length and magnitude has never been undertaken before, but I believe it will work."

The president sighed heavily into the phone. "It better. Well then, as Admiral Farragut once said in the heat of battle, 'Damn the torpedoes and full steam ahead.' ''

# CHAPTER TEN

LANCE TIEMANS LIKED TO KEEP IN SHAPE.
He played hockey, baseball, raquetball, and rode his bike
several times each week around the Oakville area. He
would ride away from his parents' bungalow, where he
was staying on leave from his air force duties and me-
ander up and down the quiet suburban streets. He especially enjoyed riding in the country a few miles to
the north. Today, however, he was riding into nearby
Mississauga, the next community east of Oakville.

It was a perfect morning for bike riding; no wind to
fight and the sun was warm on his bare legs. He stopped
on the corner of two busy residential streets to get his
bearings. For the last ten minutes he had noticed a dark
Chrysler hardtop following his turns, but keeping at a
safe distance. When he stopped suddenly at the edge of
a sidewalk, the car pulled over to the curb a block away.
Tiemans glanced behind him at the car, partially hidden

behind other cars parked on the street. Then he looked to his right and noticed a back alley only fifty feet away. He reasoned that if he turned into the alley, he'd come out on the next street. From there, a left turn would take him to the street he wanted. He checked for the umpteenth time to see if the brown envelope was tucked into his belt under his baggy sweatshirt. It was still there.

With a quick kick of his right foot, Tiemans was off. When he came to the alley he turned fast and barreled down the gravel roadway as fast as he could. Two houses down he stopped short and hid behind a toolshed, bike and all. A few seconds later the Chrysler drove by very slowly, as Tiemans carefully peered out from behind the building.

Now he really had to move. He jumped on his bike and pedaled to the end of the alley. He burst out onto the street, barely missing a parked Volkswagen, then took a quick left turn at the first block; Rollinbrook Street. He had to find the house quickly before the occupants of the Chrysler spotted him. Once the car made its way around the crescent, it would be on Rollinbrook too.

The first house on the left was number 555. Tiemans rode past a few more homes until he came to 547, where he quickly turned into the long driveway of a large two-story brown brick home. Attractive awnings covered the front windows and a white picket fence surrounded most of the yard. He ran his bike up to the back gate and jumped off before he actually came to a stop. He closed the gate behind him just a split second before the Chrysler drove by. He had lost them.

Tiemans dropped his bike on the grass between the garage and a set of winding patio stones that led into the backyard. He walked ahead cautiously until hecaught sight of the back of an overweight man sitting in a white lawn chair by the swimming pool. The man had a drink in his hand and was scribbling on a notepad. He wore a white T-shirt, lime-green Bermuda shorts, and thongs on his feet.

"Ben Spencer?" Tiemans asked hesitantly, once he was ten feet away from the relaxing figure.

The man almost jumped out of his skin. "Geez, you scared the living daylights out of me! Yeah, I'm Ben Spencer. Who are you and what do you want?"

"Lance Tiemans. Remember me?"

Spencer took off his sunglasses and stared at Tiemans for a moment. "Oh yeah, sure. I remember you. You were on the Arrow ground crew. But why did you sneak up on me? What's going on?"

"I need to see you for a minute." Tiemans looked toward the house. "Is there anyone else around? Can we go inside?"

"There's no one here. My wife and kids went to visit some relatives in London for the Dominion Day holiday."

Spencer led Tiemans into the house and down a short flight of stairs. Toys and comic books littered the uncompleted rec room. A door off the rec room led to a small office that Spencer had been using for himself. The first thing Tiemans noticed was the now-famous photograph of the Arrow dismantling that Spencer had taken from the helicopter. The picture was blown up and expensively framed. There was also a desk and chair, a phone, a typewriter, an overloaded bookcase, and some messy paperwork.

"Well, what's so important that we had to come into the house?" Spencer asked.

Tiemans licked his lips. "I've got a story for you that will blow the lid off Canadian journalism. It's the biggest thing since the Gouzenko affair."

"I'm all ears." Spencer had heard this kind of talk

before. He sat down on the edge of his desk and motioned the technician to the chair.

"Thanks. I love that picture of the Arrow torch scene behind you."

Spencer studied it for a moment. "I do too. That's the last the country saw of a great airplane."

"You're wrong."

"I'm wrong?"

"Right now, Arrows are being assembled, tested and flown, at a rate that would make your head spin. I know, I've seen them. I've touched them. This is such a hush-hush project that probably only a few big shots in the government know about it." Tiemans clenched his fist and brought it up even with his face. "I've seen Iroquois engines and I've worked on them, taken them apart. The Arrow and Iroquois projects are still very much alive."

The writer folded his arms. "I don't believe a word of it. Thousands of people would have to be involved in something like that. No way it could be kept secret. What are you, some kind of kook?"

"Kook, eh? Well, feast your eyes on this."

Tiemans showed Spencer the contents of the envelope stuffed inside his sweatshirt. There were two eight-by-ten glossy black-and-white photos; one showed two Avro Arrows with U.S. markings side by side on a tarmac, on the other was a perfect line of twelve Arrows with RCAF logos, battle camouflage, and squadron letter markings. Spencer couldn't believe his eyes. The Arrow wasn't dead? He was speechless.

"One hell of a story, isn't it, Mr. Spencer? The Arrow lives." The writer nodded, still in shock. He recalled his meeting with Robertson at the restaurant when the technician had told him the RCMP wanted the fuselage and wing blueprints. Now it all made sense. Or did it? Why didn't they need the blueprints anymore?

Then Spencer thought of the Russian bomber, the Tu-95 Bear. Could it be that it was shot down because it got too close to an Arrow fighter base in the Far North? Of course, the North, away from prying eyes.

"Where were these taken?"

"The Northwest Territories." Tiemans noticed that the writer had nodded his head as if he knew in advance where the location was.

"But why are they being built secretly?"

Tiemans shrugged. "I can't figure that one out. As near as we at Collins can figure . . ."

"Collins? What's that?"

"A completely new NORAD base. That's where I'm stationed now."

"Really?"

"There are several new bases up there. We share them with the Americans, and you wouldn't believe the size of them. First class all the way, especially TUNDRA."

"Hold on. What's TUNDRA?"

"The main base, the headquarters of the entire fighter base operation in the Territories."

"I just can't believe a huge project like this could be covered up."

Tiemans stood. "You've heard of the Manhattan Project, haven't you?"

"You mean the building of the A-bomb during World War II?"

"That's right. You know, there were nearly three hundred thousand technicians working on it, and nothing leaked to the press. It involved nineteen states and Canada, twelve hundred contractors, twenty-five universities, and over two billion dollars. The left hand didn't have a clue what the right hand was doing; it was one massive cover-up. There's nowhere near that number of people involved in this program."

"How do they build the Arrows?"

"Small parts are manufactured in different plants across North America and flown into the assembly plant, twenty miles south of TUNDRA. The people building the small parts don't know what they're really building. They never see the whole aircraft and so don't know it's the Arrow. Only the workers at the assembly plant see the finished product, and they're sworn to secrecy. From the assembly plant the completed Arrows are flown to TUNDRA for final testing. It's not that overwhelming really. Actually, you had a large hand in the success of the program. The publication of your photographs on all the international wire services dispelled any rumors that began to fly."

Spencer walked away from the desk, taking the pictures with him. "Amazing," was all he could say. Then, "I noticed in this one picture of the two Arrows that there's only one man inside the cockpits. I thought the Arrow was designed for a pilot and navigator, a two-man crew."

"They changed it. Less aircrew to worry about for security leaks. It's a one-man fighter, just like the F-104 Starfighter. I'll tell you another thing. Look at the picture behind you, the scrapping shot you're so proud of." Tiemans walked over to the wall and pointed at the eleven-by-fourteen photo. Running his finger along the side of the somewhat fuzzy shot, he stopped at the two fuselage pieces that were lying innocently on the tarmac.

"See those pieces?"

"Yeah."

"Look very closely at the way they're cut. Don't you think they're chopped off rather jagged?"

"I don't know," replied Spencer, as he got closer to the photo. "I never really looked closely."

"Metal doesn't come apart like that; it comes apart in even pieces. That's wood in the photo, plywood."

"Wood! Are you telling me those aircraft were fakes?"

Tiemans laughed. "Don't you see? All those planes in the photo," he pointed abruptly, moving his fingers to shape a large circle, "all those Arrows are wood mockups. The CF-100s on the right are the only real aircraft in the picture. The public was had and so were you. That's how they got away with it."

Spencer stuck his face right up to the photo. "It's been right there all this time and I didn't notice a thing. This . . ."

"Now, let's get down to business," Tiemans interrupted.

"Business? What business?"

"I know exactly where TUNDRA is and I know exactly how you can get in there undetected and back out again. But I want something from your paper in return. This is going to be the biggest story in Canadian history and it would be one heck of a feather in your cap if you wrote it."

"What do you want?" Spencer asked suspiciously.

"One hundred thousand dollars in a Swiss bank account and a plane ticket to Zurich. And I want it by Friday or the deal is off."

"That's only two days away. You're nuts!"

"You think so? Maybe you can't get the money, but your paper can. Get somebody over here right now or I'm going to another paper."

Spencer didn't hesitate. For something this big he'd have to go right to the top, to the owner of the paper, W. G. Gordon. Grabbing the telephone book from the top of the bookshelf, Spencer fumbled through it to find the number for Gordon's home. He dialed and was relieved to get an answer.

The voice on the other end was gruff. "Hello."

"Mr. Gordon, this is Ben Spencer."

"Yes, Ben, what can I do for you?"

"I'm sorry to call you on the holiday, but this is very important. I have a man here who has disclosed some startling information to me. There's a catch, however."

"What's that?"

"He wants something for it, if you know what I mean."

"I think I do."

"I can't explain too much over the phone. He says he wants a representative of the *Tribune* here within an hour or he'll go to another paper."

Gordon cleared his throat. "What do you think, Ben?"

Spencer looked at Tiemans, lounging against the wall. "I think he's on the level, Mr. Gordon."

"I've trusted your judgment in the past, Ben. All right, I'll be right over."

The Gordon family had controlled the *Toronto Tribune* since its inception in 1884. William Guy Gordon was the third generation to own the daily. He was a handsome, gray-haired man, almost six feet tall, in his late forties, a bachelor who loved the ladies, it was said. The *Tribune* staff knew him only as Mr. Gordon.

"Yes, Mr. Tiemans, I think I can get you the money." Gordon tugged at his neatly pressed white slacks and patted his golf shirt. He was slim and fit, and looked ready to shoot a round of golf.

"You better get it fast, no later than Friday," Tiemans demanded. "I want it in a Swiss bank account and I want confirmation so I know it's there. And I want an airline ticket under an assumed name, destination Zurich."

"Just hold on a minute. First off, I believe you. The pictures certainly look authentic, there's no doubt about that. But there might be some serious repercussions."

"Like what?" asked Spencer.

"The American and Canadian governments are obviously involved in something with a top-secret classification. If security measures are as tight as you say they are, Mr. Tiemans, we could be in serious trouble for exposing this story to the public. Are you sure you can get into Switzerland?"

Tiemans smiled. "Don't worry, I've got connections, I'll get in. Nobody will touch me, not even the prime minister or the president of the United States. I plan to stay there."

"I gathered that," Gordon grunted.

"Mr. Gordon," Spencer spoke up, "we've ignored government threats before. How about the Liberal sex scandal we uncovered in Ottawa three years ago, and how about the picture I snapped of the Arrow torchings? No one from the media was supposed to be there. Let's do it again. The public needs to know what really happened to the Arrow. I'll slip up to the base, take a few shots and get out. It's warm enough up in the Territories now to camp in the woods until I get the best shots of the place and the aircraft. Tiemans knows how I can get on and off, don't you?"

"If you know what you're doing, you'll be on and off before they know what hit them."

Gordon still didn't know what to make of it. "How are you going to get up there?"

"Sammy Hughes knows a pilot at the Island Airport, the one who flew the chopper over the Avro plant during the torching. He once told me that he makes the occasional trip up to northern Manitoba and the Territories. You know, those hunting and fishing expeditions that people take." Spencer nearly said "rich people," but caught himself in time to avoid offending Gordon. "Anyway, on these jaunts he flies a Catalina Flying Boat which can fly there and back without refueling.

We'll pay him a tidy sum to keep his mouth shut. He can fly low to avoid the radar and drop us off at the nearest lake. Then . . .''

"Wait a minute, Ben, who's us?"

"My wife and I."

"Your *wife* and you? You and Claire?" Gordon's mouth dropped open.

"Mr. Gordon, if we get caught by the base security, we'd look innocent with Claire along; just a couple of campers. Besides, she can help me with all the equipment."

Tiemans was getting impatient. "I want the money first or no directions."

"Don't worry, you'll get your money," Gordon said.

Spencer smiled. "You mean we'll do it?" he asked.

Gordon nodded. "But just you, Ben. There's no way your wife's going, no bloody way!''

RCAF Station Collins, NWT, Friday, July 3
0405 Hours (0605 est)

"Have a seat, Kapolski."

Smartly dressed in his uniform, Flight Lieutenant Kapolski saluted his commanding officer, Squadron Leader Wilkinson, who stood in front of a large chalkboard that was covered with a black cloth.

Wilkinson and Kapolski were the only souls in the briefing room. The nearly fifty chairs were vacant and the fluorescent lights above their heads gave the room a greenish cast and made it appear almost sinister.

Kapolski was very curious about this meeting. For the past month he had been sent on several high-speed, low-level photo-reconnaissance practice missions. Moreover, when he landed back at Collins, he used a specially constructed ground-based version of the mirror approach, which was found on navy aircraft carriers. He also had used arresting wires that were spread across the runway. This was another part of recovering aircraft used by the navy. During his photo-reconnaissance operations, he was required to skim over local RCAF bases at treetop level at speeds approaching Mach 1 and snap infrared pictures of parked aircraft along the dispersal points. He couldn't make any sense of these wacky operations.

Wilkinson stood erect and overpowering, despite his short height and medium build. He appeared tense.

"Flight Lieutenant Kapolski," Wilkinson said, looking down at the pilot, "within the next few hours you will be sent on an operation of national and international importance, far beyond standard operational procedure. These orders come from the top military planners in North America, from NORAD. For the past four weeks you have been trained for this crucial operation. You will be sent to photograph a secret test-fighter base, and following this will land on a U.S. Navy carrier. Here is your target."

Wilkinson took several seconds to pull back the black cloth. "Here, in the Soviet Union," he said, motioning with a pointer he had picked up on the board's edge. The long map, several feet in length, showed a wide patch of the northern tip of the world; the western half of the Northwest Territories, west to the Russian Pacific coastline.

Kapolski couldn't believe his ears. *Russia?* He was flying to Russia? Surely Wilkinson didn't mean he was going to fly from the Northwest Territories to the Soviet Union; surely he would fly from Korea?

"I realize this must be a shock to you," Wilkinson continued calmly, "but we have our reasons, and I will not be able to give you a full explanation. I can tell you, though, that you will be flying from this base and using a specially modified Arrow.''

Kapolski scratched his cheek. ''An Arrow over enemy territory, sir? From here?''

''Yes, an Arrow,'' Wilkinson smiled, ''and from this very spot. It might seem, at first, that we're out of our minds, but we're not. The Arrow's all-out speed and your experience will get us through. As you can see from the map, you will be inside Soviet territory for less than three hundred nautical miles; that's round trip. Then straight back in the same direction.'' Wilkinson again pointed to the map. ''I want something to be very clear—this is no suicide mission. Once you are inside enemy territory the operation will move fast, and you'll be so low to the ground that the Russians won't realize what hit them until it's too late. I plan to see you back here in one piece, with an intact aircraft. Command has every confidence that you will pull this off without a hitch.'' Wilkinson let his hands rest by his side, the pointer's edge dragging on the floor.

Kapolski's original shock at hearing his orders had worn off, and he was starting to look at the operation in a more realistic way. Could he really pull it off?

''As far as flying in from a point in Korea or Japan, that's out of the question. It would mean more security problems. We don't want an Arrow spotted on any runway out there. Also, we don't think any fighters that we have stationed out there can do the job. We believe only the Arrow can.

''With drop tanks and high-energy JP-4 fuel, you will be able to fly nearly two thousand miles at a speed of Mach one-point-five. You will radio on ultrahigh frequency to KC-135 Stratotankers for midair refueling. There will be at least one of these aircraft in each of the five sectors I've outlined in green on the map. Your call sign throughout the operation is PAPA-CHARLIE-ONE-

FOUR. The call signs for the other crafts and the carrier are in the guide.''

The C.O. walked over to his left, to a desk against the wall. He picked up a thin, eight-by-eleven-inch manual and gave it to the pilot. ''This operation, step by step, mile by mile, with detailed maps, is all in this. You just have to flip each page as you go along. It has all the turning points, headings and so on that you will need.''

Wilkinson paused for a few moments as Kapolski skimmed through the guide. ''Now, let's go over the route.'' He walked back over to the map and started reading the operational information sheet that was attached to the right side of the map. ''You will cruise the entire distance at forty-five thousand feet to avoid visual detection from airliners and so on, except when you descend to meet the tankers and when you reach Hokkaido Island in Japan. You will fly at a heading of two-one-five degrees from Collins to Umnak Island in the Aleutian chain. This is your first turning point, code-named ALPHA. The distance is just under seventeen hundred miles. You will refuel just after reaching sector two; the call sign is KILO-X-RAY-TWO-NINER. You drop your tanks and head two-four-six degrees for a point one-six-zero degrees longitude. Here,'' he said, pressing his finger on the map, ''five hundred miles off the Russian Kamchatka Peninsula, is your second turning point, code-named BRAVO. By that time, you will have covered three thousand miles and have been in the air three-point-five hours . . .''

Kapolski kept flipping his notes as Wilkinson read on, explaining explicitly the turning points and other data.

''Once you're over the northern section of the Sea of Japan you should be down to water level because there are radar masts on the Russian coastline, along the

Sikhote Alin Mountains. This is where it gets tricky and you have to be on your toes. From your turning point on Hokkaido you will steer exactly two-eight-three degrees and your pre-Initial Point, ironically, will be a large radar mast eight miles off to your right, plainly visible because of its height. Stay low and it won't pick you up, visually or electronically. You should be able to fly straight through a wide mountain pass there. You will fly over forest for one hundred miles to a coal mine, your I.P. Your path will cross the mine tracks leading into the side of a set of foothills. The base is twenty miles beyond, slightly to port. The heading is marked in your guide, of course. Approach the base at Mach point-nine-five, one hundred fifty feet, over the buildings on the right, to avoid any air traffic. Start shooting one thousand feet before the base and continue till a thousand feet after. Turn back as tight as you can, you're going to have to pull some G here, in order to fly back the same way. Keep your turn down to four miles or less. Then give it full throttle to get out. Fuel consumption is the key here because you can't refuel until you're back over Hokkaido.''

Wilkinson paused for breath. ''On the other side of Hokkaido will be a U.S. aircraft carrier, with the call sign ORIENTAL. You will land there, have your pictures developed in their lab, and return with the pictures back to Collins. The stop aboard the flattop will enable you to rest before starting back. The operation from beginning to end should last approximately twenty-four hours, including your rest period. This would be cut short if any emergency arises. You should be over enemy territory for only thirty minutes. An operation of this magnitude has never been conducted before, but we believe it will succeed. Do you have any questions?''

''What if I run into mechanical problems?''

"Your Arrow is fitted with a destruct button, a ten-second delay switch, which gives you time to bail out. If you have to bail out over enemy territory, you have the option of taking a cyanide capsule which will be placed in your left glove."

Kapolski swallowed. "What if I'm bounced? Should I fight?"

"No. You won't be armed. You've got speed, so use that and hustle your buns out of there."

"What about the weather in the Aleutian area and the Sea of Japan? Weather-wise, it's one of the worst regions in the world."

Wilkinson could sense that Kapolski wanted all the cards on the table. "Don't worry. According to meteorological reports from our friends in South Korea, we're okay for thirty-six hours; clear for most of the way except for some scattered cloud over Alaska. Choppy seas are expected over the Sea of Japan, which is to our advantage. We're moving on this now because meteorological reports haven't been this favorable over there in two or three months and we want to take advantage of it. Another thing, it's important that you're tracked on our radar, in this case by Airborne Early Warning Super Constellations. Your Identification Friend or Foe signal will be a special constantly flashing blip. Leave it on until you hit Hokkaido on the way in, and cease after Hokkaido. Stay on your headings and you won't get lost. After that," Wilkinson stopped deliberately, "you're on your own. If there are no more questions, let's get the show on the road."

Kapolski smiled at his C.O. "No sir, no more questions."

"Good. Takeoff time is set for 0625 hours. Good luck."

60 Miles Southeast of Tundra Headquarters,
NWT, 0513 Hours (0713 est)

"We're going to land soon, so let's get the gear together." Ben Spencer and his wife, Claire, were watching through the starboard blister of a Catalina Flying
Boat, when they felt the plane drop slightly.

One hundred and fifty feet down, evergreens blurred
past them in a steady stream. The sun cast long shadows
across the clear lakes that they passed; there wasn't a
ripple on the waters.

They were tired from the long, slow trip through most
of the night, and a little airsick from the buzzing drone
of the engines. Claire yawned. "We didn't stop for refueling, did we?"

Spencer chuckled. "Are you kidding? These babies
can stay airborne for more than twenty-four hours."

Spencer reached behind to get his large knapsack. He
rummaged through it to make sure he had his camera,
dried foods, sandwiches, a small two-man nylon tent,
a set of wire snips, and assorted pens and papers. "Do
you have the change of clothing?"

Claire surveyed her equipment. "Check," she answered mechanically.

"Sandwiches and drinks?"

"Check."

"Compass?"

"Check." She yawned again. "We went through all
this before we left."

"I know, but I just want to make sure it's all here.
Well, I guess we're all set."

RCAF STATION COLLINS,
NWT, 0601 HOURS (0801 EST)

With his helmet and operational guide in hand, Kapolski walked across the floor of the readiness hangar,
his flight boots sounding heavy on the concrete. He
stopped for a moment near the ladder of the specially
modified Arrow. As two members of his ground crew
looked on, he made a visual walk-around check of the
entire aircraft. Then he asked to see the L-14 manual,
an updated service report of this particular aircraft. He
read the top page of the binder to check on the maintenance work that had been done in the last few days.
He saw that the hydraulic pressures were checked, the
brakes were replaced, the engines were given a successful twenty-hour inspection, the ejection seat was
armed with two 20mm cannon shells, and the tires were
all new. When he was satisfied, he handed the manual
to one of the sergeants and climbed the wooden steps
to the cockpit.

This was no ordinary Arrow, for it had been fitted
with a camera pod built into the belly, a tail hook, a
refueling nozzle on the nose, and two 450-gallon drop
tanks that hugged the fuselage under each wing. It had
a dull coating of green camouflage paint over the entire
top surface and sky-blue paint underneath. Kapolski
paused at the top of the ladder to look across at the
nose of the fighter. Then he eased into the cockpit.

One of the ground crew preparing Kapolski for his
photo-reconnaissance flight was the replacement for
Lance Tiemans, the civilian who had not returned from
his leave. Kapolski missed Tiemans and his expertise,
but he'd had little time to wonder what had happened
to him.

The replacement climbed up the ladder in order to
help Kapolski strap himself in. At the top of the ladder,

he grinned and asked, "Going somewhere?" Kapolski glared coldly at him. "Mum's the word, right?" the sergeant said, as he connected the pilot's oxygen supply.

This lifeline gave oxygen to the pilot and also inflated his reptile-like G-suit. The sergeant then attached the survival kit, containing a dinghy, to Kapolski by means of a rope. Next, he tied the leg restraints around Kapolski's ankles to keep his legs locked, just in case he had to bail out into the turbulent slipstream.

The sergeant helped the pilot into the harness. One pair of straps came down on his shoulders, another went around his hips, and a third fit between the legs. The whole thing locked into a central socket above his crotch, and once strapped in, Kapolski could barely move. He was glad the Arrow was a comfortable fighter to fly. Unlike the forward-positioned seat of the CF-100, which gave most pilots a backache after only a few minutes in the air, the Arrow's soft seat was set back at just the proper angle.

Kapolski dropped the helmet over his head, put his sunglasses in place, wiggled his hands into his flying gloves, and hooked up his oxygen and radio wires. He was locked in. Next, Kapolski pulled out the pin that armed the ejection seat. He placed the pin, with its long red flag, inside the pilot's panel. The sergeant descended the ladder.

As the pilot and crew ran a final series of checks, the hangar doors, front and back, opened slowly, almost as if by magic. It was a bright, cloudless morning. Another Arrow had just landed and they could see it crossing the runway in front of the forward door.

Kapolski switched the power on and the cockpit lights blinked. He glanced at the gauges and switches before him, many of which wouldn't come into play until he was in the air: artificial horizon indicator, accelerometer, skin temperature indicator, cabin pressure altitude gauge, Mach airspeed indicator, and so on.

Less than a minute later, the sergeant pulled out the three red-flagged undercarriage pins, rolled the ladder away, slapped the camera pod for good luck, and walked in front of the aircraft on the starboard side to give the thumbs-up signal for Kapolski to start the engines. The front hangar door had been fully extended and the other ground crew sergeant walked towards the opening and peered out. He turned back to face the pilot and signaled with his thumb.

Kapolski watched as the ground crew put their ear protection in place. As a standard safety precaution, the closer of the sergeants stood ready with a fire extinguisher. Kapolski started the engines.

The operational hangar shook violently from the revving force of the mighty Iroquois engines, each with twenty thousand pounds of ear-splitting thrust. Kapolski took his time checking his instruments, then closed and locked the clamshell canopy by hitting a switch on his left, just forward from the throttles. The ground crew checked the ailerons, rudder and speed brakes in unison with the pilot. They disconnected the power cart and pulled the chocks away. They both gave their final thumbs-up signs and Kapolski returned the gesture.

Flight Lieutenant Bogdan Kapolski of the Royal Canadian Air Force rolled the Avro Arrow Mark II through the hangar doors and out onto the perimeter track. The exhausts glowed red hot and smelled of burnt jet fuel, a glorious aroma to the nostrils of any ground crew.

Kapolski crawled slowly along the track. He switched on his radio. "GOLDRUSH, THIS IS PAPA-CHARLIE-ONE-FOUR TAXIING FOR I-F-R DEPARTURE."

"PAPA-CHARLIE-ONE-FOUR, TAXI VIA FOXTROT. HOLD SHORT OF TWO-SEVEN. NUMBER ONE FOR DEPARTURE,

ONE IN THE CIRCUIT. BINGO THIS FREQUENCY. GO BUT-
TON SIX, ENTERING FOXTROT.''

"WILCO GOLDRUSH.''

Kapolski obeyed as directed and lined himself up at
the edge of Runway 27. Over the pilot's head another
battle-camouflaged Arrow, with landing gear extended,
dropped from the sky like a mighty bird and proceeded
westward. The wheels touched and the chute popped.
Kapolski tugged at his harness as he watched the other
craft steer off the runway. His harness was tight enough
and the oxygen mask was resting properly against his
face.

"PAPA-CHARLIE-ONE-FOUR IS CLEARED TO THE RAW
SILK AIRSPACE RESERVATION AS FILED. TROUT LAKE TWO
DEPARTURE, MAINTAIN ANGELS FOUR-FIVE. CONTACT
TUNDRA CONTROL AFTER DEPARTURE.''

"PAPA-CHARLIE-ONE-FOUR, ROGER.''

"PAPA-CHARLIE-ONE-FOUR CLEARED FOR TAKEOFF.''

Kapolski shoved the engines up to 80 percent RPM.
Despite the protective foam rubber on the inside of his
helmet, the explosion pounded his ears. He turned on
the emergency fuel pump, then made a last check of
the gauges and instruments. He cracked the engine
throttles on the left to maximum and released the
brakes.

"PAPA-CHARLIE-ONE-FOUR ROLLING.''

In an instant the aircraft was tearing at the concrete
runway with enormous force. Kapolski felt the familiar
thrill as the power pushed him firmly back in his seat.
Five thousand feet down the runway the aircraft eased
off the surface and leaped into the air. There was no
turning back now.

# CHAPTER ELEVEN

"YOU MEAN TO TELL ME WE DON'T HAVE TO pay a cent for this trip?"

"That's right, we're on assignment," Ben Spencer told his wife.

"Well, you sure picked the sticks."

"What did you expect for free?"

"You still haven't told me what this assignment is all about."

"You'll find out soon enough. Let's just enjoy being together for now."

Claire only shook her head and finished her sandwich. She was hungry after the all-night flight. She glanced across at the calm lake and its scenic, rocky shoreline.

Spencer was impatient to get going. He got his equipment together in his knapsack and slung it over his back. Claire was still resting on a large rock at the

186

water's edge, but she stood up too and reached for her knapsack. They were both heavily dressed in denim jackets and pants, knitted sweaters, and hiking boots.

"Ben, why were we flying so low the last hour or so?"

"So radar wouldn't detect us," he answered calmly.

"Radar? Out here in the middle of nowhere?" Claire laughed out loud. "Ben, what are you up to?"

"Let's get going," Spencer said, turning to his wife.

"Where are we going?"

"You'll see. Hand me the compass."

Claire loved mysteries. Thinking that Spencer had prepared some kind of surprise or adventure for her, she stopped asking questions and walked along quietly with her husband.

They walked northwest through a dense forest of spruce trees for a few miles until Claire flopped down to the ground. "I'm tired," she gasped. "And my feet are sore. I'm not used to wearing hiking boots."

"Me neither. Let's rest here for a while."

They were in the middle of a small clearing about fifty feet across. "Are you sure you know where we are? There's nothing but trees everywhere."

"Yes, I know where we are. The compass is right on and we'll be there soon." They heard a jet aircraft approaching. "Duck!" Spencer shouted, grabbing his wife and forcing her behind the trunk of a nearby tree. A jet fighter raced overhead full-throttle from the northwest. A few seconds later, another aircraft of the same type and heading in the same direction flew over them.

"They were very low," Spencer said, looking up after the second aircraft zipped by. "I could see the markings on the planes." He wasn't kidding, she thought, they must be only a few hundred feet up.

Claire was puzzled. "There must be an airport near here. I thought we were in the middle of nowhere."

"Now, I wouldn't be on assignment in the middle of

nowhere, would I?'' He spoke softly. ''There's a fighter base beyond this clearing that's so big, it'll . . . Anyway, you've got to see it.''

''We're not supposed to be here, are we?'' Claire asked. Spencer grinned and took Claire's hand while they crossed the clearing.

They walked back into the heavy bush and were hidden from the fighters that roared overhead at regular intervals. Spencer thought they were probably practicing circuits-and-bumps, but he couldn't tell for sure because the trees were too thick to see any distance away.

''There's the fence.''

They had come to a partial clearing, just a few feet away from a six-foot-high barbed wire fence. Some dead branches crackled under him as Spencer knelt down and removed a small set of wire snips from his knapsack.

''What are you doing?'' Claire asked, shoving her hands into her pockets.

Spencer threw the snips at the fence.

''Good, it's not electrified.''

He ran over to the fence, picked up the tool, and knelt down again. He winked at his wife and started cutting out a large area several feet square.

''What are you doing, Ben?''

''What does it look like I'm doing?''

''It looks like you're cutting through the fence.''

''You're very observant.''

''Are you crazy? That fence is there to keep people out. We could get arrested for trespassing. It could be dangerous too, if the airfield is close by.''

''It's okay, honey. This fence is to keep other people out, not me. I'm on assignment.''

Once they were through the fence, the Spencers saw another fighter come towards them, this time only fifty feet off the ground. The aircraft screamed overhead and the ground thundered beneath them as the pilot lit the afterburners.

Claire waited till it had flown over before she attempted to speak. "Hey, that looked like the Arrow, that plane you're always going on about in the Tribune."

"You've got it. That was an Arrow all right, and so were the other planes we saw. Claire," he said, grabbing his wife by the shoulders, "this is going to be the story of the century. The Arrow was never scrapped. It's still being built and the whole program is top secret. I just need to get some photos here, then we'll meet the Catalina back at the lake, and home we go. Then I'm going to write a story that will blow this thing right open."

"So that's what this little escapade is all about."

"Now you know."

"How did you find out about it?"

"It's a long story. I'll tell you when we get home."

"Ben?"

"Yeah."

"I'm scared. What if we get caught?"

"Don't worry, we won't. We'll be in and out before anyone knows it."

"I hope you're right."

"Stay low and keep near the trees, there's another clearing up ahead. Let's go."

"I have a feeling I don't have much choice."


OAKVILLE, ONTARIO, 1102 HOURS (EST)

From a telephone booth in front of Rommer's General Store on the northern outskirts of Oakville, Lance Tiemans called a taxi. Then he sat down on an old unpainted bench to the side of the store and waited.

His plan was working out perfectly. In the left breast pocket of his brown corduroy sports jacket was a document stipulating that $100,000 in Canadian funds had been deposited into a Swiss bank account, number LTR1667849, in Zurich. In the other breast pocket was a Trans Canada Airline ticket to Gander, Newfoundland, where he'd connect with a European airline for a flight to Zurich, Switzerland, via London and Paris.

Tiemans tried to relax. He was wearing a pair of dark sunglasses, just in case security agents were still snooping around. Though he hadn't noticed any following him the last few days, he thought he'd been clever to call the cab to this deserted area, instead of to the house. He'd decided, too, that he would wait until he was safely in Switzerland before calling his parents and girlfriend. He hadn't yet worked out what he was going to tell them.

In less than twenty-four hours Tiemans would be in Switzerland and $100,000, half a million francs in Swiss currency, richer. He reasoned that he didn't owe anything to the government or to A. V. Roe. He wasn't a traitor; he was only looking out for number one. Besides, the public had a right to know what its government was doing. Once the *Tribune* broke the story, Ben Spencer would become a national hero, and the *Tribune* would sell a lot of newspapers.

Everything had gone smoothly, especially at the end. Tiemans had simply slipped out the front door while his parents were working in the garden and walked the few blocks to the store. In a few minutes a cab would whisk him to Malton Airport, approximately thirty miles away. Looking back now, it all seemed too easy.

OVER THE ALEUTIANS, 0404 HOURS (1104 EST)

Alaska, the forty-ninth state of the United States of America, was the largest state in the Union, with nearly six hundred thousand square miles of ice and rock, and a total population of just under two hundred thousand. Far to the north, near the Arctic Circle, the Bering Strait separated this great land from the Soviet Union. Two small islands in particular, Big Diomede, USSR, and Little Diomede, Alaska, were only two miles apart.

Kapolski's flight path didn't come anywhere near the Diomede Islands. He was ordered to fly southwest, along the Aleutian chain, where the U.S. government had recently installed an extension of the DEW Line. The radar sets on these islands were picking up Kapolski's IFF signal.

Kapolski was on a heading of 215 degrees. His airspeed was Mach 1.5, his altitude forty-five thousand feet. He reset the IFF button, making sure it was in the ON position. Without it, he would not be tracked by the Airborne Early Warning Super Constellations in the North Pacific. It was these monster aircraft of the U.S. Navy that would feed position and heading information to the crews of the KC-135 Stratotankers that were circling over these lonely waters.

With the Arrow's fully computerized Fly-by-Wire system engaged, Kapolski merely had to put a half pound of pressure on the control column and an electric contact within the column's base would close, thus sending a signal to the control servomechanisms by way of amplifiers and electronics. In essence, the aircraft could fly by itself.

This system, Kapolski knew, would neatly take care of an engine failure. Instead of sideslipping and rolling, common when engine failures occur in other aircraft, the Fly-by-Wire would keep the aircraft steady. Still, Kapolski hoped there wouldn't be an incident, not over the Pacific Ocean or the Soviet Union at any rate; he needed the power. If any trouble resulted from a system malfunction at takeoff or landing, the Arrow was fitted with a manual override, something Kapolski still liked to use. It reminded him of the good old days of the unsophisticated Hurricanes and Typhoons.

The complexity of the Avro Arrow was phenomenal, a stunning modern invention. It had thirty-eight thousand parts. The wiring could extend over eleven miles and it had enough tubes to furnish two hundred television sets. There were eight hundred separate fuses, switches, relays and terminals. The air-conditioning system, capable of producing twenty-three tons of ice per day, had a refrigeration capacity equal to fifty domestic air conditioners. This system was capable of changing the air in a twenty-by-twelve-foot room with a ten-foot ceiling ten times in sixty seconds. This air-conditioning unit was essential aboard the Arrow to neutralize the air friction of supersonic speeds, where skin temperatures, even at high altitudes where temperatures reach fifty below Fahrenheit, can exceed forty degrees above the boiling point of water. To obtain these supersonic speeds the Arrow utilized approximately twice as much power as was needed to drive the great *Queen Mary*.

The bright northern sun beamed through the canopy and Kapolski felt confident. His mind was ready and alert. He was glad to have the special softly padded pilot seat that was installed for this trip; otherwise his butt, back and legs would be killing him by now. He wondered how the American P-51 pilots of World War II had managed to escort the Flying Fortress and Liberator bombers to Berlin and back on those daylight raids, a good eight-hour trip from English soil. They must have been terribly uncomfortable in those sardine cans.

OAKVILLE, ONTARIO, 1110 HOURS (EST)

Lance Tiemans stood up when he saw a car approaching. It wasn't a cab, though, it was a Ford sedan. When it got close to the store, it pulled over, off the road, and hit a puddle of dirty water.

The passenger window was rolled down. "Hey, watch it!" Tiemans screamed to the two men in the car. "You got mud all over my pants!"

Both men got out of the car and walked over to Tiemans, who by this time was getting a little nervous. The driver was of medium height and build with blonde, wavy hair; the other was taller, slim, with black hair and piercing eyes. Both wore conservative business suits.

"Lance Tiemans?" asked the tall man.

"Yeah, I'm . . . no. No, I'm not. Wait a minute, who are you guys?"

Both men flashed RCMP intelligence badges.

"Where are you going?" one of them asked.

Tiemans became indignant. "None of your damn business!"

The dark-haired agent grabbed Tiemans's lapel, and in one motion reached in his pocket and grabbed the envelope containing the plane tickets. "You're due back at Collins," he said sternly, as he studied the tickets. "What are you doing with plane tickets to Newfoundland and Europe?"

Tiemans could only stand there in stunned silence, his heart pounding. The other agent grabbed the Swiss bank statement from his other breast pocket.

"Well, well, a Swiss bank account for a hundred thousand dollars. I think you better come with us, Mr. Tiemans, because you have a lot of explaining to do."

OVER THE ALEUTIANS, 0413 HOURS (1113 EST)

Several small islands twinkled below Kapolski's Arrow in the glorious sunlight that shone through the scattered light cloud. The ice and snow on the occasional mountain peak reflected the sun's rays to a glossy brilliance. At this height of nearly nine miles above the ocean surface he could only partially comprehend the sensation of his aircraft flying faster than the speed of sound. What would it be like at sea level?

Over his port wing Kapolski saw the vast blue of the Pacific, stretching as far as he could see. Wilkinson had been right: it was clearing up. Ahead was water and more water, broken up by a few dots of solid ground.

Kapolski was getting low on fuel and would need a hookup shortly, within twenty minutes for sure. This would be his first midair pit stop. He had been watching a contact on his radar screen for several minutes and knew it was out there. He flipped to the next page of his guide, held it up on the sun side of the fighter, and scanned the paper for the code words and radio frequency to contact the tanker in sector two.

He selected the channel and pressed the R/T button, just down from the throttles.

"KILO-X-RAY-TWO-NINER, THIS IS PAPA-CHARLIE-ONE-FOUR. I'M APPROACHING BINGO FUEL. OVER."

"PAPA-CHARLIE-ONE-FOUR, ROGER. ON HEADING TWO-ONE-FIVE. ANGELS THREE-THREE. COMMENCE DESCENDING. MAINTAIN COURSE AND WE SHOULD HOOK UP IN TEN MINUTES. KILO-X-RAY-TWO-NINER, OVER."

"KILO-X-RAY-TWO-NINER, ROGER. SEE YOU IN TEN."

NEAR MALTON AIRPORT, ONTARIO
1108 HOURS (EST)

Tiemans was desperate. He knew that unless he could escape now, he'd spend the next few years in jail.

As the sedan sped down a side road towards the freeway that led into Toronto, Tiemans thought of what he might do. He had to get out of the country in a hurry. Going over the border into New York State, only fifty miles away, wouldn't suffice because the authorities would be after him there too. He had to get out of North America, and to do that he'd have to get to Malton Airport. He already had his tickets; if he could shake the two men in the car, he simply board his flight to Gander. They'd have to be out of commission long enough for him to fly to Gander, stop over for an hour to change planes, and fly out on Swissair. Once he was in the air over the Atlantic, he'd be home free.

But how was he going to get rid of the agents? Murder? He'd never even imagined doing anything like that before. He didn't even know how to fight with his fists. Then again, he'd never been in a desperate situation like this before. Could he kill two men?

The sedan stopped at a set of lights at a T-intersection. The car idled smoothly, and Tiemans waited for the right moment to spring into action. He was in the back passenger seat, handcuffed, and the dark-haired Intelligence officer was sitting next to him, with his gun resting on his leg.

"Are you going to take the four-oh-one into Metro?" the agent turned to look in the direction of the driver.

"Yeah, it's closer from here."

*Now!* Tiemans thought. In a wild, desperate move Tiemans lunged and slugged the agent next to him across the face with his handcuffed fists. He grabbed the gun that the agent was holding and stuck the pistol in the man's ribs.

"Okay, you in the front, do anything stupid and jerk-face here in the back gets it in the stomach. Throw your gun in the backseat, gently, or I'll pull the trigger on your friend."

The driver reached between the seats and dropped his gun onto the back floorboards. The other agent, dazed and bleeding from his left eye, slumped against the window.

The light changed to green, but the driver didn't move the car. Luckily, there were no other cars behind them. This road was seldom used; it was one of those out-of-the-way roads that the provincial government had no business putting traffic lights on.

"Okay, Blondie," Tiemans said, holding the gun at the agent's head. "Get out of the car."

WEST OF THE ALEUTIANS
0440 HOURS (1140 EST)

Kapolski pushed his oxygen mask aside and shoved a portion of a candy-bar-shaped fruit concentrate into his mouth. He was now breathing in pure oxygen thanks to a device called a regulator that automatically distributes the right amount of oxygen cabin air depending on the pilot's altitude. With the mask back in place, he munched away as he looked ahead at the rear view of the four-engined Boeing KC-135 Stratotanker. The drogue line attached to the Arrow's front-end probe reminded him of a baby's umbilical cord. It was his life line to the jet-powered tanker that was his mother ship.

He was thirty-three thousand feet over the Pacific Ocean, at an airspeed of Mach 0.70. The fuel link was pushing the high-octane fuel into the fighter at high speed by means of special pumps and a coupling apparatus. Once the fuel tanks of the Arrow registered the full thirty-three hundred gallons, he would pull away.

He grabbed another concentrate and wolfed it down. He was hungry. As he swallowed a good gulp of orange juice from a plastic cup, Kapolski's thoughts sped back to World War II again. The operations he flew were, for the most part, boring. Sometimes nothing would happen for a half-hour or longer, until he reached enemy territory or when he met the enemy bogies over his home ground during the Battle of Britain. Then, in a split second, sheer terror would erupt. *Me-109s spotted at six o'clock low . . . flak off starboard side . . . the Hun out of the sun . . .* Then the return trip and more boredom. So far, this reconnaissance trip was boring too. But he knew that once he dropped altitude and screamed into enemy territory, the boredom would be displaced by sheer exhilaration. Then there would be some tense moments on the final run and back out. The one aspect of the return trip he knew wouldn't be boring was the carrier landing, something he'd never tried before.

Kapolski checked his fuel gauges and saw that the tanks were nearly full. Then he glanced down at his map of the Aleutians. He was three hours away from the Soviet border.

MALTON AIRPORT, ONTARIO, 1201 HOURS (EST)

From his window seat on the DC-8's starboard side, Tiemans watched the busy airport traffic. The jet engines hummed smoothly for several minutes and Tiemans knew they'd pull out shortly.

The plane was only half full of passengers and Tiemans was happy to have two empty seats on his left. He didn't feel like talking to strangers right now. He was busy thinking, congratulating himself on putting one over on his superiors. Within a matter of days, the *Toronto Tribune* would break the biggest news story in Canadian history, and he'd be thousands of miles away in Europe, a rich man.

Hopefully, the RCMP agents wouldn't come to until he was safely out of the country. He'd knocked them out, tied them up and left them in the trunk of their own car, in a parking lot a half mile from the airport. He didn't have the nerve to kill them. He'd retrieved his tickets and bank statement and made his flight just in time.

He picked up the *Toronto Tribune* that had been resting on his lap and flipped through the first section, checking the news headlines. He stopped for a moment to feel for his bank statement in the pocket of his jacket. Still there. Without that $100,000, he'd be nowhere.

TUNDRA HEADQUARTERS,
NWT, 1025 HOURS (1225 EST)

"I can't believe the size of this place."

Claire pushed her hand through her long blonde hair. "It's fantastic, but I still think we should get the hell out of here."

"I've seen fighter bases before, but nothing like this one," Spencer said. "We've got to get closer so I can take some pictures."

Spencer and his wife were squatting behind some pine trees, just inside the fenced compound. To their right and left, a few thousand feet away, were several long runways, and beyond that were building complexes, hangars and maintenance structures.

The wind started to pick up, so Claire zipped up her coat. "It's getting cold."

Spencer grunted. "Well, we're a long way from Florida up here." He reached into his shirt pocket for a cigarette.

"Ben Spencer, you told me you'd quit smoking!"

"I did, I did. I only have the odd one now and again. It calms me when I'm nervous."

"If you're so nervous, then let's get out of here."

"No way. This is going to be the story of the century," Spencer answered, lighting his cigarette.

"If we get away with it."

Spencer ignored the remark. "There go two more Arrows side by side, or side by each, as your mother would say."

Claire pretended to be angry. "You leave my mother out of this. She was nice enough to look after the twins while we're running wild in the bush." Though she was still frightened, Claire was just as excited about the story as Ben was. She wouldn't dream of backing off now.

They watched the planes pick up speed and blast off to the east, the ground vibrating even after the planes were out of sight over the tree line.

In front of the hangars, about a half mile away, several Arrows were being readied for flight by a handful of ground crew, who appeared ant-like from the distance. Spencer busied himself taking notes of the layout and snapping some pictures with his telephoto lens.

"Let's see if we can get closer to the hangars. We can scoot around the right side of the complex and still stay hidden in the trees." He exhaled some smoke from his cigarette.

They got their equipment together and crawled further into the heavy bush.

"Hold it right there, you two, and put your hands behind your heads. Now!"

Spencer and his wife, startled, looked up to see the barrels of two .45 automatics pointing at them. Two uniformed men were advancing on them from about thirty feet away.

"I said, get your hands up. Move!" The Spencers obeyed.

"What are you doing here?" one man asked, as they stepped closer. Spencer could see their red armbands and white lettering. AFP, Air Force Police.

"We're camping," Spencer answered sheepishly, his cigarette dangling from his mouth.

"Campers, eh? How did you get into the compound?" The guard's voice was relaxed. "This is a restricted area."

The Spencers didn't answer.

One of the men walked behind Spencer. "Cover me." He searched through Spencer's knapsack.

"Don't worry, I'm not packing a rod."

"Shut up and keep those hands behind your head." The guard had found the wire cutters. He snatched Spencer's cigarette from his mouth and stamped it out on the ground.

"Okay, you two," said the other guard, "march, and don't stop till we say so. And keep your hands up."

After a short walk into the clearing, they were taken to a jeep and driven along a wide piece of asphalt that wound its way around the outer fringe of the runways. Spencer noticed that the buildings were painted a brown-green camouflage, probably to hide them from enemy aerial photography. He also saw four Arrows in front of a long hangar, all armed with missiles descending from their bellypacks.

The jeep stopped at a two-story building where the Spencers were whipped inside at gunpoint, into what appeared to be a large auditorium. There was a long stage where the Canadian and American flags hung as a backdrop and several doors leading off one wall. There didn't seem to be a soul in the building.

The Spencers were ushered inside the first room. The only furniture was a dull-green metal desk surrounded by wooden chairs. The MPs closed the door behind them and they were left alone.

"What now, Ben?" asked his wife.

"I don't know. I guess I'll have to talk my way out of this one."

"Yeah, sure. What are you going to say?"

"I'll tell them the truth; that I came here to write a story from a hot tip."

"What if they don't believe us?"

Spencer hugged his wife. "Don't worry, the worst they can do is hang us."

"What!"

"Relax, Claire, I'm only kidding."

Spencer was joking to hide his anxiety. He realized they might be in deep trouble. But then again, maybe not. He was a reporter, and a reporter's job is to hunt down stories. What could the authorities do to them?

The door jolted suddenly open to reveal a tall man in an American Air Force uniform, a four-star general. Spencer was amazed. A four-star general way up here in the Northwest Territories? The man's eyes tore through Spencer's. As Spencer stared back, he thought there was something familiar about the general's high cheekbones and protruding chin. His hair was brown with a tinge of gray, his face chubby but youthful. He stood with his feet planted wide apart, his hands clasped behind him.

It couldn't be him, Spencer thought, could it? After all these years, just a little older, a little chubbier, a little grayer; it was "Steady Eddie," the B-29 pilot, now Edmund Schult, the supreme commander of NORAD. Spencer had read several months before in a news release that Schult had been appointed head of NORAD.

"Commander Schult, I mean General Schult, you've come a long way from piloting a B-29 Superfortress."

"Yes, I suppose I have. So have you."

The general's voice was cool. "Well, Mr. Spencer, here's your wallet." The general stepped into the room and dropped it on the table. "None of your ID states that you're a reporter with the *Toronto Tribune*. Why not? Don't members of the press carry ID in Canada?"

The general turned to the guard at his post by the door. "You may close the door, Sergeant."

"Yes, sir," replied the sentry.

As he reached for his wallet, Spencer winked at his startled wife. "Ben, you mean this man was the pilot on that bomber mission you're always telling the kids about?"

Spencer grinned. "Yeah, and Bradley even shaved."

The general smiled. "I see you still have a sense of humor. You're also still living dangerously, aren't you."

"Dangerously? How?"

"Come off it. You wrote a great firsthand story of that Tokyo raid. You risked your life all during the war, but it worked out well for you; you made a name for yourself in journalism. You ignored our 'no media' instructions for the Malton scrapping of the Arrow and now you've cut your way into a restricted zone. It's really unfortunate that you two have wasted your time traveling all this way for nothing. There will be no story. Campers, eh?" The general looked menacingly at Spencer. "Campers don't cut their way through barbed-wire fencing." He shook his head.

"How did you know who I was?"

"As soon as you were picked up, I was telephoned. When I heard your name, I knew right away who you were. We've all heard about you in the States. Even the president is amused, for some reason, by your columns."

"I'm flattered."

"The picture you took of the Arrow scrapping on the Avro tarmac was a beauty, something we never counted on. But it certainly worked in our favor."

"What's the big secret with the Arrow?"

"You know I can't tell you that."

Claire had been quiet up until now. "You caught us, now what are you going to do with us?"

"I ought to have you two arrested."

"Look, General, I'll make a deal with you," Spencer said.

"I don't think you're in a position to make deals, but go ahead, I'm listening." Schult looked amused as he folded his arms.

"Let us off and we won't breathe a word of this to anyone, not to friends, relatives, or even the paper. I'll tell the *Tribune* that this base was just a hot tip that turned sour, just a rumor. As far as I'm concerned, this base doesn't exist." Spencer placed his hands in his pockets, waiting for a reply.

The general pretended to consider the offer. "Won't your paper be awfully angry about giving away a hundred thousand dollars to an informer for nothing?"

Spencer's head jerked forward. "How did you know about the money?"

Claire's face went white. "One hundred thousand? You never told me about that!"

"We picked up Lance Tiemans just before his plane took off from Malton Airport. He was carrying his Swiss bank account on him and plane tickets to Zurich. It's really too bad because Tiemans's technical knowledge of the Iroquois engine was essential to us. You two are lucky you aren't in his boots; he'll be thrown into a military jail for a long time. Now," he paused, "you two come with me."

Tundra Headquarters, NWT, 1154 Hours (1354 est)

An armed guard opened the steel door to the underground operations room. It took a few seconds for the Spencers' eyes to adjust to the semidarkness of the black-walled area.

Commander Schult had led them into an enormous room that was 150 feet long, 100 feet wide, and nearly twenty feet high. Rows of adjoined consoles ran parallel almost the full length of the room. The first row of consoles and seats were raised slightly from the floor, the second row raised even higher and the last row, the glassed-in area from which the general directed the defense, was raised the highest, and seemed to dominate the room. Attached to each console was a monitor, a telephone, and a keyboard with alphabet and other miscellaneous buttons. Some of the staff were speaking into their receivers, while others were typing on keyboards. Even though only half of the desks were occupied, there was a steady wave of organized bustle.

A dozen telex machines, along the wall on the right, were pounding away. Straight ahead, against the far wall, were four twenty-by-thirty-foot projection screens, all showing different areas of North America, complete with lines of latitude and longitude in Mercator map form. Different colors, numbers and alpha codes blinked constantly on and off on these displays.

The projection screen on the left showed a general view of Canada and the United States, with a row of clocks on top to depict the appropriate time zones. The second screen flashed a close-up of the Northwest Territories, and the other two displayed the Pacific and Atlantic seaboards.

"This is the operations room," said the general, after allowing his visitors sufficient time to eye the massive room. "NORAD has a similar room at our head-quarters in Colorado."

"Why would NORAD have an operations room up here in the Arctic?" asked Spencer.

"Mr. Spencer, I'm not at liberty to answer that question for you. I'm sure," Schult continued, "you've noticed our new computer projection screens in front of you. Each one shows a different view of our NORAD air defense system. The lines of bright orange lights show our three lines of ground radar detection. Each light depicts one station. The DEW Line, which stands for Distant Early Warning, is the most northerly, two hundred fifty miles above the Arctic Circle. This elaborate organization, made up of fifty radar sites that extend three thousand miles, has cost over six hundred million dollars to build. It's maintained by six hundred American and Canadian technicians who work around the clock. This system is of utmost importance to us because if we are ever attacked from the north it gives us time to react and plot strategy. Depending on the speed of the enemy aircraft, it gives us four to six hours before any major Canadian or American cities are reached. The men operating this radar line along the top of the world face some of the worst weather conditions anywhere in the world. Temperatures can hit seventy below and winds can reach over a hundred miles per hour.

"Six hundred miles south of the DEW Line, south of here, is the Mid-Canada Line, which runs along the fifty-fifth parallel. It extends twenty-six hundred miles north of the U.S.-Canada border. The Mid-Canada Line, also called the McGill Line because several University of Montreal scientists were involved in the planning of it, is financed by the Canadian government. The Pinetree Line, on the international border, is financed jointly by Canada and the United States.

"Any one of these radar sites can relay information concerning enemy targets to the technicians here in our operations room. This information is fed into our computerized SAGE system, that's Semi-Automatic Ground Environment. This computer is almost human, only better, limiting the chance of error to almost nil. By calculating the data, SAGE gives readouts on a projection screen as to how we can act and react to every move the enemy makes. Faced with an air battle, SAGE considers every option and gives us the best tactical decision in a split second. This computerized system eliminates the need for the old plotting table. Up until just this year, we used a vertical twenty-by-thirty-foot transparent plotting board; the plotters used the back and the controllers used the front. Now, you have to take into consideration that all this happens once we've identified a wave of enemy planes. Most of the time, our ground radar stations pick up a passenger plane or a single Russian reconnaissance . . ."

"Like the Tu-95 your CF-100 shot down," Spencer interrupted. "That was somewhere in this vicinity."

"Yes, Mr. Spencer, like the Tu-95 we shot down. It was a most unpleasant incident, but we had no choice." The writer could sense that the general did not wish to discuss the Bear incident. "SAGE can also solve navigation problems, give us weather systems to avoid, and so on.

"Another aspect of our detection screen is Airborne Early Warning. We have at our disposal a considerable number of Lockheed Super Constellations, each with a crew of thirty-one men, that fly north and south, back and forth, along our Atlantic and Pacific seaboards. These planes are loaded with six tons of radar equipment and can detect enemy aircraft over the horizon, actually giving us more reaction time, in case of an enemy attack, than the three stationary early warning radar lines. These aircraft fly continuously in what we call an umbrella system, whereby no amount of airspace in our vicinity is not surveyed at any given time. The crews work, eat, and sleep aboard these high-altitude aircraft.''

Spencer listened attentively to the general while Claire's eyes scanned the room, studying the communications equipment.

"We also have underwater sonar devices that are able to detect enemy submarines hundreds of miles away, as well as another DEW Line installation across the thousand-mile-long Aleutian chain. So you see, we have all points covered. We are also working on a ballistic missile warning system that will be deployed sometime in 1960. One of these stations will be in Greenland.

"In addition to all of these electronic communications, we have the Ground Observer Corps, or the GOC, as we call it, just in case the radar lines are sabotaged or knocked out. There are fifteen thousand full-time observation posts and twelve thousand partially manned posts in Canada and the United States. These are operated by personnel who are specially trained in spotting aircraft, friend or foe, and relaying the information to the proper authorities. Four hundred thousand men and women are involved in the GOC alone.

"As for fighter-interceptors, the RCAF has the subsonic CF-100 Canucks, and the U.S. Air Force has the supersonic Lockheed F-104 Starfighters, and the Convair F-102 Delta Daggers. Coming up, we have the Voodoos and the Delta Dart.''

"And the Arrow," added Spencer.

"Yes," the general said, without so much as a smile, "the Arrow, and I believe, along with many others in NORAD, that it is, right now, the best fighter-interceptor in the world, bar none. Its fire-control system includes a new heat-seeking missile that's capable of destroying any enemy aircraft, regardless of how much evasive action it takes." The general's eyes met Spencer's.

"We have three conditions of air readiness: white,

for a possible air attack; yellow, for a probable air attack; and red, for an imminent attack. I, or my assistant commander, Air Marshall Hugh Phillips of the RCAF, have the authority to call any one of these conditions of readiness. I can also invoke Conelrad, Control of Electro-Magnetic Radiations. This procedure involves getting all commercial radio and television stations off the air in order that enemy aircraft do not have the added advantage of using signals from the towers as navigational aids."

"You have quite an organization," said Claire, smiling.

"Yes, we do. There are two hundred thousand men and women involved in NORAD; approximately one-tenth of them Canadians. The air marshall and myself are accountable to the Joint Chiefs of Staff of the United States and the Canadian Chiefs of Staff Committee.

"Now, Mr. and Mrs. Spencer," the general continued sternly, "I want you to understand that the odd civilian has been given permission to view the inside of one of our operations rooms at Colorado Springs. Articles have even been published about our NORAD setup, once they pass the NORAD censors. So what you are seeing is really nothing new to the public. However, *this* particular room in the Territories does not exist. Do I make myself clear?"

"Yes, sir, you are very clear." Spencer answered, and Claire nodded.

"Now, I will arrange suitable overnight accommodation for you in the barracks. Although the sun never sets here in the summer, try and get some sleep. You will be awakened at 0400 hours and report to me at 0500. Then I will decide what I'm going to do with you."

The general motioned for one of the two guards near the door. He whispered something to him, then turned back to the visitors. "You will not be allowed outside the barracks. Till tomorrow, then," he said, abruptly.

As the guard led them down the long corridor, Spencer had a thought. If this elaborate system of radar detection and computer operation was so good, how did that Tu-95 get through? And why did the general show them the operations room? Was it just for old time's sake?

Shortly after the Spencers were ushered out, the general was handed two reports just torn from a telex. One was from a Super Constellation one thousand miles west of the Aleutian Islands.

*TUNDRA HEADQUARTERS*
*7. 4. 59.*
*0620 (1220 MST)*
*PAPA-CHARLIE-ONE-FOUR SIGNAL RECEIVED. HEADING OF 218 DEGREES. POSITION: 46 DEGREES 36 MINUTES NORTH LATITUDE, 159 DEGREES 53 MINUTES WEST LONGITUDE, APPROXIMATELY 950 MILES EAST OF HOKKAIDO, JAPAN.*

The other, sent only three minutes later, was from Pearl Harbor.

*TUNDRA HEADQUARTERS*
*7. 4. 59.*
*0623 (1223 MST)*
*ORIENTAL HEADING 345 DEGREES. PRESENT POSITION 42 DEGREES 16 MINUTES NORTH LATITUDE, 148 DEGREES 45 MINUTES WEST LONGITUDE. 90 MILES SOUTHEAST OF HOKKAIDO, JAPAN.*

The NORAD commander folded the telexes. For the first time, the very first time, he had second thoughts about OPERATION KLICK. Would it really work?

# CHAPTER TWELVE

HERE WE GO, KAPOLSKI THOUGHT, AS HE eased the control column forward after the final refueling tanker banked away. He had 350 nautical miles to go to his target.

Most pilots would have been dog-tired after seven and a half hours in the pilot's seat, but not Kapolski. So far, his cruise over the Pacific Ocean had been effortless and uneventful. His signal dictated to NORAD that he wasn't to be touched. He had used the relief tube twice and managed to catch a few winks after setting the supersonic machine on auto. Now he was fully awake and ready for whatever dangers he would have to face inside enemy territory.

The altimeter read nine thousand feet, then eighty-five hundred . . . The minutes ticked away. The thick green vegetation of the Japanese island reached up to him. Enemy territory was now only two hundred miles and twenty minutes away. He adjusted his helmet and sunglasses as he peered over the Arrow's nose at the Sea of Japan, the watery separation between Japan and the Soviet Union. Hokkaido Island, at thirty thousand square miles the second largest island of Japan, was below him. Kapolski dropped the Arrow through the clouds that started to appear. The island seemed to be sparsely populated; all he could see was dense forest and the occasional road. At this low altitude he could feel the subsonic speed of the aircraft. The hills and valleys whizzed by in a steady stream at over 610 knots. Six thousand feet now.

The light on the radar-sensing indicator blinked blue. He was being tracked on radar, but by who? Was it the Russians or was it ORIENTAL, off the southeast tip of Hokkaido, picking him up on its long-range equipment? It didn't matter. He couldn't do anything about it anyway. If it was the Russians, he'd soon be low enough to disappear right off their scopes.

North of Hokkaido's tip, only fifty miles across the Soya Strait, was Sakhalin Island, USSR, where the Soviets had naval and air manpower and equipment on alert. They were in the range to pick him up. Northeast of Hokkaido, almost right on Japan's doorstep, were the Kuril Islands, also owned by the USSR. That meant more radar and more fighter-interceptor strips. Kapolski knew the importance of staying two hundred miles clear of these built-up military sectors when coming off the Pacific run.

By the time he'd reached Hokkaido's western coastline and found his landmark, he had already dropped down to 1,000 feet. Now he was over the Sea of Japan, and the altimeter was spinning counterclockwise 800 . . . 700 . . . 500 . . . 400 . . . 350 . . . Easy now, he thought, don't pile it into the drink . . . 250 . . . 175 . . . easy, easy . . . 150 . . . 100 . . . 80 hold it there. He sped up to just under Mach 0.95, 1,000 feet per second. Ahead lay the Sikhote Alin Mountains of the Soviet Union and beyond that was Siberia. He checked his heading; 283 degrees, right on course.

Intelligence had been right on about the weather. The seas were choppy, the best water conditions for operating invisibly on enemy radar. There was some cloud but it was perfect down on the deck. Kapolski was lucky today because this region, like the Aleutian chain, was notorious for bad weather. A cold current in these waters usually made the climate more foggy, more stormy, and colder than other places with the same latitude.

Kapolski crossed the imaginary halfway point that divided the Soviet Union and Japan. Less than ninety miles to enemy territory. Kapolski checked his heading again. The misty outline of a mountain range appeared ahead. Then he saw his landmark, the radar mast, on the right, miles off still but very clear, the top jutting through the low coastline mist. Intelligence was right on again. Kapolski now had the Arrow skimming only seventy feet off the water. He kept his eyes open for the gap in the mountain range. The seconds ticked by. There it was, about five miles straight ahead. The densely forested gap appeared to have a slow rise off the water, perhaps a hundred feet.

Kapolski was breathing heavily into his oxygen mask, now regulated for pure cabin air. He eased the column back slightly and the fighter started climbing. Within seconds he would be over Russia. The gap appeared to be wide enough, a half mile across, he guessed. But would it be easy to follow through? He knew he was flying by the seat of his pants from here on in. As he came closer to the gap, he pulled back on the stick some more, then edged it to starboard. From one mile away he aimed for the center of the gap and held his breath.

He made it through with a hundred feet to spare below the aircraft. He was inside Soviet territory now, but was he undetected? He quickly glanced down at the binder in his lap and flipped to the next page. He read his guide:

YOUR I.P. IS A COAL MINE, 100 MILES AHEAD. HEADING 272. FOLLOW GAP THROUGH.

The mountains to either side of the fighter echoed the blasting thunder of the Iroquois engines. There was thick taiga below and blue sky above. He crossed a river so quickly that it appeared to be a mirror reflecting the sun's rays. Kapolski was exhilarated to be flying so low and so fast. The flora reminded him of the Canadian North; thick forest, zero population, not a road anywhere. He scanned the sky above. No aircraft.

A winding railroad track disappeared into the mountainside off his port side. It was the coal mine. He saw the rail cars and some tall structures. The gap was easier to pass through than he had thought. The geography of the land started to level out and there was still no sign of life. Kapolski felt sensational. This crazy mission was going to work!

With only three minutes to go till target, Kapolski checked the IFF signal. It was off. He eased the nose up slightly till he reached 150 feet. His speed was still just under Mach 1. His right hand gripped the column that contained the shutter release for the camera pod. He took one last look at the route map. For the last ten miles it was scaled down to four miles per inch. He confirmed a bridge and a dirt road on the map. The road tucked into some low hills off port. He read the guide again:

THE BASE IS TWO MILES BEYOND A SET OF HILLS.

He had no sooner read that, than he was over the hills and could see the base beyond. He dropped the guide to the floor.

It seemed so easy. There were still no enemy aircraft

in sight. Kapolski's blood raced. He had caught the Russians by complete surprise.

Built into the Arrow's belly, just below and back from the pilot's seat, was a cylindrical camera pod with a forty-degree forward oblique camera and three panoramic lenses hooked to an automatic exposure control. This unit was the latest in photo-reconnaissance equipment, supposedly far ahead of Russian technology. Several feet of Kodak Plus-X film were ready for exposure. Kapolski caught a good look at the base as he raced pell-mell towards it. He was surprised at the size of the layout.

He gripped the moulded stick; his skin stuck like glue to the inside of his glove. His right eyelid twitched. Several hundred feet before the first building he pressed the release button with his right forefinger. He shot over some hangars where a few scattered aircraft were parked outside. A dozen fighters, maybe. Too fast to count. Delta-winged fighters, from what he could tell. The tower was on his left. One aircraft was on the taxi strip, either coming or going. At a forty-five-degree angle to Kapolski's left was a runway, and another crisscrossed it to form an X. There were at least forty camouflaged fighters roasting in the Siberian sun. They too looked to be delta-winged. Kapolski held his finger firmly on the camera button.

Kapolski wondered how tight the security was down there. Were there watchdogs? Guards? Gun towers? He wished the shutter button would release bombs and blow up the entire complex.

A few hundred feet beyond the last hangar he released the shutter. He shoved the column to starboard and banked ninety degrees to the right, giving extra power at the same time.

Kapolski's Arrow was now through Mach 1. He could feel the increased centrifugal forces of the G-turn against his body, despite the operational G-suit. He tensed his neck and stomach muscles to maintain consciousness, but blood still drained from his head downwards, and the skin on his face pulled down until he looked like a bloodhound hunting dog. Kapolski was nearly blacking out from the force of 7-G. Now experiencing tunnel vision, he focused on the trees 150 feet below him.

Kapolski was careful to keep his speed at just over Mach 1, in order to shorten the radius of his turn to only two or three miles. He knew that at Mach 2 it would take the aircraft several more miles to complete the turn and he couldn't afford that. He had to return the same way he came in.

On the final edge of the turn Kapolski straightened out. He eased the stick back, sending his aircraft into a slight climb up to three hundred feet.

All jet fighter pilots were instructed in the use of supersonic bangs as a military tactic, but no one in the RCAF had ever been in a position, until now, to use them against the enemy. Kapolski had no choice but to get out of there as fast as he possibly could.

Kapolski picked up the mountain gap fifteen miles east of the base and followed it through at three hundred feet. The lush forest below him was a gray-blue blur. The machometer quickly reached Mach 1.1 . . . Mach 1.2 . . . Kapolski's blood was racing as fast as the aircraft. The Arrow's supersonic boom left a trail of destruction like a hurricane. Trees were nearly uprooted, a line of telephone poles was sent swaying like a row of palm trees, dust and rocks were spewing in all directions.

The mining development inside the gap was thrown into confusion. Once-neat piles of coal and rubble exploded as if dynamite had been set off under them. The railcars rocked on their tracks. The windows in all the

buildings shattered and tiny glass particles flew through
the air. All this time, a sonic trail followed the fighter.
BOOM! BOOM! BOOM!

Kapolski lifted the Arrow to clear a range of foothills
he had not remembered flying by on the way in. He had
veered off course. The mountains loomed up ahead and
Kapolski pulled back on the stick, sending the fighter
into a steep climb. He swallowed hard into his oxygen
mask as he cleared a broad-peaked mountain with only
fifty feet to spare. He skimmed along the top of the icy
range and was soon out over the Sea of Japan. Kapolski
nosed the aircraft down, closer and closer to the beck-
oning waters. Then he leveled off.

He flicked on the highly sensitive airborne radar to
wide sweep and picked up four high-speed targets to
the rear. They had to be Russians. Damn it! This was
no time for a dogfight; he was outnumbered and without ammunition. He needed speed, speed and more
speed to outrun them. The altimeter read four hundred
feet, too high. He eased the stick forward to until the
Arrow was tearing twenty feet over the now choppy
sea. Then he applied full military power. The weather
had changed. The sky and water were turning a murky
gray. The Iroquois engines were whining in his ears,
gobbling up fuel at an alarming rate. At eight hundred
knots, Kapolski was roaring over the Sea of Japan at
fifteen miles a minute, one mile every four seconds.

He was over international waters now, but didn't let
up. At this speed and height, the red-hot exhausts
sprayed the water into a steaming, twisting rooster tail
several hundred feet long. One pursuer broke off, probably due to lack of fuel. But the other three followed at
a distance. Were they armed? Did they have photo
equipment aboard?

One of the Russians, blinded by Kapolski's rooster

tail, got too close to the water. He hit the water surface, then the nose struck, and finally the entire aircraft somersaulted several times. At such a speed and angle, the force of hitting the water was equal to smashing into a cement wall. Within seconds, pieces of metal splattered an area five thousand feet long. It was then that the remaining two aircraft broke off.

Kapolski was greatly relieved to see his radar free of blips. He climbed gradually to twenty-seven thousand feet, switched the IFF back on and slowed to cruise speed. He had been in the air nearly eight hours, and the fatigue from being in confined quarters for so long hit him now. His knees and lower back were starting to ache; the leg harness felt like a set of leg irons, and he was only at the halfway point of his mission. This must be how the World War II P-51 pilots had felt on their long-range escort missions. He looked at the fuel gauges and saw that he was riding empty. The supersonic speeds had sucked the tanks dry.

Kapolski consulted the map on his knees for the sector 5 tanker.

"OSCAR-VICTOR-ONE-NINER, THIS IS PAPA-CHARLIE-ONE-FOUR. I'M APPROACHING BINGO FUEL. THIS IS CRITICAL. OVER."

They had to be within range, thought the pilot. He saw a large blip on the wide sweep of his radar, but then it disappeared. On a heading of 094 degrees, he saw a dark cloud buildup to the south, the general direction of the blip.

"OSCAR-VICTOR-ONE-NINER, THIS IS PAPA-CHARLIE-ONE-FOUR. DO YOU READ?"

No answer. Kapolski called for the backup tanker but there was no response; it had to be out of range. Where did the main tanker go?

Kapolski didn't like the look of some cumulonimbus thunderclouds off the starboard wing. He was nearly out of fuel, with a storm knocking at his door. He had an awful, heavy feeling in the pit of his stomach. If he didn't latch onto a tanker in the next few minutes, he was certain to run out of fuel before reaching the carrier.

EAST OF HOKKAIDO, JAPAN, 0720 HOURS (1720 EST)

Sixty-five miles off Hokkaido's shore, the radar controllers of an American aircraft carrier, the *USS Truman*, were preparing to bring in a mysterious fighter aircraft. A photo-reconnaissance mission, that's all they were told. It was top secret, code named OPERATION KLICK, and only essential personnel were told that this fighter had to be recovered, no matter what.

Suddenly, without prior warning, the weather patterns south and over Hokkaido turned foul. A thick, gray cloud mass clutched the air above the water surface east of the Japanese island, taking the ceiling down to a thousand feet and closing by the minute. A storm was brewing, threatening to move north-northeast.

The operations center of *Truman* was inside a large, dimly-lit cabin on the second deck. Several screens, or tote boards as they were called, ran at right angles to the deck and were manned by sailors with grease pencils, ready to mark plots on the see-through Plexiglas displays. Plotting tables, twelve in total, were set up throughout the room, and were also manned. The cabin had stored up heat from earlier in the day when the air temperature was over eighty degrees, and some of the men were becoming sweaty and irritable. The outside heat joined the heat generated by the radar equipment. The air-conditioning wasn't functioning properly, and the room felt like a furnace.

The officer in charge of flying operations, Commander Matthew Stocker, sat on a high chair in the middle of the cabin. His white uniform was vibrant in the overall red lighting of the room and made him stand out among the enlisted men. The other sailors, dressed either in the working blues with dungarees of the lower ranks or in the khaki brown of the petty officer ranks, were fanned out in all parts of the room. They were all wearing headsets and listening intently for any contact with the pilot of OPERATION KLICK. These men were fully experienced in the Carrier Control Approach. No other planes were flying in the ship's vicinity, as all *Truman*'s aircraft were safely aboard.

Stocker looked over the shoulder of Chief Petty Officer Stu Reiff, whose eyes were glued to his radar display. "Three sweeps, then shut her down."

"Aye, sir."

"Anything?" Stocker asked after the first sweep.

"No, sir," answered Reiff without looking up.

The commander frowned. He was worried about the mission and the sudden change in weather. "He should be in contact by now. Try calling him again."

"Aye, aye, sir," responded Reiff. "PAPA-CHARLIE-ONE-FOUR, THIS IS ORIENTAL. DO YOU READ? PAPA-CHARLIE-ONE-FOUR, PAPA-CHARLIE-ONE-FOUR, THIS IS ORIENTAL. DO YOU READ?"

In the silence that followed, the commander asked, "Do you have the right frequency?"

"Yes, sir. Three-three-zero-point-five megahertz."

Reiff sat stripped to the waist and hunched over his display, his legs straddling the boxlike machine. A little overweight, he felt the searing heat of the room and was sweating profusely. For the past two hours he had been drinking ice water right out of the pitcher. He looked away from the glowing orange display, swallowed some more water, and wiped his mouth with the back of his hand.

"Third sweep passed, Commander."

"Okay, shut it down. We don't want the Russians to pick up our signal." The commander unbuttoned his collar, took a deep breath, and stood up.

The plotters and technicians relaxed. Sighs and the movement of feet could be heard, mixed in with the sound of pounding teletypes. A sailor dressed in dungarees and white hat opened the door that led to the companionway just as another sailor came in and handed a message to the commander. One coming, one going. This activity went on all day.

Stocker looked at the message. "Tell them, nothing yet."

"Aye, aye, sir." The sailor left.

Reiff felt a cool breeze coming through the door as it opened. It was a great relief compared to the inside heat of the room. The storm front had to be getting closer, he thought, but the heat of the room still hadn't diminished. He wished he was outside inhaling some of the cool North Pacific air.

The commander received another message, this time an updated weather report. He scanned it quickly.

"Ten seconds to radiate, sir," a voice called out.

Stocker folded his arms and adjusted his headset properly on his ears, so he could listen in. "Okay, get ready," he called out.

"ORIENTAL, THIS IS PAPA-CHARLIE-ONE-FOUR. DO YOU COPY?"

Kapolski was almost in a state of panic. He knew he was on the right frequency for contact with the ship. He had run out of fuel two minutes earlier, approximately forty nautical miles from the prearranged meeting position with the carrier, but there was no answer. He'd hit the ram air turbine switch and was now on

auxiliary power only. Why wasn't the ship answering?
Was the storm killing all reception?

"ORIENTAL, ORIENTAL, THIS IS PAPA-CHARLIE-ONE-
FOUR, PAPA-CHARLIE-ONE-FOUR. DO YOU READ? DO YOU
READ? OVER."

"I have him, Commander," announced Reiff. "PAPA-
CHARLIE-ONE-FOUR, THIS IS ORIENTAL. WE COPY." He
slapped the side of his radar set in excitement.

"ORIENTAL, THIS IS PAPA-CHARLIE-ONE-FOUR. I NEED
SPECIFIC LANDING INSTRUCTIONS AND FAST. I AM ON
BINGO FUEL. REPEAT, BINGO FUEL. OVER."

"SQUAWK IDENT, PAPA-CHARLIE-ONE-FOUR. MODE
TWO, CODE TWO-SIX," Reiff said quickly. Procedure
called for Reiff to delay in asking the pilot for a position. He had seen the aircraft's oval globe in the upper
left-hand corner of his radar set as soon as he received
radio contact. A few seconds later, Kapolski's IFF signal burned into Reiff's display in the form of two lines
to one side of the oval. It's him, Reiff thought. Papa-
Charlie-One-Four is only a few minutes away, but out
of fuel; a bad situation for the aircraft and the carrier.

"Forty miles out, Commander, and coming our
way," called a sailor from the other side of the room.

With the wave of a finger, Stocker motioned to one
of the sailors standing beside him. "I want a message
sent to the White House and to NORAD. Tell them
we've made contact with Papa-Charlie-One-Four. Tell
them he's out of fuel, and that we have no choice but
to bring him in dead-stick.

"Reiff, notify Papa-Charlie-One-Four that he's coming in as is, dead-stick. Making a pass will be too dangerous. Bring him right in."

"Aye, aye, sir." Reiff turned back to his radar display.

All the technicians in the operations room had heard
the orders. The president was involved, and NORAD.

They were bringing in a pilot without fuel, something unheard of. Something big was up.

"PAPA-CHARLIE-ONE-FOUR, THIS IS ORIENTAL. WE ARE GOING TO BRING YOU IN DEAD-STICK. YOUR PIGEON IS ONE-SEVEN-ONE DEGREES AND I WILL VECTOR YOU TO A FIVE-MILE GATE," announced Reiff into the headphones.

"I READ YOU, ORIENTAL."

"Five seconds till silence," a voice rang out.

"PAPA-CHARLIE-ONE-FOUR, THIS IS ORIENTAL. RADIO AND RADAR SILENCE WILL COMMENCE IN FIVE SECONDS. DO YOU COPY?"

"ROGER, ORIENTAL."

"Hit it!" called the commander.

Kapolski had a moment's breathing space now that he had made contact. He had landed dead-stick one other time in his air force career; it was during a horrendous bomber escort trip in 1944, at the height of the RAF bombing of Germany. But he knew that landing without fuel on land, where there was more room to maneuver, was much easier than landing on the shorter confines of a carrier.

He surmised that Oriental had probably not picked up his signal earlier because they were on communication silence for short periods. Oriental's signal wasn't strong, but it was there, nevertheless. Russian waters were only a hundred miles away, and the Russian Navy was more than likely trying to pick him up right now. He hoped they wouldn't be able to establish a firm position. He also knew that Oriental's Tactical Air Navigation, a strong UHF radio signal that could guide a plane right to the deck, would not be functioning. There was a method to this madness. Any operating TACAN signal could easily be tracked by the enemy, who would go after the incoming aircraft. With no fuel, he'd be at their mercy.

Kapolski turned the craft ten degrees to starboard as he'd been ordered and dropped the nose slightly to a heading of 171. The machine responded sluggishly. Several seconds later, he heard the same reassuring voice of the ship's controller on the Carrier Control Approach. The signal was weak, barely readable.

"PAPA-CHARLIE-ONE-FOUR, THIS IS ORIENTAL. OVER."

"ROGER, ORIENTAL. WHAT HAPPENED TO THE TANKER?"

"I DON'T KNOW. IT DISAPPEARED OFF OUR SCOPES AND A BACKUP IS OUT OF RANGE. DON'T WORRY, WE'LL BRING YOU IN."

"I'M IN YOUR HANDS. THERE'S A STORM FRONT TO STARBOARD, ALMOST RIGHT UP MY ASS."

"WE COPY. WE'VE BEEN TRACKING THE STORM. YOU SEEM TO BE IN THE EYE OF IT. DO YOU HAVE AUXILIARY POWER?"

"AFFIRMATIVE."

"ROGER. WHAT'S YOUR PRESENT SPEED?"

Kapolski glanced at his controls. "TWO HUNDRED AND FORTY KNOTS."

"HOW'S SHE FLYING?"

"SO FAR, SO GOOD, ORIENTAL. ALTIMETER, AIRSPEED INDICATOR, TURN AND BANK, OPERATIVE. I HAVE RUDDER CONTROL BUT IT'S SLUGGISH. JUST ENOUGH TO DO THE JOB. SPEED BRAKES WORK FINE. AILERONS ARE PARTIALLY OPERATIVE. STICK CONTROL ISN'T BAD, SO THE ELEVATORS AND TRIM TABS MUST BE FAIR, OVER."

"I READ YOU. YOUR ALTITUDE IS NOW ANGELS TWO-FIVE, SO ACCORDING TO A GLIDE PATH WE'VE WORKED OUT, YOU'RE RIGHT ON TRACK. KEEP THAT AIRSPEED STEADY AT 230 TO 240 KNOTS. AND DON'T DROP TOO

FAST. TWO THOUSAND FEET PER MINUTE, FOR NOW, SHOULD DO IT. ORIENTAL ON SILENCE FOR THIRTY SECONDS. OVER.''

''I COPY, ORIENTAL. OUT.''

Kapolski looked over his right shoulder. It was then that he saw a flash of lightning that descended to the water just a few miles off. There were no violent winds yet, but he knew they were coming. He had to get this bird down in a hurry. If the storm front hit before he could land he'd have to bail out. It was next to impossible to fly an aircraft in such turbulence with no power; it would be crazy to even attempt it. Even bailing out in such weather had its drawbacks. If the chute opened in the middle of the storm he'd go for a wild ride in the up- and downdrafts, much the same way that water droplets travel during a fierce rainstorm before they turn into hail. He had heard of a pilot during World War II who had bailed out in a thunderstorm and when he finally touched ground, he was all iced up like a large chunk of hail, and very dead. Besides, even if Kapolski could let down safely in the water, who'd pick him up? Nobody else was crazy enough to fly in this dreadful weather. Also, the film would be lost. Kapolski's mind was racing over possibilities, but he remained calm. At least no one was shooting at him.

When it came to gliding, the Arrow had an advantage over other modern military aircraft because of its durable delta-winged construction. Kapolski knew the best glide speed for the plane's frame was approximately 230 knots, and he was doing his utmost to keep it there by using the speed brakes like a throttle. He also knew the Arrow had an imposing over-the-nose view. It hadn't posed a problem during practice runs in Canada's northland, but there had been more room to maneuver there.

Kapolski couldn't see anything at all through the solid

THE LAST FLIGHT OF THE ARROW 225

mass of dark, dirty clouds. He began to feel some turbulence in the air.

"PAPA-CHARLIE-ONE-FOUR, YOU'RE DOING FINE. COME LEFT TEN DEGREES FOR TRACK CORRECTION. DO YOU READ, PAPA-CHARLIE-ONE-FOUR?" The ship's signal was much stronger now.

"ROGER, ORIENTAL. LEFT TEN. I CAN'T SEE A THING." Another flash of lightning was followed by another crack of thunder. "THE STORM'S GETTING CLOSER NOW. HOW FAR TO TOUCHDOWN? OVER."

"TWENTY-EIGHT MILES."

"ROGER. CALL YOUR CEILING."

"EIGHT HUNDRED AND CLOSING."

Inside the operations center, Commander Stocker hit the communications switch for all channels, and his voice echoed throughout the carrier. "ATTENTION ALL PERSONNEL. WE HAVE AN AIRCRAFT APPROACHING OUR CARRIER. HE'S APPROXIMATELY THIRTY MILES OUT AND COMING IN WITH ZERO FUEL. IT'S IMPERATIVE THAT THIS AIRCRAFT RECOVERS. THIS CARRIER IS NOW UNDER FULL ALERT. CLEAR THE DECK. GIVE THE AIRCRAFT LOTS OF ROOM. DECK CREW, RIG THE BARRICADE. THIS IS NOT A DRILL. I REPEAT, THIS IS NOT A DRILL."

WASHINGTON, D.C., 1725 HOURS (EST)

In the bomb shelter below the White House, Jeffrey Kolb raced down the hallway leading to the president's underground Oval Office.

"Mr. President, Mr. President!" Kolb shouted, as he ran past two guards and burst into the room, waving a telex. "Papa-Charlie's been sighted coming out of Japan."

The president rose from his chair and read the sheet

intently. "Hmmm, less than forty miles from ORIEN-
TAL. And a storm about to hit. Out of fuel. What, out
of fuel!" The president's eyes rested on the defense secretary. "Oh, sorry, Jeffrey, take a seat."

Kolb sank into a soft leather chair, while the president sat on the edge of his desk. His eyes were focused
on the door, and his forehead was wrinkled in thought.
Kolb could tell from the president's face that his superior sensed disaster. "He's out of fuel. How could that
happen, with all the refueling points?"

"He missed the final tanker. How that happened
hasn't been confirmed yet. There's something else we
must consider."

"What's that?" asked the president.

"The chances of this pilot, an air force pilot who has
never landed on a carrier before, landing successfully
in a storm and with no power are very slim. What scares
me most is that, as far as I know, a navy aircraft is not
brought aboard when it's out of fuel. It's just too risky,
for the pilot, the deck crews, and the carrier itself. The
pilot ditches in the sea and they pick him up later."

"But he's got the film aboard."

"I know that," responded Kolb. "Of course, they
have orders to bring him in no matter what; we need
that film. Still, it doesn't look good. I hope he's got
something in that camera pod that's worth all this. And
I hope this pilot, whatever his name is . . ."

The president thought for a moment. "Kapolski."

"Yes, Kapolski. I hope this Kapolski is as good as
NORAD says he is. He won't have the option of a wave-
off; he's only got one crack at bringing the Arrow in."

East of Hokkaido, Japan
0730 Hours (1730 est)

The tall, almost skeletonlike Commander Stocker stood up in the middle of the operations center. "Gentlemen, I have received a message from the president of the United States. He has been informed of every phase of this mission. He knows what we're faced with here and he has informed me that every crew member will receive his personal thanks if we get Papa-Charlie-One-Four down without mishap. And I'll add to that by saying I'll buy all of you the thickest, juiciest steak and the tallest glass of beer you've ever seen, when we reach port. Now," he announced, sitting back down in his chair and adjusting his headphones, "back to work."

Reiff's mind started to race. This had to be a top priority mission if the president was being informed of its progress. Obviously, this aircraft was coming from Russia. Had it been photographing Soviet military installations? The pilot must be top-notch to be trusted with this mission. What kind of aircraft was he flying? The pilot had a European accent. Was he a Soviet defector stealing a Russian aircraft?

Commander Stocker bolted from his chair and walked over to the tote boards. As the fiery red light reflected off the glass, he watched the sailor marking the aircraft's location on his own side. Stocker's eyes met the sailor's for a moment through the Plexiglas. The ship was less than twenty miles from the aircraft. The markings glowed in the dimly lit room. Six minutes till touchdown, if the storm didn't cross the plane's path first.

". . . BECAUSE OF THE LOW CEILING, THE LANDING SIGNALS OFFICER WON'T TAKE OVER UNTIL HE HAS A CLEAR VISUAL OF YOU COMING IN, WHICH WILL BE AP-

PROXIMATELY ONE MILE OUT. HIS CALL SIGN IS 'PADDLES.' DO YOU READ, PAPA-CHARLIE-ONE-FOUR?''

"AFFIRMATIVE," answered Kapolski, as he held on to the control column with his right hand and the speed brake switch with his left. The thirty seconds of radio silence passed slowly.

"PAPA-CHARLIE-ONE-FOUR, THIS IS ORIENTAL. YOU ARE NOW FIFTEEN MILES FROM THE GATE AND AT ANGELS ONE-EIGHT. ALTIMETER TWENTY-NINE FORTY-FIVE. DOES YOUR ALTIMETER CONFIRM? OVER.''

"DEAD ON, ORIENTAL.''

For the next several seconds, Reiff and Kapolski discussed whether or not Kapolski should lay off the speed brakes for a time. There was a danger of his coming in slow and short. They ruled out the idea because Kapolski was afraid the aircraft might stall. Then there was more radio silence.

"PAPA-CHARLIE-ONE-FOUR, THIS IS ORIENTAL," Kapolski heard the now-familiar voice breaking the interlude. "YOU ARE TEN MILES FROM THE GATE, BUT YOU'RE ABOUT FOUR HUNDRED FEET TOO HIGH. DROP YOUR NOSE A TOUCH. IN THE NEXT FIVE MILES WE WANT YOU DOWN TO ANGELS ONE-TWO. DO YOU COPY?''

"I COPY, ORIENTAL.'' Then "COME ON, BABY. WE'VE BEEN THROUGH A LOT TOGETHER. GET ME DOWN.''

He eased the control column forward, gripping the upper portion with enough strength to almost break the mechanism in two. His hands were sweating inside his gloves. He had been through a lot in his air force career. Like a cat with nine lives, he'd survived World War II, Poland, the Battle of Britain, D-Day, Korea, the CF-100s, the Arrow. Was his time finally running out? What he was about to do was one of the trickiest, deadliest procedures ever conducted by a pilot. Even a navy pilot wouldn't attempt to land a twenty-three-ton aircraft without any power on an aircraft carrier with a storm at his back.

The clouds were turning very dark now, as the storm front was catching up with the Arrow. All the cockpit lights and gauges were lit as if it were nighttime. A slow drizzle splattered the cockpit window and a black cloud bank completely surrounded the fighter. It was only a matter of time till the storm hit with all its fury.

"PAPA-CHARLIE-ONE-FOUR, THIS IS ORIENTAL. YOU'RE DOING GREAT. FIVE MILES FROM THE GATE. AT THE GATE I WILL GIVE YOU A VECTOR OF TWO-TWO-ONE DEGREES. THEN IT'S RIGHT DOWN THE PIPE. SILENCE IS NOW LIFTED THE REST OF THE WAY AND WE WILL BE IN CONTINUAL CONTACT. DO YOU COPY, PAPA-CHARLIE-ONE-FOUR?"

"I COPY, ORIENTAL." Kapolski observed that the altimeter was at eleven thousand feet.

"PAPA-CHARLIE-ONE-FOUR, THIS IS ORIENTAL. DROP YOUR GEAR AND ARRESTER HOOK AND STAND BY FOR TURN TO FINAL APPROACH."

"ROGER."

Kapolski brought the nose up, but the aircraft responded sluggishly. He was concerned he'd stall, so he dropped the nose again. At his present speed of 230 knots he was taking a big chance, but he reasoned he didn't have much choice; it was either too fast or nothing. He could drop the gear just shy of the carrier on the final approach, but by that time he would have enough to worry about, so he hit the switch connected to the landing gear doors and crossed his fingers. Immediately, he felt a tearing, pounding jar from beneath the floor. Several more thumps followed further back in the aircraft and vibrated into the cockpit. Kapolski gritted his teeth until they hurt. The nose wheel landing gear door, which faced the slipstream head on, flat side out, must have torn loose. The door must have banged along the bottom of the fuselage as it broke off the aircraft. Now, he heard the landing gear falling free and he gave the aircraft a slight jiggle at the column to make sure they were locked into place. The green light on the landing gear position indicator blinked that everything appeared all right, minus the nose gear door, however.

"PAPA-CHARLIE-ONE-FOUR, THIS IS ORIENTAL. YOUR FIVE-MILE GATE IS IN FIFTEEN SECONDS. OVER."

"READY WHEN YOU ARE, ORIENTAL. DO YOU HAVE A MAINTENANCE SHOP ABOARD? OVER."

"AFFIRMATIVE. WHY?"

"I'VE SUFFERED SOME DAMAGE TO THE NOSE GEAR. I THINK THE DOOR JUST BLEW OFF."

"WE'LL GET THE SHOP ON ALERT." A pause. "HERE IT COMES, PAPA-CHARLIE-ONE-FOUR. VECTOR STARBOARD HEADING TWO-TWO-ONE. YOU ARE NOW FIVE MILES FROM THE DECK. LESS THAN TWO MINUTES TILL TOUCHDOWN."

"ROGER, ORIENTAL. TURNING TWO-TWO-ONE." Kapolski eased the control column to the right. He felt the aircraft labor, but it was still responding.

"ARE YOU VISUAL? OVER."

"ORANGES SOUR, ORIENTAL," answered Kapolski as he glanced down at the altimeter: 2,500, 2,400, 2,300 . . .


"Sir," called out one of the radar plotters, "I've got a bogie. Distance: thirty-two miles. Heading: one-eight-five degrees. Speed: eight hundred fifty knots."

"What? What's his altitude?" Stocker responded immediately.

"Angels ten, sir," came the immediate answer.

Stocker concluded that the bogie had to be a Russian fighter, probably from one of their bases in the Kuril Islands, a hundred miles to the north. They must've gotten a fix, despite the *Truman*'s radar and radio silence. Now they really had trouble!

"Sir, he's descending. Angels nine."

"Will he converge on Papa-Charlie's glide path before he reaches the ship?"

The plotter made a split-second calculation. "It'll be close," he said, speaking into his mike, without looking away from his screen. "At their present speeds the intercept will probably be over the deck."

Reiff turned to Stocker, four feet away. "Commander, should I contact Papa-Charlie to be on the alert for an unidentified aircraft?"

"No. Papa-Charlie is powerless to do anything anyway. He can't take evasive action and he's not armed. If we inform him of the possible danger he might panic. He has enough to worry about right now and so does the deck crew. We've got just over a minute to go. We'll have to sit on it and I hope and pray Papa-Charlie makes it in before that, whatever it is out there, does something stupid. I wonder if that bogie knows he has us."

Stocker quickly calculated that the bogie was traveling nearly sixteen nautical miles a minute. "How far out is Papa-Charlie now?"

"Three miles, sir. A minute and approximately twenty seconds away."

"And the bogie?"

"Twenty-five miles and about a minute and a half, as near as I can tell."

"Relax, boys," said the commander reassuringly. "Steady as she goes."

The landing signals officer and his assistant, in bright orange-and-white-striped coveralls, stood on their platform on the port side of the carrier's stern. They were scanning the sky intently through the drizzle for the aircraft they heard about at the briefing only an hour before. Behind them, several deckhands were getting the crash equipment ready from behind the superstructure. The barricade was up. Most of the deck personnel were already well away from the fighter's intended path, just in case it went astray during its recovery.

"This is crazy, Frank," said the senior LSO. "How am I supposed to bring in an aircraft under these conditions? Visibility is down to five hundred feet, it's raining, and the plane is now out of juice. Bone dry! And get this; according to the boss the nose gear might be damaged. Has the navy gone nuts?"

The assistant put his hood up to keep his face and hair dry. "Why doesn't he just ditch the thing alongside?"

"Well, Joe, we've got orders to recover this guy no matter what, and we're not supposed to ask questions." The LSO was holding onto the radio-telephone with one hand and edging his foot towards the cutoff switch that transferred control of the landing once he established a visual.

"Looks like the deck is starting to pitch," Joe said, looking across the deck as Frank kept his eyes glued astern. They both felt the wind at their backs.

"We want it down in the stern for him, seeing that he has no power."

"You're right." Frank paused to scan the sky. "Here he comes, Joe!" The senior LSO spotted the battle-camouflaged fighter less than a mile away, bursting through the clouds in the northwest sky.

"Good Lord, what is it?" Frank didn't recognize the enormous delta wings and pointed nose. It had no navigation lights on; "lamps black," as it was known in navy lingo.

Joe quickly hit the foot switch. "PAPA-CHARLIE-ONE-FOUR, THIS IS PADDLES. DO YOU READ?"

"I READ, PADDLES, AND I SEE THE SHIP. BRING ME IN. OVER."

"OKAY, JUST RELAX. COME LEFT AND WATCH YOUR SPEED. YOU LOOK TOO FAST. DO YOU HAVE A MEAT-BALL?"

Kapolski stared through the Plexiglas and saw the helicopter that acted as a plane guard. It was fifty feet off the water surface and a thousand feet to starboard, astern of the ship. He applied the speed brakes and watched the airspeed indicator drop down from 180 knots. His eyes rested on the Optical Glide Path Indicator, three thousand feet away.

"PAPA-CHARLIE-ONE-FOUR, DO YOU HAVE A MEAT-BALL?"

"AFFIRMATIVE."

"LEFT A LITTLE, PAPA-CHARLIE. LEFT. MORE LEFT. YOU'RE HIGH. BRING IT DOWN."

Kapolski had done extensive training in the Territories with the Optical Glide Path Indicator. He'd practiced and practiced using the four-by-four-foot concave aluminum image with green datum lights on either side and red wave-off lights on top. Several times during practice he had been waved off, but he knew that there would be no wave-offs this time around. Kapolski knew too that from this point on, the LSO did the talking and he did the listening, obeying every command. As the bright lights reflected on the polished image, Kapolski saw that the center of the lights formed a large fiery dot, the shape of a meatball. But it was above the line of the datum lights and that meant trouble, for the meatball had to be even with the datums to achieve a proper landing.

"FULL SPEED BRAKES, PAPA-CHARLIE-ONE-FOUR."

Kapolski was coming in too high, but he couldn't seem to get the fighter down fast enough. The buffeting wind was bouncing the aircraft around like a balloon. Kapolski saw the copter disappear below and behind him.

"YOU'RE TOO HIGH. YOU'RE TOO HIGH!"

Kapolski was only three hundred feet away from touchdown, barreling in at nearly 170 knots. He saw that the runway deck lights were on. The LSO was still screaming at him to get the aircraft down. The ship's stern was starting to drop. Luckily, the ship's speed was steady at thirty knots, away from him, in addition to the twenty-knot wind over the deck.

"NOSE UP. UP!"

Joe and Frank had a good view of the fighter now. They stared in awe at the dual set of landing wheels at all three points of its tricycle landing gear. They'd never seen anything like its long needle nose and tall tail fin, its clamshell canopy, its gigantic wings. There was absolutely no engine sound from this aircraft that looked like a huge metal eagle with her wings spread full.

Kapolski watched the deck through his port side, then quickly switched to the starboard as he frantically tried to visually align the mighty machine so that he would land smack on the center of the yellow line. The meatball was still too high on the mirror.

Kapolski saw the two LSOs in orange whiz by on his left. He took a deep breath as the deck rushed up towards him. This was it. In a stunning impact that rattled his backbone, he hammered the aircraft down in a controlled crash. The main gear hit before the fourth arresting wire, missing it cleanly.

As he saw the ocean ahead, Kapolski knew the nose was still too low for the wires to catch. The barrier raced towards him. He closed his eyes and cursed in Polish. Then he felt a tug that nearly jerked his head off his shoulders. The sixth and last wire had caught the tail hook. It felt like the shoulder straps were going to strangle him, but he couldn't do anything but sit tight and ride it out. Then the Arrow finally slammed to a stop and rolled slightly back, the front end bobbing up and down several times before stopping.

Kapolski took several deep breaths as he leaned to the port side and looked through the cockpit window. To his astonishment, he had stopped only a few feet from the ship's angled deck edge, well left of the yellow line down the middle. The last arresting wire had been stretched out to its furthest point. He whipped his helmet and leg strap off and opened the canopy as soon as he saw a deckhand place the ladder in the aircraft's port side.

The pelting rain felt exhilarating after eight hours in the cockpit. He rubbed his arms and inhaled the salty smell of the ocean. The air temperature, he guessed, had to be somewhere in the mid-sixty degree range.

He was quickly met by another deckhand who climbed the ladder. "Sir," he said, with astonishment, "I never would have believed it if I hadn't seen it for myself."

Kapolski grinned. "I sure wouldn't want to do this every day."

With the help of the deckhand, Kapolski disassembled himself from his gear and climbed down the wooden ladder. He stopped on the last step. Several men were already scurrying around in order to get the aircraft below. For a brief moment Kapolski thought he heard an aircraft overhead. Then he felt a slight shaking of the ladder. Surely, no one else could possibly be flying in this weather. He glanced up at the clouds, but couldn't see anything resembling an aircraft. Shrugging, he jumped the last step to the deck.

"GET THAT AIRCRAFT OFF THE DECK AND GET IT BE-LOW. LET'S MOVE IT! GET THAT PILOT OUT OF THERE!"

# CHAPTER THIRTEEN

OTTAWA, ONTARIO, 1740 HOURS (EST)

"BANZAI!" YELLED DEAN STEDMAN, RIP-
ping the telex paper off the machine. "He did it! He did
it!" The defense minister of Canada danced a jig before
his startled boss and two RCAF noncommissioned officers. "Listen to this: *1648 HOURS EASTERN STANDARD
TIME. PAPA-CHARLIE-ONE-FOUR RECOVERED. CAMERA
POD INTACT. AREA SOCKED IN BY STORM. ORIENTAL.*"

"This calls for a celebration," said the prime minister.

Stedman knew his superior was a teetotaler. "A celebration?"

"Yes, a celebration." The prime minister left the
room and reappeared with a box of cigars, a large bottle
of champagne, and four glasses.

Stedman was startled. "Well!"

The prime minister laughed, his voice booming
through the room. "Dig in, men."

"Thank you, sir," said Stedman, pulling out a pack

236

of matches. In less than a minute all four men were puffing away.

"Now, let's drink up." The prime minister poured champagne for the group. "To Flight Lieutenant Bogdan Kapolski," he said, hoisting his glass level with his chin, "the best damn pilot in the air force."

"To Flight Lieutenant Kapolski," bellowed the other three in perfect harmony.

Back in his office after the celebration, the Tory leader was concerned. "Dean, what do you think those pictures show?" he asked.

Stedman belched. "Excuse me, too much champagne."

"I'll say, you drank nearly half the bottle yourself. Well, what do you think?"

Before he had a chance to speak, the telephone rang.

"Yes," the prime minister said, sitting down to answer it.

"Sir, it's Salisbury from communications. I've just received a telex from ORIENTAL." The sergeant cleared his throat.

"*1851 HOURS EASTERN STANDARD TIME. THE STORM HAS CLEARED AND PAPA-CHARLIE-ONE-FOUR READY FOR LAUNCHING.*"

The prime minister nodded. "Thank you. Let me know when he's off."

"Yes, sir."

The prime minister replaced the receiver and looked at his defense minister. "They're ready to launch him."

Stedman frowned. "Why so soon?"

ABOARD USS TRUMAN, 0939 HOURS (1939 EST)

The hot glow of the twin Iroquois engines' exhausts blasted across the flight deck, leaving behind a wobbly, hot mirage at the rear. Kapolski moved the Arrow forward by utilizing plenty of throttle and riding the rudder-pedal brakes. The smell of high-octane fuel enveloped the deck as the catapult director, dressed in blue, straddled the catapult shuttle run. He was giving Kapolski directions for proper positioning by using above-the-waist hand signals.

By motioning with their hands below the waist, a set of signals meant specifically for the chock men, the director and his crew, also in blue and fitted with safety phones, worked together to prepare the mighty aircraft for the catapult takeoff. There were roll bars built into the deck to center Kapolski on the catapult if he couldn't position himself exactly.

Kapolski's heart went out to the chock men, the unsung heroes of the flight deck. They were often called deck apes because they used ropes and muscle power to maneuver aircraft across the deck. They were out in all kinds of weather, inhaling burning jet fuel and enduring the vibrations of high-powered engines, but day after day they performed their jobs. They were men who were proud of their jobs and proud to be in the U.S. Navy. Kapolski thought of his own dedicated ground crew back at Collins, and he wondered whether Lance Tiemans had returned.

With his manual open in his lap, the pilot reread the instructions for a successful launch:

*1) Obey all signals.*
*2) Use more than enough throttle while taxiing.*
*3) Stay off the brakes.*
*4) At the signal, give engines full throttle.*

*5) If gauges appear normal, salute officer and lock head back against headrest.*

Kapolski was thankful that this flattop was one of the longer ships in the U.S. Navy, otherwise he might not have made it aboard. The maintenance shop below deck worked above and beyond the call of duty by digging up a nose-gear door from a salvaged navy fighter to fit the Arrow. The slab was cut, shaped and fastened into place in sixty minutes, a minor miracle to say the least. Ninety minutes after touchdown, the Arrow was gassed up, repaired, and ready to go.

The storm front, with winds gusting to nearly fifty knots, had blown through in a hurry. Below deck, Kapolski had had a bite to eat and a short nap, until the photo-reconnaissance pictures were returned from the lab. The navy kept one set of pictures, plus the negatives, and gave Kapolski another set of eight-by-ten-inch prints to fly back to TUNDRA.

While aboard ship, a couple of navy pilots had questioned Kapolski about his mission, but he had remained tight-lipped; name, rank and serial number only. *Flight Lieutenant Bogdan Kapolski J23198.*

The storm was now moving northward over the Kuril Islands, and the Russian military bases were socked in. Kapolski was given orders to launch as quickly as possible, in case the Russians were crazy enough to try something again. But first, the carrier was conducting a radar search of one hundred miles.

From the cockpit Kapolski could see nasty, dark clouds to the north. Two men beneath the aircraft connected the holdback lines and the bridle line between the shuttle and the aircraft. Once the hookup had been completed, the director handed matters over to the flight deck officer who was in charge of the launch. He was dressed in a yellow top and cap, and stood on the right side of the aircraft.

When the safety chocks were lowered, the flight deck officer gave Kapolski the signal to release the brakes. The Arrow rolled forward and took up the bridle tension, which brought the nose into an upwards attitude. The FDO gave Kapolski the thumbs up. Then he waved a green flag, the signal for full throttle.

Kapolski pressed forward on the throttle and listened to the roaring engines echo throughout the cockpit. His eyes shot to the takeoff checklist on his right, knowing full well that all was in order. When he glanced outside he noticed that a large number of sailors were standing along the outer reaches of the deck to watch the show. Kapolski then brought his head back to rest against the headrest, keeping his eyes on the FDO. The takeoff force of the catapult alone was equivalent to nearly 5-G and Kapolski wanted to be ready. The FDO was waiting for his salute. They never saluted before takeoff in the air force, but this was the navy.

Kapolski saluted. The FDO turned and peered down the deck to make sure the Arrow would be launched during a bow pitchup. Patches of blue sky were appearing now through fluffy clouds, the wind was twelve knots.

Kapolski remembered to keep his head well back and not attempt to fly the plane off the deck; the force of the steam-driven catapult would spring him into the air. The FDO dropped the flag, and the catapult engineering chief pressed the launch button.

Kapolski felt a sensation he had never experienced before. No takeoffs from the ground had ever been like this. He felt his skin and mouth pull back on his face from the G-forces, as the aircraft raced along the deck at full-throttle. The Arrow was cradled in a giant slingshot, and it sprang loose from the catapult's grip just before it reached the ship's bow.

Once over open water, Kapolski brought the stick back towards him, as he climbed gradually at tremendous speed. Five miles off the ship's bow, he started banking to starboard at an altitude of one thousand feet in a wide, disciplined turn. He wanted a little fun before he left *Truman*'s vicinity.

Following the turn, he straightened the fighter out and dropped to an altitude of one hundred feet; then he pushed the throttles forward. He could still see the carrier and was attempting to line up with it so they would converge on parallel paths approximately two hundred feet apart.

Within seconds Kapolski was nearly even with *Truman*. At a speed of five hundred knots, and at a distance of four hundred feet off the ship's bow, he suddenly eased the fighter over, lit the afterburners, and performed an upside-down wave. The last the sailors on the deck saw of the fighter were two glowing, red-orange balls of fire, rising swiftly into the sky.

# CHAPTER FOURTEEN

THE PRESIDENT, JEFFREY KOLB, AND GENeral Schult were all hunched over the photo-reconnaissance pictures of the MiG-K Skyjacker that were taken the previous day over the Soviet Union.

The president was studying the glossy, black-and-white photos with a magnifying glass. He leaned back in his chair. "Your pilot did an excellent job, General, an excellent job."

"Thank you, sir. We got the best man to do the job." General Schult had been ordered to Washington on a B-52 bomber that flew to the Northwest Territories out of North Dakota. He hadn't slept in nearly twenty-four hours and looked it.

"You certainly did get the best. How he ever got that fighter onto the carrier dead-stick is beyond me. But why did he miss his last refueling point?"

The general put his hands behind his back. "The

242

tanker in that sector was struck by lightning and went down, no survivors. Pieces of wreckage were found four hours later by a *Truman* fighter aircraft. The backup tanker was out of range for Kapolski.''

''I see. Now tell me something about this particular shot.'' The president pointed to a photograph on his desk.

''Of course, sir.'' The general walked around to the president's right.

''These are infrared pictures, are they not?''

''Yes, sir.''

''What are these white spots behind the engines of the aircraft?'' The president pointed to a line of nine MiG-Ks in the right-hand corner of the picture. To the rear of the engines, the ground was white. The ground behind six MiG-Ks pointed in the opposite direction, on the left side of the picture, was dark.

''They're hot spots, Mr. President, from engine heat. The aircraft in that line on the right had their engines running just previous to Kapolski snapping the pictures. The engines of the aircraft on the other side of the photo probably hadn't been running for several hours, perhaps days.''

The president nodded. ''This is one hell of a big base.''

''I agree.''

The president turned his swivel chair to face Kolb. ''Jeffrey, is the Russian informer safe?''

''Yes, sir, he is. He's out of Washington. He was more than happy to get out now, instead of waiting until the end of the month. He and his wife will be given new identities and new residence in California. The last information we received from him was the location of the five other MiG-K fighter bases inside Siberia.''

''That information is all contained,'' the president nodded toward a set of telexes on his desk, ''in these sheets, is that correct?''

"Exactly."

"Well then, Jeffrey, send in the ambassador." The president stood up and faced the door.

The ambassador seemed to have lost some weight since their last meeting. Chenkovsky's face looked longer, his cheekbones were more prominent, and his skin color was almost anemic.

"Mr. Ambassador, please have a seat."

"No thank you, Mr. President," Chenkovsky answered, eyeing the photographs on the president's desk, "I prefer to stand like the rest of you."

The president introduced Kolb and Schult to the ambassador, who simply nodded at the two men.

"Mr. Ambassador, your country is still building the Skyjacker. Why?" Without letting the ambassador reply, the president went on. "According to our reports, there are a total of six massive MiG-K fighter bases in Siberia. We also know that the Soviet Air Force plans to attack North America on August 1. What do you say to that?" Chenkovsky stared at the three men and cleared his throat, as the president continued. "We have obtained photo-reconnaissance pictures of your main base and we plan to release them to the international news agencies."

The ambassador's mouth curled into a sneer. "I don't want to spoil your little Fourth of July celebration, but if you release those pictures, we'll release our pictures of the Arrow bases in northern Canada."

The three Americans were paralyzed.

The ambassador grinned. "I think I'll have that seat now, Mr. President."

"By all means," the president grunted.

"Mr. President," Chenkovsky continued, "we know everything about the TUNDRA project. We know where every one of your seven bases are. We know they're just as big as ours. And we have photographs, too, from the ground. Good, clear, black-and white-photographs.''

Schult glanced at the president. ''I get the feeling that we are about to make a deal,'' said the NORAD commander.

Chenkovsky spoke up. ''This time my country proposes that the USSR and NORAD both demolish their respective fighter projects for good. We can send groups of high-ranking officials into each other's countries to observe the total destruction of the Arrow and the MiG-K. There would be no need to involve the news agencies. This is my premier's proposal. The ball is in your court now. I will wait to hear from you.'' The ambassador nodded curtly and left.

Schult spoke first. ''Let's go to the news agencies anyway. What if they do divulge the existence of the Arrow? It will harm them more than us. They were going to attack us, remember.''

''I know, but they won't attack us now.''

''The president's right, General,'' said Kolb. ''I think we better work together with the Russians on this.''

Schult closed his eyes for a moment. ''I think we're going to be sorry.''

''No,'' the president said to Schult. ''If we go through with your idea, our reputation will be irreparably damaged.''

''But . . .''

''No buts.''

# CHAPTER FIFTEEN

Spencer puffed on a cigarette and stared out one of the windows of the barracks. A line of nine Arrows was being inspected. He had been watching the area, about a hundred and fifty yards away, for the past several minutes. Men were coming and going, carrying tools and placing them on the ground. Two dump trucks pulled up. Off to one side, a group of ten men in civilian clothes were watching the activity. Spencer thought it was strange that they weren't wearing a service uniform of some kind. A guard was staring coldly back at him from the yard outside the window and there were two more assigned to the Spencers in the hall. Spencer turned and inspected the room for what seemed like the hundredth time.

There were two beds side by side and two sets of large lockers in the approximately twelve-foot-square room. Overlooking the beds were two large windows, with the blinds pulled up, allowing the sun's rays to lighten the room.

"I don't particularly like their choice of colors," Spencer said. "Everything on this base is olive green; it looks like a prison."

Claire was sitting on a bed watching her husband pace the room. "We're under guard, aren't we? So I guess we are in prison." She was angry that Spencer wasn't worried about the predicament they were in. "We've been here for five days!"

"I know, dear," he said calmly. "There's nothing we can do but wait." He gently touched her trembling shoulders. "Don't worry, we'll be out of here soon."

"We've been here five days, and only one change of clothing. There are guards all over the place to make sure we don't make a move. Are you sure the general contacted our family, like he said he would?"

"He said he would, and I trust him."

There were footsteps in the hall, then a tap at the open door.

Spencer turned. "General Schult."

"Look towards the hangar area, you two." Claire joined her husband by the large window. "What do you see?"

Spencer turned white as a ghost. The nine Arrows he'd been watching a few minutes before were now being dismantled by a work crew of perhaps thirty men. "What are they doing?"

The general frowned, recalling his meeting with the president. "They're destroying every Arrow on this base with acetylene torches. For good this time. By tomorrow, every Arrow in the Territories will be completely destroyed."

Spencer's mouth hung open. "But why? You pretended to scrap it in February, and now you're scrapping it again. Why?"

"Never mind why. Your time is finished here. I wanted you to see this final dismantling before we send you back to Ontario. As far as you're concerned, there was no Arrow after February 20. The issue is dead. The entire Arrow affair is classified. Is that clear?"

The Spencers saw that the general meant business. They both nodded.

The writer pointed toward the group of ten men standing to one side of an Arrow. "Who are those people, the ones out of uniform?"

"That's none of your business," Schult replied calmly.

OVER NORTHERN ONTARIO, 1112 HOURS (EST)

The DC-3, with thirty TUNDRA pilots aboard, was still two hours out of Ottawa. They were about to receive their relocation orders following the final Arrow dismantling. Wilkinson had informed the pilots, in no uncertain terms, that everything they had done in the past several months in the Northwest Territories would have to be blotted from their memories. The Arrow was gone for good; there was no trace of it left anywhere, they were told.

The men were in a somber mood, except for Flight Lieutenant Bogdan Kapolski. Kapolski was still on a high after his photo-reconnaissance mission into the Soviet Union a week earlier. As he watched the steady pattern of Canadian Shield trees, rocks and lakes five thousand feet below, his thoughts drifted back to the mission. He had actually flown, at supersonic speeds, an Iroquois-engine-equipped Avro Arrow, a fighter that wasn't supposed to exist, from the Northwest Territories into the Soviet Union to photograph a foreign military installation for NORAD. He had landed the mighty machine without any fuel on a U.S. carrier off Japan. And he couldn't tell anyone, ever! Who'd believe him anyway?

Kapolski was ready to retire from the Royal Canadian Air Force. He'd accomplished something great, but the Arrow was gone now. When Wilkinson had informed the pilots at Collins that the Arrow bluff would finally be put to rest, Kapolski was shocked. Why the bluff in the first place? It didn't make sense.

He had taken his photo-reconnaissance Arrow to its absolute limit. He had smashed two jet airspeed records in a matter of hours. The first was at low-level, over the Sea of Japan, when his airspeed indicator read Mach 1.4, and the second was over the Pacific Ocean, at an altitude of nearly fifty thousand feet. Kapolski fed full power to his fighter and hit Mach 2.8. These earth-shattering events would never be recorded in *Aviation Week* or *Canadian Aviation*. There would be no news releases, no pictures, nothing.

In the years to come, perhaps near the end of the century, the events of the TUNDRA Project would probably be declassified and made public, Kapolski thought. Would anyone then believe his involvement in it?

Kapolski needed to look ahead to his future. He thought of starting a business somewhere; maybe a small farm or a fishing tackle shop on the West Coast. He had always liked fishing. Or maybe a bowling alley, or pool hall; a place where he could relax and tell air force stories to anyone who cared to listen. He had no relatives or close friends to go back to. He'd be starting out all over again. He'd have to make new friends, maybe even find a new wife. Was there a place for a disillusioned former RCAF pilot with an outstanding war record?

OTTAWA, ONTARIO, MONDAY, JULY 13
1003 HOURS (EST)

Dean Stedman was drinking coffee in the prime minister's office. The windows were open, the sound of robins singing filled the sun-filled morning. But the room was full of gloom and doom.

The two men were standing by the window. "Well, it's finally done; the Arrow hacked to death by acetylene torches, and under the watchful eyes of the Russians, of all people," Stedman grumbled.

"The last message came through this morning. The Arrow is indeed history," said the prime minister. "We had no choice. I hope you're not blaming me?"

"No, of course not. We had no choice whatsoever." Stedman sighed. "But I sure hope we got their aircraft too."

"It's been confirmed through American sources that the MiG-K is also history."

"Good. I guess we'll have to keep going with our interceptor defense. The CF-100s will have to suffice until we can purchase some Voodoos and Starfighters," Stedman said with a frown.

"And don't forget the Bomarc missile. This whole Arrow business made the Tory government look very bad. Now, the Bomarc is turning out to be a dud. And don't say, I told you so."

"What can I say? In recent tests, the Bomarc has shown itself to be totally unreliable against high-speed aircraft. There are several M.P.s who insist that we should set an example for a nonnuclear world by deploying a conventional warhead on the missile."

The prime minister pointed to a bag of mail on a chair. "I'm getting thousands of letters. Most of them are from workers in Ontario who lost their jobs in February when we scrapped the Arrow. We couldn't pick them all up for TUNDRA. The theme of most of the letters is that I have destroyed not only an advanced aircraft, but also the Canadian aeronautics industry to boot. Many of the A. V. Roe and Orenda high-tech engineers are now in the United States with NASA, McDonnell Douglas, Boeing or Pratt & Whitney. Some have even gone to Australia. I got a strong backing from these people in the last two elections, but I won't in the next one. You know, it's ironic.''

"What is?" Stedman asked.

"A former Liberal cabinet member told me that if the Liberals were still in power, the government funding of the Arrow never would have gotten this far. They would have terminated the Arrow and Iroquois program two years ago." The prime minister shook his head. "If that had happened, we wouldn't be in the mess we're in now. I remember a conversation we had in this room, about a year ago.

"About what?"

"You said that destroying the Arrow would cost us votes. You may be right.''

Stedman put his hands in his pockets and walked towards the door. He stopped halfway across the room. "Will the TUNDRA Project ever be declassified?"

"Yes," the prime minister answered quickly. "It's been decided that NORAD will release it all, even Kapolski's flight into the Soviet Union, in thirty years' time. I probably won't be around then. Hell, I'd be in my nineties. But you'll be in your sixties. When that story breaks, it'll cause one hell of a stir." The prime minister lifted his head proudly. "Maybe then the public will realize that I tried to do the right thing.''

## About the Author

Daniel Wyatt lives in Burlington, Ontario with his wife and two children. He is the author of TWO WINGS AND A PRAYER and MAXIMUM EFFORT: The Big Bombing Raids. LAST FLIGHT OF THE ARROW is his first novel.